ALSO BY MATT RITTER:

Plants of San Luis Obispo, Their Lives and Stories

A Californian's Guide to the Trees among Us

California Plants: A Guide to our Iconic Flora

www.mattritter.net

RAINWALKERS

A Novel

Matt Ritter

Pacific Street Publishing
San Luis Obispo, California

For information about special discounts for bulk purchases, please contact Pacific Street Publishing at info@pacificstreetpublishing.com.

To request the author for a speaking engagement or book signings, please contact Pacific Street Publishing at info@pacificstreetpublishing.com.

Ritter, Matt.
    Rainwalkers : a novel / Matt Ritter. — Second U.S. Edition
        p.   cm.

ISBN 978-0-9998960-2-0 (paperback)
ISBN 978-0-9998960-3-7 (e-book)
This title is also widely available as an audiobook.
Library of Congress Control Number: 2019938188
Second Edition: June 2020

Printed in the United States of America

10 8 7 6 5 4 3 2

Thank you to James Coffey, Jenn Yost, Sam Baber, Kyle Nessen, Mike Garrett, and my family.

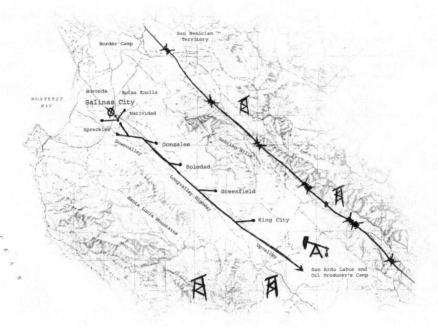

CHAPTER ONE

Willie Taft buried his wife of twelve years in a sandy bank above the Salinas River. She had cooled to the temperature of the soil by the time he took the last hesitant handful of sand and carefully scooped it onto her pale face. He tried to rise, but pain and outrage contorted his body, and he pounded the ground until his knuckles burned and tears dripped over the wound on his bloody cheek.

She deserved so much better, and Will couldn't bear to leave her. All that love, all that life, led to a hurriedly dug, shallow pit. *Why her and not him?* He wanted to scream the question but didn't for fear of being discovered. He knew they'd be close behind him, and he didn't have much time.

Will rose and looked at her sorry little mound of sand one last time. He wanted to mark her grave, maybe one shiny river stone to commemorate her beautiful life but knew he couldn't. He collected a few dry branches, covered the mound, then hustled along the bank through the willows to avoid detection.

It hadn't rained in two days, and now clouds were rolling in from the lower Valley. The temperature was dropping. Will scanned the sky. Somewhere far above, satellites that no longer sent nor received communications orbited in the vast emptiness of space, ghosts of a vanished world. Thin stacks of white chimney smoke rose in the distance. As he ran along the riverbank, the tide of adrenaline ebbed, and his hunger and thirst grew. The bone-deep pain in his cut face was setting in, and Will knew he had an hour, maybe two, to find shelter.

He stood on the levee in the dark. In the field below, a tin-roofed farmhouse glowed faint yellow. Smoke billowed from the chimney at one end, and a single light cast a glow on a stack of split wood on the front porch. He could smell the rain and had to take his chances.

He attempted to brush the soil off his denim and tucked in his shirt. He came up the stairs onto the porch and knocked softly. After a long time, a woman came to the door.

"Yes?"

"Excuse me, ma'am. I'm wondering if I could trouble you for something to eat," he said while sweeping his bangs off his sweaty forehead.

The woman didn't answer. He waited while she stared, shaking her head slowly.

A man's voice came from behind her. "Rose, come away from there. Who is it? Can we help you, son?" asked the man as he pushed past his wife.

"Sorry to her, sir. I was walking by and saw the smoke from your chimney. It's been an awfully long time since I had a bite to eat."

The man thought for a moment, then looked him up and down.

"Hadn't had nothing to eat, huh?"

"No, sir."

"It's past our supper, but Rose could scare you up something." He looked at his wife, who said nothing, but raised an eyebrow. "Alright," the man said, "you come on in and sit down, but you're going to have to remove them boots."

The front room was warm and lit in sepia tone by a single lamp. At one end, was the door to a well-lit kitchen in which sat an old wooden table, from where the couple had just risen.

"Come sit with us in the kitchen," the old man said to Will.

The woman went to the stove while the man brought a third chair from the living room. She put a full glass of buttermilk in front of him. He looked up at her, thanked her with a nod, and drank half the glass in two gulps. The cold buttermilk tasted so good that his eyes were still closed when he set the glass back onto the table.

"Thank you," he said under his breath.

"Name's Grover, and this is Rose."

"Pleased to meet you. I'm Will; Will Taft."

"That's a serious looking cut on your face, son. Fresh, too. How'd you come by that?"

Will hesitated a moment. "I was coming up from the creek a ways back and hit a willow branch."

The old man eyed him carefully, then said, "Fine if you don't want to tell, but ain't no tree ever cut a man like that."

Grover waited, but Will just took another gulp of buttermilk. The sound of batter sizzling on the frying pan broke the silence.

"After you eat, you can get it cleaned up."

"Thank you, sir."

"What are you doing walking through these parts? Since the war's been on, we haven't seen many young men."

"I'm headed back to Gonzales. My wife and I were collected, separated from our daughter."

"There you go," Rose said, dropping a plate in front of him. It was the first time she'd spoken, and her voice was much lower than Will expected.

"Thank you, ma'am. Smells great."

Rose didn't sit down. "We know what you are. Grover's got a soft spot for your kind, but you're going to have to move on after you eat."

Will was eating ravenously and didn't look up. "I understand," he said with a full mouth.

"Rose, will you please fetch a clean towel?" Grover asked. "Thank you."

As Rose left the kitchen, Grover leaned in close to Will. "Tell me what's going on out there. Are you with the resistance? Is the fighting this far upvalley?"

Will finished his last bite and wiped his lips with his sleeve. He studied Grover's leathery face. Hard, outdoor living had worn him down, making it difficult to tell his age, but his eyes still had a youthful glimmer of curiosity in them.

"I don't know. I've been running from the UP for two days, and my wife—" Will choked on the words, and his throat tightened as he said them. "I have a young daughter and I need to get to her as quickly as possible."

"Here's the towel," Rose said, coming back into the kitchen. "There's a wash room around back. You can use it on your way out."

"Much obliged, ma'am. And thank you for the food."

"You're welcome. Now go on and get that cut cleaned up."

Will let the water run into the sink in the washroom at the back of the house. When it got warm, he took a long breath and scooped a handful onto his cheek. A pain burned deep into his jaw while brown, dried blood washed off into the white sink. Will hadn't felt warm water in many days, and he let it run over his hands and forearms. The pain in his cheek radiated across his forehead, and his battered arms shook under the water.

Will thought again of his wife. How he'd begged her to stay in the work camp, to let him go alone. Tears formed in his eyes and he held the towel against his bloodied face.

Grover was waiting for him on the back porch when he emerged.

"Thank you for your kindness," Will said quietly.

"Here, take this. It'll help you on the road. I ain't got no use for it around here," Grover said, handing him a brown paper bag. "If you continue along the road, you'll see an old barn next to a farmhouse just up the way. That's the Taylors' barn. They never go out there this time of year. You can stay out of sight and get some rest there. Let that cut close up." He looked up at the sky and said, "The rain will start up again soon. You need to be careful."

Will shook Grover's hand.

"Good luck, son."

Will was out in the darkness along the edge of the road when he looked into the bag. In the low light, he could see half a loaf of bread rolled in a cloth, and below it was a revolver. The matte-black steel was cold in Will's callused hand. He opened the cylinder to see the dimpled ends of six brass bullets.

CHAPTER TWO

It was mid-morning when Will awoke from a night of delirious dreams. The rain from the night before had ended, and the faint putrid smell of it hung in the air. Lying still and blinking, Will gently brushed his fingertips over the wound on his aching cheek and stared up at the ceiling of the barn from his bed of dusty hay. His mouth was dry, and hunger pulled on him from a pit in his stomach. All of the previous day's agony sat like a strange half-reality in his foggy mind, blending with the fading memories of his dreams.

Will closed his eyes and saw the face of an unfamiliar child. That face morphed into another, then another, then another. The faces of twenty different children of varying ages came to him in succession, then all at once they were screaming at him. Will opened his eyes and the vision was gone, and he was once again staring at the ceiling.

Since returning from the war, Will was plagued with such visions. He had told no one about them and didn't know what they meant. They appeared like fragmented memories of events that had never happened or hadn't happened yet. He saw the faces of people he'd never met in perfect detail. He didn't care to have another vision for as long as he lived and, without exception, each time he had one, it left him with an uneasy feeling of dread.

Sitting up, he reached for the grimy paper bag that the old man had given him. Tearing a short piece of the stale bread, he began to chew, and a sharp needle of pain threaded around his cheek and shot down his neck. After a second piece, to give his aching skull a break, he took the bullets out of the handgun, spun the cylinder, and replaced each of them carefully.

Will rose and tucked the gun into his belt under the back of his coat. He was about to sneak out of the barn when he heard a diesel motor in the distance. He froze.

Moments later tires were crunching on the gravel driveway between the barn and farmhouse. He crept to the edge of the closed barn doors and peered out through a crack in the old boards.

How had they found him? Had the old man betrayed him? The wife? It was quiet in the barn, and Will could hear his pulse, a sharp thrumming against his eardrums deep inside his aching head.

He knew the light blue uniforms of the Administration's UP soldiers and had worn one himself for many years. The uniform was instantly recognizable as the only clothing in the Valley colored in any significant way. The Valley Administration supposedly had a large storage of Sudanese indigo from a time long gone. When mixed with the natural tones of the crude, unbleached Valley cotton, the dye created a patchy light blue uniform, invariably worn by each young man in the Valley at some point in his life. The same light blue that Will had once donned with pride invoked fear in most Valley residents.

He watched as two soldiers stepped down from a rusted white jeep and looked around the yard. Their uniforms looked worn and faded in the morning light. Will's instincts took over and, without thinking, he assessed their weapons, strengths, and weaknesses. Both soldiers were in their twenties, one barely so. The older of the two carried a handgun in a holster on his hip and looked tired and haggard beyond his years.

Will's mind raced through various scenarios as the soldiers knocked loudly on the front door of the farmhouse. An old woman pushed the screen door open and hunkered in the doorway talking to the soldiers. Will couldn't make out what was being said, but pulled the gun from his belt, knowing what was about to happen. He hadn't been in this specific situation before but had seen his fair share of violent conflict. His own calmness often surprised him in the face of mortal danger.

After their brief conversation, the soldier pushed his way past the old woman into the house. She let the screen door slam shut and followed him inside while the second soldier stood with his rifle on the porch, nervously scanning the yard. Moments later, the screen door opened, and a young man emerged from the house followed by the soldier with his gun drawn. Will could see the young man's face panic-stricken as he held both his hands in the air.

"Leave the boy be," Will heard the old woman scream as she followed the soldier onto the porch. "He's injured."

The boy stumbled on a stiff leg and fell down the porch steps.

"Get up," said the soldier, "or I'll shoot you right here."

The boy pushed himself back up onto his feet and limped into the driveway.

"You thought you could hide. Thought we wouldn't find you?" The soldier followed him while reaching into his back pocket for a long zip tie. "Down on your knees in front of the jeep. Hands out. Now."

While the old woman wailed, the soldier secured the boy's arms to the front bumper bar of the jeep. Going to the front seat, he returned with a long black club. He reached down and pulled the boy's shirt over his head and hit him hard on the bare skin of his upper back. The boy yelled in pain, going limp onto the ground in front of the jeep.

"Who else is hiding? You have friends from other farms who we don't know about?"

The boy didn't respond, and the soldier hit him again across the shoulders. From behind the barn doors, Will could hear the loud thuds of the club against the boy's bare back.

"Go ahead. Speak up. Where do we find the other cowards hiding?"

An old man pushed open the screen door and hobbled onto the porch, leaning hard and shaky on a cane.

"That's enough," he yelled, his old feeble voice barely traversing the yard. "The boy knows nothing."

"Shut your mouth, old man," said the soldier turning to him, the sweat on his brow reflecting the morning sun.

"He's got a bum leg. We asked him to stay here to help us. It's our fault, not his."

The soldier turned back to the boy and poked him with the club.

"Where are the others hiding?"

The boy stayed silent.

"Alright, you don't want to talk? Maybe your grandma will." Turning to the younger soldier, he said, "Bring her down here."

"No," yelled the boy, struggling under the shirt wrapped over his head. "Leave her alone."

The second grabbed the old woman and drug her from the porch to the feet of the other soldier. The boy continued to struggle against the zip ties.

Will's fists were clenched, and he was frozen behind the barn doors. *You need to get to your daughter,* he told himself. *Don't interfere. The soldiers will be gone soon, and you can move on.*

The soldier poked at the old woman with his club.

Will raised a fist to his mouth.

"Alright, that's enough," he said to himself behind the barn door.

He kicked the barn doors open in front of him and, while raising his gun, crossed the yard at a run in the direction of the two soldiers. Will was on them before they had a chance to move.

"Drop it," Will shouted at the soldier whose club was lifted. Turning to the younger one, he said, "If I see you go for that rifle, I'll shoot you where you stand. Both of you put your guns on the ground in front of you."

Will was breathing hard, and both soldiers stood with their mouths open, not moving. "Go on. Slowly now. Put 'em down," Will repeated, his voice cold and hard.

The younger soldier fumbled with the strap of his rifle, pulling it over his neck, then set the gun carefully on the porch in front of him. The older soldier didn't move, sizing Will up with the flicker of his eye. Will took a step forward and raised the gun to his head, causing him to second guess whatever plan he'd been stewing. He dropped the club onto the gravel, pulled the gun from his holster, and carefully set it on the ground.

"Move to the tree and sit with your back to it," Will commanded.

"Who are you?" asked the older soldier.

"I'm nobody. Turn around." Will removed the zip ties from the soldier's back pocket.

The two did as they were told and sat with their legs out in front on the ground below the leafless sycamore that loomed over the farmhouse yard. Will tied their arms together around the tree, then lifted the old woman to her feet.

"Do you have a way to cut him free?" Will asked her, nodding to the boy.

"Yes. Thank you," said the old woman looking up at Will through watery eyes. She limped past the old man on the porch and into the house, returning with a pair of garden clippers. While the old woman pulled his shirt back down over the boy's reddened back, Will clipped the zip tie.

The boy embraced his grandma. "Are you okay?" he asked.

"I'm fine."

"Thank you, mister," the boy said, turning to Will, cringing at the pain in his back.

As he turned to face him, Will looked at the boy for the first time. He was a late teenager, a good ten years younger than Will. He had a boy's round face, but his skin was freckled and sunburnt. His hair was the color of light straw, streaked almost white in parts. His pale blue eyes were deeply bloodshot.

"I'm Zach," the boy said, extending his hand.

"I'm Will."

Will could see the boy's eyes drift to the wound on his cheek, and he once again felt conscious of his pain.

"Where did you come from?" Zach asked, looking at the open barn doors.

"I was just passing by."

"Can we do anything to help you?" Zach asked.

"No, I need to move on." Will looked over at the two soldiers tied to each other around the tree. "And you should, too."

"What do you mean?" the boy asked with a puzzled look.

"I was in the UP," Will said. "More of them will come for you when these two don't check in." Turning to the grandma, Will said, "You have to go somewhere as soon as possible."

"We'll be fine. We have a place to hide."

"Grandma," Zach said, "will you take those guns and the club to the porch?"

"Sure," said the old woman.

"Then help Pa sit back down."

Zach nodded to Will to follow him around the back of the parked jeep.

"Are you a resistance fighter?" Zach whispered once they were out of earshot of the two soldiers.

"No, just headed downvalley."

"Downvalley? What part?"

"Gonzales."

"Gonzales," Zach repeated, looking surprised. "I've never been farther than Greenfield."

Above them, a cloud moved in front of the sun. Will looked around the jeep at the soldiers on the ground, then up to study the sky.

"I have to get going now," Will said, stuffing the handgun back into his belt.

"I'll go with you."

Will looked at him and scoffed. "No, you won't."

"Come on. I have nothing here. I have nowhere else to go. More UP will come, you said it yourself, and I'll be shipped off to the border zone, or worse." Zach paused and looked down at his leg. "My limp is getting better. I can help you get to Gonzales."

"Look, kid, I understand. I do. But there are people after me. It's dangerous where I'm headed."

"I know the old farm roads and fields between here and Greenfield."

"Where are your parents?"

"Collected several years ago." Zach looked at the ground and bit on his lip. "We haven't heard from them since."

Will witnessed the woman coax the confused old man back inside the house. Hunger pulled on the pit of his stomach, and he glanced back at the open barn doors where he'd left the brown bag with the remaining bread.

He looked into the distance, considering his options.

After he didn't reply, Zach whispered, "I can walk in the rain."

Will took a step back away from the boy and looked him up and down in surprise.

"What did you say?" Will asked.

"You heard me," Zach whispered.

"How do you know?"

"It doesn't make me sick. Never has."

"Who else knows about this?"

"My parents knew."

Will looked at the boy for a long time as if he were studying an animal in the zoo. He'd heard rumors of such people but had never met one and doubted if it were true. The screen door slammed, and the old woman came out onto the porch.

"Alright," Will said after a long pause. "Pack a bag, and don't bring a bunch of unnecessary stuff. Something you can walk with all day. One pack, with food and water in it. And bring a pack for me. We have ten minutes."

"Thank you," Zach said as he rushed past the old woman into the house to pack.

Will picked up the soldiers' weapons from the porch.

"You watch over him," the old woman said.

"I can't promise he'll be safe," Will said while hoisting the rifle over his shoulder. "It's dangerous where we're headed."

The old woman held onto Will's forearm and looked up at him. "You watch after him," she repeated.

Will nodded.

They were interrupted by a shout from one of the soldiers. "Hey, are you just going to leave us out here?" he yelled, craning his neck to look at Will and the old woman.

"Do you want me to take care of them?" Will asked.

"No, I can handle it. You two need to get going."

"Leave them there a couple of hours after we've gone before doing anything," Will said.

"I might just leave them out in the rain."

"Your choice."

The old woman studied Will, then with a smile and nod said, "Alright then, I'll help him pack some food."

Will went through the jeep and collected what ammunition he could. Zach returned with a pack for Will and another one already loaded on his back.

As Zach said his goodbyes on the porch, the clouds were rolling away. Will could feel the heat of the day rising. Behind the farmhouse, steam rose in the fields where the sun warmed the soggy earth. Will loaded the ammunition into his pack and took a bite of the stale bread he recovered from the floor of the barn. As he chewed, the pain in his cheek shot through him and ran down his neck. He gently touched the wound, and his fingertips came away wet with blood.

He thought about his daughter, alone in Gonzales, wondering where he was. His wife's pale face covered by sand flashed across his mind. Anger enveloped him like a disease. Both hands were clenched into tight fists and his fingernails bit into his palms.

CHAPTER THREE

During the night, the rain had come in waves, pulsing in a loud and deadly rhythm on the rooftops. Muddy water rose in the lower Salinas and ran over the sand bight through the low-lying salt marshes and into the cold Pacific, forming a brown mushroom cloud. Beyond the dirty billow, beyond the slow rotation of an ancient raft of plastic, in what was once called the Monterey Bay, dolphins gathered to wait for the upwelling, with no human eye to witness their healthy numbers nor human aggression to disturb their quiet community.

Ben Harrison awoke cold and alone in the predawn darkness. He had dreamed of a deep and abiding sickness that came into him in every breath and a heat in his throat that couldn't be coughed out. Lying awake, he listened to the rain on the window and wondered if it was changing. What would become of the Valley? What *had* become of the Valley in which he once believed so deeply?

The sun was rising when Ben closed the door of his apartment and walked toward the elevator. Halfway down the hallway, he stopped to peer up at a flickering fluorescent bulb. Five such lights had gone out in the last year and were never replaced. The back of his neck grew tight as he continued to stare into the blinking uncertain light, then it went out, and that small stretch of hallway was left dim. Ben looked up and down the hallway, wondering how many lights would go before someone required action.

He had a natural inclination toward scientific thought and wanted to get a stepladder, deactivate one light each day, and record the point at which any of his neighbors complained. Only through malfunction did the objects of the world expose their true nature. Would the world fall apart one light at a time, and what was it like to preside over a subtle slip into darkness?

Fourteen floors down, the elevator door opened to the cold, smoky light of the foyer where a young man stood waiting.

"Good morning, Minister," he said, standing straight and pulling on his light blue uniform as Ben exited the elevator. The guard looked like a boy barely out of his teen years. Although Ben was only in his mid-thirties, he often felt old, as the UP guards and soldiers got younger and younger.

"Good morning," Ben repeated.

"I've been advised to take you on a different route to the laboratory this morning."

"Why is that?"

"Last night, before the rain began, there were reports of resistance activity in the Boronda Sector."

Ben nodded.

"Okay, hold here," said the guard, holding out his hand.

While Ben waited, the guard walked out the glass doors into a covered parking area. He waved to an awaiting black vehicle. The car pulled forward, and the guard opened the back door and motioned to Ben. Once Ben was inside, the guard slammed the door and got into the front passenger seat.

"Good morning, Minister Harrison," said the driver as the car rolled out of the covered entrance and down an empty street.

"Good morning. It's been a few weeks."

"Well, I've had a bunch of assignments for the Manager. Glad to be back on my regular duty. How are you, sir?"

"Fine." Ben wondered how much truth the driver wanted to hear. "Things could be better with our efforts to fix the rain."

"I'm sure you'll figure something out," said the driver as he down-shifted loudly and sped through a large puddle. "As you know, we can't go through the Boronda, so the drive will be longer than we'd like."

"How long?"

"Twenty minutes, tops," said the driver.

"What's the forecast?"

"Supposed to be dry for the entire morning. Doesn't look like it though," the driver said, leaning his head down near the steering wheel and peering up into the looming clouds.

"Ahead on the right," said the guard.

"I see it," said the driver. He slowed and came around the only other car on the street, a blue sedan stopped in the middle of the lane.

"Give it plenty of room," said the guard.

In the driver's seat of the car, a man sat slumped over the wheel as if he were asleep.

"Keep moving," the guard said as the driver slowed the car. "We're not stopping."

Ben shifted in his seat, struggling to see the man through the fogged window as they slowly rolled by.

"Stop the car," he yelled.

"Sir, we were told to not stop for any reason," the guard said, turning around to face Ben in the back seat.

"I don't care what you were told. That man could be in trouble."

"Sir, it could rain any minute," the driver said, studying the sky.

"Pull over right here," Ben commanded.

The guard and driver looked at each other. "Alright, let me get out first," the guard said.

The driver stopped the car, and the young guard jumped out with his rifle.

"I have a bad feeling about this, sir," said the driver. "I'll keep the car running."

As Ben stepped out of the back seat, the smell of sulfur in the air was overwhelming. The guard had drawn his weapon and stood away from the car, frantically scanning the edge of the road and the buildings beyond with his rifle.

Ben approached the blue sedan cautiously from the front. The reflection of the gray sky on the windshield made it difficult to see the driver's seat. As he came around the side, he could see that the driver was still buckled in his seat. His mouth and eyes were wide open. Ben knocked on the window. No response. His heart raced as he opened the driver's door. Nothing inside the car moved.

"Hurry, sir," the guard yelled, looking up at the sky.

Ben picked up the man's hand to check for a pulse, but it was stiff and cold to the touch. He reached across, unbuckled his seatbelt, and pushed him forward onto the steering wheel. With the dead man slumped forward, Ben reached for his wallet in his back pocket.

The smell of sulfur intensified, and Ben felt light-headed. His throat burned with every breath.

"Sir, we need to get back into our car," the guard yelled in a cracked voice.

Ben took short quick breaths and scanned the rest of the sedan. The interior was empty except for a briefcase that sat on the back seat behind the dead driver. Ben put the wallet into his jacket pocket and reached into the back seat for the briefcase. He closed the driver's door again and headed back toward the guard.

"Quickly, get inside," said the guard, holding the back door open for Ben.

The doors slammed, and the driver sped forward. Inside the car, the air felt drier, and Ben's breath came more easily. The burning in his throat subsided.

"How do you explain that?" Ben asked as he looked through the man's wallet.

"Not sure, Minister."

"The car should have protected him from the rain."

The driver looked at the guard, who looked back at him. Neither man answered.

"He was dry," Ben said.

Both the driver and the guard looked forward, waiting for the other to speak.

"What are you not telling me?" Ben asked.

"Sir, we've heard rumors of people dying even when dry."

"Impossible," Ben protested.

"I don't know, sir. You're the expert. Just letting you know that rumors have circulated."

Ben looked at the Valley Administration identification card in the wallet. "That man worked for the Administration. You're saying he could have died in the rain while driving home last night?"

The driver shrugged. The guard watched the road ahead in silence.

Ben continued, "That man's family, if he has one, needs to know what happened. Someone needs to come back to recover the body."

"We'll make sure someone is sent out, sir."

Ben sat back in his seat, trying to collect his thoughts. He had feared this as a possibility with the rain but didn't know how it would come. He watched the mud-stained bases of tall buildings pass. Weak, dispersed light showed on their east-facing facades while black clouds accumulated above them.

They entered the city center. Tall buildings loomed above, many of which looked abandoned, but none were so. The streets were lined with hastily-built sidewalk covers, little tunnels of corrugated tin sheeting on wooden scaffolding. The street stretched out in front of them, rutted, pocked, and deserted. It had been years since anyone outside the Administration operated an automobile.

The first droplets of rain hit the windshield.

"This was supposed to hold off for another hour," said the guard. "How far out are we?"

"Five minutes. Four if I speed."

"Well, pick it up then."

"Sir, it's beginning to rain, and we've been told to take every precaution." The guard reached under the seat and retrieved a black gas mask. "Can you please put this on until we arrive, or the rain stops?"

Ben took the black rubber mask and looked at it. "What is this? This won't help."

"Here it comes," said the driver, gripping the wheel tightly.

They drove into a wall of rain, and it pounded the windshield of the car.

"Please, Minister. We've been asked to have you wear the mask if the rain started. Your cooperation is important."

Ben smelled the latex of the mask, fine white powder on black rubber, as he took his glasses off and set them on his lap. He pulled the gas mask over his head and pushed it tight against his face by holding the filter port. He inhaled through his nose and the rubber suctioned onto his cheeks.

The driver sped through the open streets, then slowed as he approached the guard tower and gate of the Valley Administration Building.

"Hurry up. Open it," the driver said under his breath.

"A gas mask," Ben said ten minutes later, standing in his lab. He was speaking to a younger man in a white lab coat.

"How did they think that would help?"

"They told me that people are dying in the rain in closed cars." As he said the words Ben felt a sickening nervousness in his stomach.

"Impossible."

"We found an Administration technician dead in his car. Stopped right in the middle of the lane, still buckled in."

Ben stared out the lab window and shivered. Stories below, rain drilled down onto the pavement. A constellation of noxious water droplets was mapped out on the lab's windowpanes, half-spheres each with a halo of condensation around them.

"Do you think it could be volatilized into the air?" Ben asked.

"I don't see how, but I suppose anything is possible now."

Ben shook his head. "What have we done?"

CHAPTER FOUR

Will and Zach crossed the mud causeway above soggy fields of black earth. Will followed Zach and watched him limp with the UP rifle tied to his pack.

The boy stopped and looked up. "It'll be getting dark soon and the rain will start. We need to find shelter." He turned around to face Will.

"Let's keep moving. We can walk in the dark." Will motioned ahead of them to push on.

"Aren't you afraid of the rain coming?"

"I am. More afraid of not making it to Gonzales soon, though."

"The farther downvalley we get, the worse the rains will become."

"I know."

The afternoon sun went down, and the smooth trunks of eucalyptus trees edging the fields turned the color of steel. They walked on tufts of weedy grass above the mud through cart paths between black expanses of partially planted fields. In the distance they could see the line of flickering yellow lights from Administration trucks high on the longvalley highway, their Doppler whirr permeating the silence.

A dispersed white cloud from the evening fires drifted upvalley, and Will could smell it over the scent of wet loam all around him. They came to a clearing where they could see lights in the downvalley distance.

"Should we stop in on one of those farmhouses? I think I smell meat cooking," Zach said.

"It's too dangerous. Any of those houses could be filled with UP sympathizers."

Zach didn't respond.

"There's no way for us to know. We should only stop when we need to," Will said, but the smell of the sweet smoke brought on pangs of hunger.

They came to a place where the path between fields narrowed and went down into a low wash. The arroyo willows arched over them on both sides, making it too dark to see well. Will walked cautiously in front of Zach and could hear his uneven steps a few feet behind. As the path climbed back up onto the levee, Will heard a quiet but distinct click to his right side.

"Hold it right there. Neither of you move." An old man with a wild silver beard and greasy baseball cap stepped out of the trees.

The old man held a crossbow with the aluminum-tipped arrow pointed at Will's chest. He aimed the crossbow at Zach, then back at Will, who turned while raising his hands. Nobody spoke, and he waited to see what the old man would do.

He spoke directly to Will. "Tell your friend to lie down that long-barrel or I'll put this arrow right through you."

Will turned to Zach and nodded, who bent and set the gun down. He came back up with his hands up.

"You two ain't unifieds are you?"

"No, we're just walking downvalley. Passing by," Will replied.

"Didn't think so. Resistance?"

"No."

The old man seemed to speak to himself. "Fools out here in the rain. I ain't picking up no more dead bodies on my property. You," he said, pointing to Zach with the crossbow, "get up here with your friend." Zach shuffled toward Will while the old man considered the two with an undisguised look of irritation. "Can't you two smell the rain comin'? You're goin' to die out here in about fifteen minutes. You can either move off my property and become someone else's problem or get under some shelter 'til it passes."

"Where do we go?" Will asked.

"Head up that way," the old man said, nodding and pointing with the arrow, "and don't go trying anything stupid."

He picked up the rifle and followed them onto the levee. They went down the other side to a wide dirt road leading uphill to a gathering of run-down buildings with farm implements strewn about.

"Go on up into that door ahead."

Will followed Zach up the stairs onto a weathered deck around a trailer set down on wooden cribbage six feet off the ground. They hesitated and looked back at the old man, who was at the bottom of the steps. From where they stood Will could see back into the Valley along the path from where they'd come. A breeze had begun to blow, and Will could smell sulfur in the air.

"Go on. Whatcha waiting for?"

Will turned the nob and pushed the hollow door open. Inside it was warm and bright and smelled of baked beans. The trailer was a one-room affair. A mattress on a frayed blue carpet was at the far end. A potbellied stove sat on loosely placed bricks. Closer to them was a small table near a window that looked over the darkening Valley. An iron skillet on the cooktop was full of something dark brown.

Will and Zach waited while the old man stomped his shoes on the doormat, came inside, and closed the door behind him. No sooner had he closed the door than the first heavy drops of rain came down on the roof and deck.

"Hear that? By now you'd be runnin' around, faces burnin', tryin' to find shelter. From where I sat eatin', I could see you comin' for a mile. You ought to be more careful. There ain't as many friendlies left in this part of the Valley anymore. Only gets worse downvalley. Grab those crates and have a seat there." He pointed to the table while laying the rifle against the wall.

"I got some of my dinner left in that skillet. Less you have a problem with it, I'll dole it out halfways."

"No problem at all. Thank you," Zach said.

The old man looked at Will, waiting for him to respond.

"Sure," Will said, lifting a hand to his aching cheek.

"You need to pull that cut together, son, or it ain't ever going to heal right. I got some strips I'll give you after you eat."

Will nodded.

"Alright, I'm gonna set down my bow and get you food. I'm goin' to ask you to remove that pistol you've been hidin' in your belt and set it down over by the rifle. You'll have your guns back before you leave."

"Sounds fair," Zach said, looking at Will.

Will reluctantly took the pistol from his belt and set it on the floor by the rifle.

The old man went to a cupboard, then to the skillet, and came back with two bowls of food. Will hadn't realized how hungry he was until the bowl was set in front of him.

"Name's Elbridge."

"Thanks, Elbridge. I'm Zach, that's Will."

They ate in silence while the old man took off his cap, exposing a thick head of poorly cut silver hair. His nose was big and round and lighter in color than the rest of his tanned face. The white and black hairs of his mustache curved over his upper lip, and he parted them with his thumb and forefinger while watching them eat. The backs of his hands were like a parched lakebed, cracked and dried, with little hexagonal islands of peeling skin. All three men looked out the window and listened to the rain as it grew louder.

"Don't talk much, do you, Will?" Elbridge asked.

Will looked up from his bowl. "Guess not."

"Where you two headed?"

Zach looked at Will, then back to the old man. "Downvalley."

"Seems like that's the wrong way to be headed, into more rain and more trouble."

"What do you mean, more trouble?" Zach asked.

"I heard they're collecting people downvalley, closer to UP headquarters. Clearing out whole areas."

"Where'd you hear that?" Will asked.

"A man came by here a few days back, walking alone, headed downvalley, too. Begging me for food. Said he'd been transferred to one of them upvalley work camps. But he escaped. Told me nearly all the people in his town had been collected."

"Did he say where he was from?" Will asked.

"Chualar." The old man shook his head. "Where you from?" he asked Zach.

"Outside King City."

"Wheat country."

"You ever been that far upvalley?" Zach asked.

The old man stared indignantly at Zach. "Son, I've been around a long time. I've been all over this Valley and outside it, too."

A look of disbelief stretched across Zach's face, and he looked to Will for confirmation that the old man wasn't to be trusted. Will studied the food in his bowl.

"You're too young to know this, but this Valley hasn't always been the way it is now, and it sure as hell ain't the only place in the world." He shook his head slowly and looked at Will. "You have no idea what's been lost. Things you only read about in what few books are left, I've seen in person."

"Like what?" Zach asked.

The old man just shook his head and seemed to get lost in thought. "If somethin's gone and nobody knows it was ever here, does it matter?" the old man asked himself quietly.

"I think it does," Will said while crushing an ant as it passed across the windowsill. The old man eyed him.

"Tell you what. Them little Argentinian ants know the rain better than any of us. I can tell how their lines change, how they get agitated when it's about to start. They seem to know in advance. Never seen 'em be wrong about it neither."

Will picked up a crushed ant and looked at it while the old man went on.

"Ain't many insects left in this part of the Valley or any animals for that matter. But them ants don't seem to have any problem with it. Saw a line of them comin' in out of the full rain just yesterday, wet as could be."

"I don't understand why the UP would be collecting more people. What are they looking for? Who will work the fields?" Zach asked.

"Like I said, I don't know. They need more people to guard that wall, I guess."

"The same thing happened to me," Will said, feeling a rare urge to speak.

Both Zach and Eldridge stared at him. "What did?"

"Last week my wife and I got pulled out of the fields and transferred to an upvalley work camp, separated from our daughter."

Both men were silent, waiting for him to go on. Will sat for a moment, collecting his thoughts. Conversation never came easily to him, and he felt like he was forcing the words out.

Finally, he said, "I heard similar rumors in the camp, that children were being left at schools all up and down the Valley. All their parents collected. It's been over a week since I've seen Helen." Will choked on the words of the last sentence. "I'm headed downvalley to get her." He could feel a dark pressure building in his chest.

"Where's your wife?" the old man asked, nervously pulling on his beard.

"We escaped from the camp together, but a guard injured her. We made it a day and a half until she couldn't go any further," Will said, staring into his empty bowl. "That was yesterday."

Nobody spoke. Zach looked away, and the old man stared up at the ceiling.

"I'm so sorry, son. Are they comin' after you?"

Will nodded. "Likely."

Through glistening eyes, he looked out the window to the wet darkness beyond and smelled the bitter formic acid from the crushed ant on his fingers. Thinking about their collection and transfer to the labor camp filled him with rage. Every promise he'd made to himself after returning from the war would now have to be broken. On that sandy bank above the Salinas, Willie Taft told his wife over and over again that he'd stop at nothing to get back to their daughter. He whispered it to her, even after she'd died.

He turned to the old man, then to Zach, both catching his eyes, then looking away. "When the rain lets up, we need to get going."

The old man knocked on the table. "You're a full two days walk from Gonzalez. It'll likely rain through the night." He rose. "You two can lie down here, get some rest until the rain stops. In the meantime, let's get that cut pulled together and get you two outfitted for the rest of your walk. If you're tryin' to get to Gonzales, you'll need every bit of help you can get."

CHAPTER FIVE

"This is where he buried her."

Three men stood on the riverbank above a willow thicket. Down the gravely slope, a partially exhumed woman laid pale and face-up in the sand.

"She died in the rain?"

"Hard to tell. Maybe from that wound on her side."

"How long ago did they escape?"

"Two days. Killed a guard on the way out, too."

Millard Fillmore brushed his long black coat over the holster on his hip and squatted on his heels at the top of the bank. The others stood nearby, watching him carefully. He ran a finger across a black clod of soil, then picked it up and smelled it. He rose and looked into the downvalley distance. He bit the toothpick, which sat permanently in his mouth, and wiggled it between his teeth.

"Willie Taft?" Millard asked.

"Yup."

"You sure?"

"Yup."

"I'll find him." After a long pause, Millard said, "Dead or alive."

"It don't matter all that much which. There hasn't been a single successful escape since I've been running that camp, and hell if I'm goin' to start allowin' it now."

"What about the woman?" Millard asked.

"We'll recover the body."

Millard turned back to the two men from where he'd been staring into the distance. "You ought to tie her to a fence pole next to the camp barracks."

The two men glanced at each other.

Millard continued, "As a warning to the other workers."

"I guess that would get the message across. A might bit extreme. Anyway, the way news travels around that camp, everyone'll know by afternoon that she died during the escape. They'll also know that I sent you to recover Taft, which ought to help dissuade folks from future attempts."

"Tracks lead downvalley." Millard pointed to the soil, but there were no obvious tracks. "Shouldn't be hard to stay on his trail."

"He's probably dead already. If the downvalley weather hasn't already killed him, I'm sure you'll find him."

"Likely."

"Well, get to it then. Bring him back, like the others. Quickly as possible."

"Yes, sir," Millard said in a sarcastic tone and walked away without another word.

The two men kept their eyes on him as he went.

"That's a tough one right there," one of the men said when Millard was out of earshot.

"I ain't met a man with a colder heart, but damn good at what he does. Decorated war veteran. Captain in the UP. You've probably heard the stories."

"Cold-blooded killer is what I heard."

"He's that, too."

"Wouldn't want him on my trail. The guy who escaped last month, I heard he only brought his head back."

"That's true. Willie Taft's the same, though."

"What do you mean?"

"Served in the UP at the border. Decorated hero himself. Rumors are he was ruthless. Guess we're lucky he only killed one guard on their way out."

"Millard's the right man for the job then."

"He'll bring Taft back, or he won't come back at all."

CHAPTER SIX

"Excuse me, Minister, the Valley Manager has sent for you."

Ben Harrison turned around from his lab bench to see a UP guard at the door.

"When?"

"He'd like to see you now, sir."

"Alright, you can tell him I'll be up in fifteen minutes."

"Sir?"

"Fifteen minutes."

"He's expecting you now."

"Alright." Ben looked at the microscope and slides laid out on his bench. "Let me get changed."

"I'll wait in the hall."

Ben went back to his microscope, carefully took the slide off the stage, and racked it on a shelf above the bench. He grabbed a second slide off the rack, mounted it on the scope, bent over the lenses, and scanned the slide.

"Still living," he said quietly to himself while taking the second slide out of the microscope.

He removed his white coat, carefully hung it on a peg on the wall, and went out into the hallway where the guard awaited him.

"Hello, Valley Manager," Ben said after an elevator ride and walk down a long sterile hallway.

"Hello, Science Minister," said the Manager, looking up from his desk. "You can close the door behind you and leave us alone," he said to the guard.

Through a wide window behind the Manager's desk, Ben could see Salinas City. High rise apartment buildings stretched out and faded into the dingy mist. It had begun to rain again.

As the guard left, Ben sat in the green metal chair facing the Manager's desk. "What can I do for you?"

"Any progress? Anything to report?" the Valley Manager asked.

His eyes were cold and remote, sunken into his pale, almost larval skin. He looked as if he didn't care about Ben's answer but was instead calculating his next move. From across his wide desk, a rotten smell escaped from the Manager's thin lips. Although they'd known each other for years, the Manager never ceased to make Ben uneasy.

"The tests aren't working. I need more rats, and I'd like to move on to pigs soon. Our experiments with the ants yielded no results."

"Remind me what you were doing with the ants."

"Several species of ants in the Valley have some natural resistance to the bacterial toxins in the rain."

"Right."

"They're the only animals that seem to be unaffected. We've made so many different solutions from the ants, but none affected the bacteria in collected rainwater."

The Manager shook his head in disappointment. "Keep working."

Ben nodded. "I had to wear a gas mask on my way here this morning. Is it true that people are dying without getting wet?"

"Nothing has been confirmed."

"I don't see how it's possible," Ben spoke to himself. "I need more rain. New samples of the bacteria. We can volatilize the rain in a chamber." He looked up at the Manager. "This is not good."

"I know. We'll get to that. I have something to report to you," the Manager said.

"What is it?" Ben asked.

"We may have found some survivors."

"Of what? The rain? How?" Ben stuttered.

"Never mind that." The Manager waved his hand in front of Ben. It was an awkward and contrived gesture as if the Manager was mimicking royal pomp. "We've found three boys, various ages. As far as we know they can be out in it for as long as they want." The Manager paused and turned from Ben to look out over the city. "True rainwalkers."

"So, the rumors were true," Ben said, trying to conceal the excitement in his voice. "Where are they now?"

"We discovered them at the school in Greenfield. We're having them transferred here."

"How did you find them?" Ben asked.

The Manager sat looking at him and didn't answer.

"Goddammit." Ben rose. "How did you find them?"

"It had to be done. This rain is killing us. There will be nothing left of our great valley, or our civilization if we don't do something."

Ben shuddered. "What are you thinking? We talked about this, we all talked about it. We agreed it wouldn't happen."

The Manager's face became stony, and he stared with indifference at Ben. "*We* agreed to nothing. You watch your tone with me. We may go way back, but I could have you replaced instantly."

"We can fix this in other ways," Ben yelled.

"Fix this? You've fixed nothing. It's you and your kind tinkering with the Valley's weather that got us into this mess in the first place. Couldn't leave well enough alone."

"My kind? The rains changed long before either of us were born. What do you mean, my kind?"

"Scientists. Trying to improve the Valley. Always meddling," the Manager said.

"This Valley wouldn't exist without the rain. Do you want to return to the hundred-year droughts?"

"Unharvested crops, dead people in the fields, soldiers who can't defend the borders, and it's getting worse. Sit down." The Manager pointed to the chair and waited for Ben to sit. "We're dying, Ben. We're being attacked at every border. The wall is constantly under siege. Castroville is underwater. The upvalley oil camps are producing less and less. I don't know what else to do. We're weakened by this damn rain."

Ben shook his head and didn't respond.

"You get your people together and figure out what makes these children special and how we can replicate that in other people."

"No more screening children. No more," Ben said, pointing his finger at the Manager.

"Don't presume to tell me how to run this Valley," said the Manager, pointing back at Ben. "We need solutions, and you're failing. We're done here."

CHAPTER SEVEN

While Will and Zach slept on the floor of the old man's trailer, clouds shuddered in the darkness on the Santa Lucias at the western edge of the Valley. It was from that purple and brooding wall that rain came each night. Up on the steep ridgeline, a forest of firs basked in moonlight above a gossamer of gloom, and silence prevailed, no bird song, no hum of insects, nor hooves sneaking across soft leaves. All gone.

Marine fog rolled down the east-facing slopes and mixed in the air with microscopic debris and man-made bacteria. Each night, the Valley basin filled with clouds that rung out like an old sponge. Artificial bacteria designed by forgotten scientists in their experiments gone wrong nucleated ice around every particle of Valley dust that fell from the sky in each rain. During their descent, the bacteria filled each raindrop with a foul-smelling airborne chemical deadly to humans but neutralized in the soil within seconds.

Before sun up, water flowed off the thin flinty soils and scented shrubs of the hillsides to the riches of black mud and shapeless clumps of plowed earth on the Valley floor. The drinking water that squeezed through the deep soils into the Salinas River was once again pure. The rain affected neither the plants nor the soil fungi, so the diverse Valley crops prospered despite, and because of, each night's toxic bathing. If such were not the case, Valley residents would have starved within weeks of the first deadly rains that ended the hundred years of drought. Instead, each morning the Valley soil took on deadly water at all sides and purified it as it ran toward the enduring river at its center.

Along the entire Valley border, out past the rolling low hills of the eastern Gabilans, a high wall ran through the dust, sagebrush, and dry grass. It was a wall without end, circling the Valley, neither beginning nor ending at any location, and broken only at the guarded border crossings. Lonely young men in poorly built lookout towers were perched along the wall, watching the sun rise and feeling the dry rattling desert breath howl in from the east. Beyond their sight, far past the golden horizon, stretched a dryness so complete that life could no longer be sustained in any of it. Dead stands of brittle creosote and the broken stems of burrobush stretched across vast expanses on the surface of what was once the western North American continent.

What was beyond the uncrossable deserts, no living Valley person knew. Two generations had passed since the Regional Breakup and little accurate history was retained. With no means of long-distance travel, no contact nor even memory of contact remained with others on the eastern edge of the continent. Life in the Valley was insular, and information was sparse. Rumors circulated the Valley, most of which were false, either accidentally or purposely designed for fearmongering about the never-ending conflict with the Valley's only known neighbors, the San Benicians.

The Salinas River was swollen and churning from the night's rain when Will and Zach descended the old man's steps. Will looked at the hazy wall of clouds in the distance. The sun was rising over the low-rolling Gabilans and illuminating the Santa Lucias to the west.

This Valley was Will's home. He'd always loved it, served it, and was nearly killed twice while defending it. Although he'd never been far from the confines of its borders, he figured it was the most beautiful place in all the known world. Except for bordering San Benician territory, which he'd been in only once and was lucky to have escaped alive, he'd only heard stories of other places in the world. Paris, New York, Europe, Asia, they may as well have been on other planets.

Even though true seasons no longer existed in the Valley, this day would have fallen in early spring, and the morning was already warming. On the foothills to the east, rows of abandoned orchards with their twisted and unpruned ancient limbs bloomed beautifully in the morning dew, each releasing a melancholy sweetness that beckoned like a forgotten lover for bees that would never return.

"You two have a long walk ahead of you," said the old man. "Couldn't have asked for better weather, though."

"Thank you for your kindness," Zach said.

"Don't mention it," said the old man, still gazing at the sky. "Looks like you're free of rain for the good part of the day. Now get movin'."

"If anyone comes asking after us, we'd appreciate you forgetting we were here," Will said, working his fingertips over the new Steri-strips on his cheek.

"You got it," the old man said as he turned back to his front door.

Downvalley they went, through the warmth of the morning. They skirted the wide arroyos and dry creek beds of the Gabilans, then trudged west through the mud of the midvalley alluvial fan. Hiding in the shrubs under a culvert beneath the longvalley highway, they watched a UP convoy rumble by. Young boys in new light blue uniforms sat shoulder to shoulder on a string of old flatbed trucks, their wind-chapped faces turned downward.

"You were in the UP?" Zach asked Will as he rubbed his sore thigh.

Will took a long drink of water, then handed the bottle to Zach. He watched the trucks disappear into the distance. "A long time ago."

Zach finished drinking. "If it weren't for my hurt leg, I'd be on one of those trucks."

Will looked at Zach. He was so young, too young it seemed to be out here with him. "Consider yourself lucky."

"Do you miss being a soldier?"

Will shook his head. "I miss being a farmer. I was a soldier because I had to be."

The diesel hum of the convoy had faded, and Will rose. "Come on. We need to keep going."

By the time the sun was low and threatening its descent over the Santa Lucias, Zach and Will were on the western outskirts of a small town. They stood near a rusty tin rain shelter in the hummocks of grassy weeds at the edge of a fallow field. The other side of the field yielded abruptly to abandoned houses and old buildings. Above them, a silver water tower with faded and chipped lettering that read GREENFIELD sat like a pewter egg endwise on a stand.

Will and Zach waited and watched from a distant stand of sheoaks but could see no activity. These were recently abandoned buildings, their carefully tended yards not yet gone to seed, but no people could be seen.

"Where is everyone?" Zach asked Will after they had stood several minutes in silence.

"I don't know," Will said, looking nervously about. "We can't be seen here. The people are gone, but there are likely UP around."

"It's like the town's been cleared out."

"Yeah, let's head through it that way," Will said, pointing to the fields skirting the town to the west.

Minutes later they were walking on a path behind a hedgerow at the edge of a field when Will grabbed Zach from behind.

"Get down," he said, pulling on Zach's shoulder.

They crouched in the ditch, watching a group of low buildings with matching green roofs a short distance away. Along one roof a banner was strung that read *Today's Learners Tomorrow's Leaders*. A UP soldier in his light blue uniform stood on the blacktop of an abandoned playground. He was yelling and pointing at something.

"Can you see what's going on?" Zach asked.

"No."

Two soldiers in light blue pants, who had removed their jackets, emerged from behind one of the school buildings. Each was turned around, walking backward, dragging a bundle along the ground, while the older soldier yelled at them.

"We have to get out of here," Will whispered to Zach. "Stay low and behind the hedges."

They were about to make a break for the trees at the back of the adjacent field when they heard someone yell at them.

"Hey. Don't move."

They turned to see another UP soldier who had been off on the edge of the field urinating because his fly was still unzipped. He looked to Will like a surprised and frightened teenager, even younger than Zach.

He nervously lifted his rifle in their direction. "Stay right there. Drop your weapons and slowly put down your backpacks. I'll shoot you if I have to."

They lifted their hands slowly. Zach reached for the rifle, which he'd tied to his backpack.

"Hey," the young soldier yelled in the cracking high voice of a child. "Slowly, put it down."

Both Will and Zach dropped their bags and backed away from the soldier with their hands in the air. The rifle sat in the soil next to Zach's bag. Will studied the young soldier. He could see how his fear and inexperience distracted him, made him make small mistakes in his movements. Will was completely still, untroubled. He looked down to see Zach's hands shaking and wanted to say to him, *this is not the moment you're afraid of.*

"Now turn around. Walk toward the school."

They came across the field, their long afternoon shadows stretched out in front, on a dirt path to the playground. The UP soldier followed Zach and Will with the gun trained on them from a distance.

"I got something," the guard yelled from behind them, getting the attention of the other soldiers standing on the playground.

"What do we have here?" asked the lead soldier as they approached. "A couple of deserters? Resistance fighters maybe?" He was clearly older than the other soldiers and wore a mocking smile. He pulled his pistol from the holster on his hip and approached Will.

"So, what do you two have to say for yourselves? What're you doing out here?" He turned to the two other soldiers who had stopped dragging the bundles and said, "You two get back to work. There's still plenty to do."

"We're headed downvalley," Will said, his voice as casual as a man describing the weather. He could feel the stiff handle of the revolver tucked into his belt against his lower back. Will kept his steady hands up where the soldier could see them. He was neither nervous nor scared but wanted to deal with the soldiers and move on as quickly as possible.

"Walking downvalley, huh?" The soldier's sardonic smile returned. "Sure, you are."

Will could feel himself growing irritated. He didn't have time for this. *Let's get on with it,* he thought. He continued to wait for the right opportunity. These men weren't skilled soldiers. They were recently enlisted teenagers who had failed to even search him for his weapon. The safety was still engaged on the rifle pointed at his back.

The lead soldier could seemingly sense the complete lack of fear in Will's gaze and spoke in a hurried and nervous tone. "Looks like we got ourselves a couple of resistance fighters. Lucky us. Nobody's supposed to be in this part of the Valley. What're you doing out here?"

"Just told you, walking downvalley." Will's voice was steady. "We're headed to UP headquarters to enlist in the Valley army. If it's fine with you, we'll be on our way."

The two other soldiers returned from around the corner of the building dragging something in a canvas roll.

"You're not going anywhere," said the soldier as he turned to watch the men dragging the load. Will glanced at Zach, who was wide-eyed and panting. The two men slid the canvas roll along the asphalt to the edge of the playground where a wide hole had been dug. They unfolded the canvas to expose the bodies of three children. They kneeled and rolled each of them into the hole.

Will's mouth fell open, and he involuntarily put one of his raised hands against it. He could hear Zach gasp.

Will took a deep breath to steady himself. He lunged at the lead soldier and was on him in a step and a half. The soldier didn't have time to lift his pistol before Will grabbed him, swung him around, and held him from behind by the neck. He knocked his handgun to the ground and, with a free hand, pulled the gun from his belt to the side of the soldier's head. Will stepped back slowly, pulling the soldier with him.

"Easy now," he said to the boy soldier who had discovered them. "You move and he gets shot right here." The boy kept his gun trained on Will. "Set the rifle on the ground. I'll let him go, and we'll be on our way."

"Don't put your gun down. You shoot this man," said the lead soldier. "Don't be a damn coward."

"No, no, easy," Will said slowly, crouching behind his captive. "You shoot and everyone dies. Put the gun down."

The soldier kept the rifle raised, shakily considering his options. Five seconds passed, then Will turned the gun from the side of the soldier's head and pointed it at the boy.

"Please, put it down."

"Shoot him," the lead soldier shrieked.

The boy made a slight movement, lifting his gun in Will's direction. Will squeezed his trigger and shot the boy in the chest, who fell back while firing his rifle into the air. Will returned the gun to the side of the lead soldier's head and whipped him around in the direction of the other two soldiers.

"You two, over here now," Will commanded.

Will nodded to the handgun at his feet and said to Zach, "Grab that gun."

Zach stared at the hole. The two soldiers at the edge of the blacktop stood paralyzed, mouths agape. "Zach," Will said again, his voice louder, "grab the gun."

Zach picked up the gun and aimed it at the two soldiers.

"On your knees," Will said, pushing the soldier he was holding down in front of him. "Hands behind your head."

Will glanced at Zach, who still wore a stunned expression. He was having difficulty holding his gun steady. "Zach, we're fine. Stay calm."

"What is this, Will?" Zach asked, his face going white.

"I don't know." Will's expression remained unchanged.

With all three men lined up on their knees and Zach with the gun trained on them, Will searched them for other weapons.

"Stay right where you are." Turning to Zach, Will said, "Keep the gun on them. Shoot if they move."

Will walked to the soldier he'd shot, who was motionless on his back. He picked up his rifle, put it over his shoulder, and kneeled next to him. The boy's watery eyes were wide open, staring upward. The afternoon sky had come into them. Will felt for a pulse in his neck and found none. He let out a long sigh, then turned back to the other men.

He went to the hole at the edge of the playground. Down in that hole, crisscrossed in all directions, were the bodies of twelve children. Will held his hand to his mouth. The dead children seemed to range in age from toddlers to bodies that were as old as his daughter.

An icy shiver went through his spine as he quickly scanned the pile for any who looked like her. *She couldn't be here. She's still in Gonzales. Still alive.* He walked around the corner of the building and saw five more children lined up on a canvas tarp, ready for transport to the hole.

With the pistol still in his hand and the rifle around his shoulder, Will approached the three soldiers on their knees. He could feel sweat accumulating on his brow. His face was hot, his mouth had gone dry, and a deep burn radiated from his wounded cheek. A familiar rage grew in Will's mind, but he had learned how to suppress it.

"What's going on, Will?" Zach repeated his question as Will returned. "Why are those kids dead?"

Will approached the soldiers from behind and yelled, "What is this?"

Nobody spoke.

Will kicked the lead soldier between his shoulder blades, and he went down on his face.

"Speak." Will's voice boomed. "What happened to these children?"

Will grabbed him by the shirt collar and lifted him back up into a kneeling position.

"We were following orders," the soldier said with a look of confidence in having done the right thing. There was soil on his lips, and he spat onto the ground in front of him.

Will came around to face the soldier and kneeled to speak to him. "What have you done?"

"What they told me to do. My commander took the survivors, and we were left here to clean up. Get them all buried."

"Survivors?"

"Three of them."

Will looked up at the hole, then scanned the school buildings. He felt as if they were being watched.

Will shook the gun in the soldier's face. The desire to hit him was overwhelming. He wanted so badly to punish him, to knock the cocky look from his jaw. As a young man, Will's temper consumed and controlled him, but he'd learned during the war to squelch it, to channel it. He reached back and slapped the soldier with the butt of the gun, who rolled over and went limp on the ground.

Will drew a slow breath, stepped back, and said, "Stay where you are. Face-down on the ground. If I see you move, I'll come back and shoot each of you."

Zach backed away.

"Go grab our bags out in the field," Will commanded.

As Zach hobbled off to retrieve the bags, Will returned to the boy he'd shot. This wasn't the first person Will Taft had killed, not by a long shot, but he could remember everyone. He'd always told himself that each of them, the UP guard at the labor camp, the San Benician soldiers on the other side of the border, deserved it. Kill or be killed. Will checked again for the boy's pulse. His eyes had turned cloudy, and purple blood solidified around the open bullet hole above his sternum.

Will reached down and carefully zipped the boy's fly. "I'm sorry," he said under his breath, then rose and followed Zach downvalley.

CHAPTER EIGHT

Millard Fillmore followed two tracks along a windrow of ancient trees, past the bluish-green patches of horehound, and across a sandy bank. They were as clear to him as if someone had painted orange arrows on the ground. One man was limping. The other was a larger man with a purposeful step, heavy on the heel. These were Willie Taft's steps. He'd seen the same tracks many times before, followed them across the border.

He'd parked on the edge of the highway and walked until he picked up the tracks again. Where the footprints went down into the wash and crossed the sandy flat, he stopped. There was a third set of tracks, a troubling set. They were slight, nearly invisible, made by someone patient who had waited and watched.

It was late afternoon when he entered the thicket where he'd wait until dark to proceed. He reached into his pocket for a small metal canister, then squatted on his heels. He removed the soggy toothpick from his mouth, its blond wood frayed along the margins, and carefully put it back into the canister before extracting a new one, then he waited, surveying the many slight imprints in the hardened mud in front of him and watching the sky.

After the sun was down below the dark mass of the western Santa Lucia, Millard rose in the brown dusk. He crept up out of the wash onto the bank where he could see a collection of broken-down buildings in the distance. He saw an old man open his door, come out onto the landing, then go back inside.

Another half hour and it was dark. In the downvalley distance, a stormy darkness grew like a great sourceless vacuum of sounds and light. Millard could feel it sliding and rolling in thick sheets in his direction. It would rain soon, and he needed to hurry. He climbed the dirt path to the group of buildings on the hill. Pausing under the weeping canopy of a Peruvian pepper, he bent to pick up its shriveled pink fruit. He crushed the spicy bead between his fingers and breathed in deeply. He watched the trailer for ten more minutes before creeping through the darkness toward it. At the bottom of the steps to the trailer's door, he froze.

"Something didn't seem right. I didn't see you leave the trailer, though," Millard said without turning around.

"Don't know how many times I told you not to assume what you're seeing is real. Go on now, set that piece of yours on the ground. Then get up those stairs, or I'll put an arrow in your back."

Millard slowly pulled back his coat, extracted his handgun from the holster, and with the handle held between his thumb and forefinger, bent to set in on the ground.

"Now up the stairs."

Once he was inside and halfway across the room, Millard turned with his hands up to face Elbridge.

"Didn't think I'd ever see you again," he said as Elbridge shut the door.

"And yet, here you are, trying to sneak up to my doorstep."

"This is a business call."

"Business? You're in the business of killing people. You have no business here."

"I'm looking for a man. Escaped from the San Ardo Labor and Oil Producer's camp two days ago. You know that I know he was here, with a gimpy companion. I intend to have you tell me where they were headed."

"Doesn't matter to me what you intend to have me do."

"Look, old man. I have a job to do. I'll bring him back, dead if I have to."

"Not with my help, you won't."

"Who's the gimp?" Millard asked. "Did you arm those two men? Do they have weapons with them?"

The old man didn't answer, just stared at him along the line of his arrow.

"Alright, this is the way it's gonna be? You aren't gonna tell me anything about them? I'll find them one way or another. You're just delaying the inevitable."

"What if I put an arrow in you right now?" The old man raised the crossbow.

"You and I both know killin' me would be more trouble than it's worth to you. You got something on these two men? I know the large one, Willie Taft. He isn't a resistance fighter. Can't figure why you'd be helpin' them."

The old man grew irritated.

"You best leave those two boys be. Something terrible is happening in this Valley, and you're just helping it."

Millard looked down at his pistol, which Elbridge had placed in his belt. "Alright, you going to let me have my gun back?"

"Nope. I never suspected you'd turn into such a rotten bastard, huntin' folks for money after everything I taught you."

"How about you let me walk away then?"

Elbridge glanced out the window. "We got about a half hour 'til that rain comes. I'll let you go in about twenty-five minutes."

Millard shook his head. "Well, if you're going to send me out into the rain, how about you let me have a glass of water first?"

The old man looked to the sink. "You can get it yourself. There's well water on the counter."

Millard took two steps to the kitchen counter where he found a heavy mug in the cupboard above the sink. Methodically, he picked up the pitcher and slowly poured the cup three-quarters full. He lifted the mug to his nose, smelled it, then drank it down, swallowing loudly. Millard filled the cup a second time, this time almost to the brim.

In one swift motion, he hurled the full mug at Elbridge while ducking. The arrow stuck into the cabinetry just above his head. He lunged at the old man, who threw the crossbow at him and fumbled for the handgun in his belt. Before he could lift it, Millard was on him and swatted it away, then swung the old man around in his arms and held him in a chokehold. Millard went for his pocketknife and flipped it open with one hand on the side of the old man's neck. The tip of the knife dug into his skin, and a thick droplet of blood came forth onto his white beard.

"You were like a son to me," Elbridge said, struggling against the hold.

"Shouldn't have let me go for the water. Your kindness was always your weakness."

"Let me go," the old man pleaded.

"How soon 'til that rain really comes?" Millard asked him.

"Don't know. Less than an hour. Now let me go."

"I'll ask one last time, where were those two men headed? Don't be a fool."

"A fool? I tried to teach you everything, and this is all you became. You could have been so much better. You're the fool."

Millard dug the knife deep into Elbridge's throat. He felt a warmth on the back of his hand and saw a fine mist as blood sprayed from the old man's neck. A gurgling sound came from his open mouth, and his body went limp. Millard let him fall into a crumpled mass on the ground.

As Elbridge struggled for his last breaths, Millard kneeled next to him and whispered into his ear, "You're the only fool. Always too proud and too kind." He stood, recovered his pistol, and went to the sink to wash his hands.

Out on the trailer's wooden landing, Millard surveyed the down-valley sky, trying to calculate the time needed to return to his jeep and how long until the rain returned. He holstered his pistol, buttoned his coat, and sprinted off the deck and down the path toward his vehicle.

CHAPTER NINE

Science Minister Ben Harrison left his laboratory in the Valley Administration building in the early afternoon carrying a black leather bag. The bag wasn't heavy, but he let it rub against the side of his knee as he walked down the long hallway to the elevator for a ride down to the second floor.

Upon exiting the elevator, a tall, thin military officer greeted him with dark hooded eyes and sunken cheeks still visible beneath a short salt and pepper beard. Ben was also tall and had always been skinny, so as they shook hands the two men looked like gaunt pillars of a high bridge.

"Good afternoon, Minister."

"Colonel Adams, good afternoon. I wasn't expecting to see you here."

The colonel took his time to respond. He was a dignified, stoic, and thoughtful man. Although only in his forties, he was aged far beyond his years, a witness to the deaths of a thousand young men in too few years.

"As you know, this project has become a high priority for the Valley Manager. It was one of my units that collected the children. If you'll follow me this way, we have them waiting for you in a room down the hall."

"How are things going on the fronts?" Ben asked as they walked.

The colonel stopped and looked at him, then shrugged and looked away.

"I've known you a long time, John," Ben said. "You're the highest-ranking military officer in the Valley. What's happening?"

"Things are not as good as I'd hoped. Our efforts in the border regions need reinforcing. The Valley exclusion wall takes constant maintenance. Frequent rains have crippled us. The only saving grace is that they've also affected our enemy's ability to push forth into our territory."

"How long do we have?" Ben asked.

"Until what?"

"Until we have to contract our borders until we're invaded. Until we're overrun," Ben said.

The colonel looked down the hallway and considered the question. He spoke in a hushed voice. "I don't know. That may depend on you. We operate the best we can under the circumstances. You need to find a way to stop this incessant raining. It's getting worse by the week and has been for the last few months."

Ben didn't speak; he shook his head, letting the colonel know he'd been heard.

"Is there any progress toward a solution?" the colonel asked.

"We're trying. Our recent experiments have failed."

The colonel took a step closer. "I believe in you, Ben. Always have. We came into this administration together, and we can fix this together. Find a solution."

For a moment, the colonel held his gaze on Ben, then turned down the hallway, leaving him to follow.

Colonel Adams opened the door on a windowless room with a couch, a table with two chairs, and a stainless-steel sink in the corner. Two young boys sat on the couch, playing cards between them. A third boy, much younger than the other two, sat at the table drawing on a piece of brown paper.

"Boys," the colonel yelled, "this is Science Minister Harrison. He's also a doctor, and he's here to make sure you're healthy. Do as he says."

"You can call me Ben," Ben said as he set down his black bag, grabbed the free chair, and pulled it in front of the couch. "What are your names?"

The oldest boy spoke first. "I'm Jacob, that's Kyle, and he's Micah," he said, pointing to the young boy at the table.

"How old are you, Jacob?"

"Eight."

Ben looked at the second boy on the couch, who continued to stare down at the cards.

"Kyle's seven, but he doesn't talk much," Jacob said.

They turned to Micah, who looked up from his drawing at the table. "I'm five," he said, then he looked directly at Ben and asked, "Do you know where my mommy is?"

Ben sat silently looking at the boy, figuring his answer. "Micah, I don't know where she is, but we're trying to find her."

Ben glanced at Colonel Adams, who stood stone-faced. He felt a sickness in the pit of his stomach and a hard knot forming in his throat. Faded memories of his own mother came back to him. He was the age of the middle boy when he was taken from her. He drew a deep breath and swallowed.

"Colonel Adams, would you mind if I had time alone with these boys? I'll get them checked out."

"I'll wait in the hallway."

"Thank you."

When the door had closed, Ben looked at the youngest boy and said, "Micah, come over here and sit with us on the couch."

The boy put down his pencil, rose, and looked Ben over. "You're going to get my mommy to come here?"

"I'll try."

Micah crossed the room and sat between the two older boys after they had collected the cards.

"What's in your bag?" the oldest boy asked.

"A stethoscope and some other doctor's stuff. Oh, hold on, I also have something else in there." Ben reached for his bag, pulled out three suckers, and handed them to the boys. The second boy took the sucker without looking up at Ben. "Go ahead, you can have them now."

Ben watched the boys unwrap the candies and look them over.

"What is it?" the youngest boy asked.

"It's a candy, you lick it. Go ahead. I think you'll like it."

The oldest boy was the first to try it. He licked it carefully, then with eyes lit up, put the whole sucker into his mouth. The other boys watched him. He nodded to them and said, "It's good."

"How are you feeling?" Ben asked the oldest boy.

"I want to go back home," he answered, holding the sucker out of his mouth and studying it.

"Where is home for you?"

"Greenfield. The school, I guess."

"So, you didn't get sick when you were out in the rain?" Ben asked, choosing his words cautiously.

The boy's face grew stiff. He looked down at his lap where he held the sucker. After a long silence, he said, "I felt nothing."

The boy shrugged and didn't look up at Ben.

"You're fine now." Ben put his hand on the boy's knee, and he flinched.

"I don't want to go back into the rain," Micah said, his voice muffled by the sucker in his mouth.

"Did the rain make you feel sick, Micah?" Ben asked.

The boy shook his head.

"Well, you're not going to have to go back."

Just then a knock came on the door. Ben rose and opened it. A young man in a lab coat was waiting outside.

"Come in."

"Boys, this is Theodore. He works with me in the lab here in the Valley Administration Building. He'll help you."

"Can he get my mommy to come here?" Micah asked.

"I'm going to try right now while you talk to Theodore. Then I'll come back in a while."

Theodore followed Ben into the hallway. The door closed behind them, and the colonel joined them.

"They're younger than I thought they'd be," Theodore said.

"The elementary school in Greenfield."

"Where are these kids' parents?" Ben asked the colonel.

"I don't know. Dead or in an upvalley camp."

"Do we have the full names of the children? Can you find the parents?" Ben asked.

"I can try. The Valley Manager said nothing about bringing their parents here."

"Don't worry about that. I'll take care of it. You send word of the names of these three to the camps and see if we can find their parents." Turning to his assistant, Ben said, "We need to run the tests on them immediately. We need to draw blood."

"Sure."

"And take your time. Those boys have been through a lot. Start by feeding them."

"Of course," he said, then opened the door and reentered the room.

When the door shut again, Ben looked at the colonel.

"Are you under orders to find more children?" Ben asked.

The Colonel hesitated, then stared at Ben. "I'm not at liberty to speak about any ongoing operations, Ben."

"What? John, come on. How long have we served together?" Ben asked.

"Many years, but I have my orders from the Manager, and you do, too."

"You realize what you're doing, right?"

The Colonel looked down at his polished black shoes and seemed to hesitate before speaking.

"Do you mean what *we* are doing, Ben?" he asked in a loud whisper, looking up and down the hallway. "You're a part of this."

Ben said nothing.

"We're facing defeat. Not just at the border zones, but our entire Valley could be overrun. You need to find a way to stop this incessant rain or we'll find a way to operate in it. And that's what the Manager is doing." Speaking in an accusatory tone, he asked, "What have you been doing?"

"Planes are flying the downvalley airspace tomorrow with a different seeding formula we just finished creating."

"Do you think it will work?"

"Not likely." Ben let out a long and involuntary sigh. "The seedings have stopped affecting anything."

"Do you know why it's getting worse?"

"I don't. Potentially there's been a new mutation. We've run tests, collected the bacteria in every different type of cloud, killed everything from rats to pigs in the rain, and still can't figure out what's changing."

"Something needs to happen soon."

"We'll figure this out. These children hold the answer."

"I don't like it any more than you do, Ben. It's despicable. This isn't the Valley I grew up serving."

"Me neither."

The colonel looked nervously over Ben's shoulder down the hallway. "Maybe there's a better way, and maybe it won't always be like this, but for now we're desperate. Sacrifices must be made. The Manager has his plan, and I'll do everything in my power to protect my men and the people of this Valley."

"Even the children?"

The colonel didn't answer.

"There's got to be a better way," Ben said.

"I hope we can find it."

Colonel Adams stood tall and straight and looked at Ben.

"For the Valley," he said.

"For the Valley," Ben repeated.

The colonel did a ceremonial turn on his heels and stiffly walked away.

CHAPTER TEN

The Salinas Valley is in a place once called Northern California. A long, narrow swale created over millennia by the collision and subduction of the Pacific Plate under the Continental. A river cuts a deep trough along the Valley floor, running downvalley from the rolling hills of San Ardo in the south, eventually falling into the Pacific far to the north. The Valley's deep and rich soils are the result of eons of erosion from the steep Santa Lucias on the Valley's western edge, combined with the slow slumping of the straw-colored Gabilans along the east.

The first inhabitants of this remarkable place arrived fourteen thousand years ago, a band of disconnected survivors wandering in from the cold north, wild and superstitious. The Valley became a Native American oath to fertility, bisected by a well-worn path down its center. Souls waiting for the taking; warring, violent, yet peaceful in their own way, but not at all prepared for what was coming. They had their stories and legends, all of which eventually came to pass.

Along their path from the south came a marauding band of dried up European foreigners attempting trickiness at first, and when that didn't work, brutal, unmatched force. From the path grew a road, the Camino Real, connecting the religious hovels, new pueblos, and presidios. The Valley was forever changed. The Camino went from San Miguel Arcángel to San Antonia de Padua to Nuestra Señora de la Soledad to the San Carlos Borroméo de Carmelo before leaving the Valley north to San Francisco.

In the times between the religious missions and before the rains, the camino was named U.S. Highway 101, but that name had no soul and didn't last. At the end of the one-hundred-year drought, after the death of two hundred million trees and the regional breakups, the

Valley Administration replaced Highway 101 with the longvalley freeway, raising it high above the Valley floor, isolating it from any farm road intersections. An unbroken bridge, the freeway floated above the Valley, between the work camps and oil fields in the south to the downvalley headquarters of Salinas City in the north.

Halfway between its origin and destination, the longvalley freeway crossed above the old town of Gonzales. The same well-worn route that connected that original pueblo to all the rest still ran through that town, but it ended abruptly in a field of broccoli and beyond that corn, then grapes, then lettuce, then cotton.

The residents of Gonzales, who worked the endless surrounding fields, never had access to the longvalley highway as it ran over the top of their town. They could hear it and look up from the muddy fields to watch official vehicles and military caravans sweep by. The fruits of their labor were pulled up a guarded ramp, the only access to the highway from Gonzales, to be set on the edge, loaded and carried downvalley to Salinas City. Each week a single trailer was lowered down the ramp for the town Manager to disburse its vital contents.

In this way, Gonzales did not differ from any of the old midvalley pueblos. They were isolated, peaceful, and the day-to-day agrarian lives of the residents, at least those who didn't disappear in the night, was quiet and easy. It was easy, at least, until the sickening rains became more frequent in the crowded downvalley areas, then life got hard throughout the Valley.

Shortly after the rains worsened, there was more activity on the guarded longvalley ramps as residents of Gonzales and other towns on the Valley floor started being collected for work in the upvalley labor and oil-producing camps. Families were separated as teenage boys were collected for compulsory UP service while their parents made one-way trips up the guarded ramp, never to be seen again.

A school sits on the western edge of Gonzales, two blocks from the Native American path that originally ran through the Valley. For many years that school serviced the children of the families who worked the fields. When the older people of Gonzales began to be collected, the school became a refuge for the orphaned children. The gymnasium filled with cots where the children, ranging in age from five to fourteen, slept. Those same children ate together in the cafeteria. The few parents and grandparents left in the town did what they could to help with the orphaned children, but the responsibility of day-to-day care fell on the schoolteachers when there were any left.

Mary McElroy stayed with the children. She was one of five teachers at the school before the collections began and soon became the only remaining adult at the school. Her husband, who was in charge of loading the ramp trailers, didn't come back from work one day, only two months after they were married. Mary went looking for him, pounding on the ramp's guard station door but was given no information. Eventually, the Gonzales town Manager received word that Mary's husband had died in an escape attempt with several others on the outskirts of the San Ardo labor camp.

All Mary had then were the school children, and she loved them dearly. Each night the children would gather around her in the gymnasium to hear her read aloud and say her soft-spoken words of hope and encouragement, before returning to their beds to silently pine for their parents. Each night Mary would close the book she was reading, look up at the ever-increasing circle of children around her, and say the same words, and some students mouthed the Valley prayer with her.

> *Let us hope that tomorrow brings sunshine and*
> *the rain is light and short.*
> *Let us hope that tomorrow we are rejoined*
> *with our families.*
> *Let us hope that Gonzales, and the Valley beyond,*
> *stay peaceful and prosperous.*
> *Bring us sunshine, respite from the rain, and our*
> *loved ones home safe.*
> *For the Valley.*

Mary would finish and all the children, in their tired little voices, would repeat, "For the Valley."

Before being collected, Will and Hannah Taft arrived at the school each afternoon to retrieve their daughter Helen, always fresh from the fields, smiling and laughing. One afternoon they didn't arrive. Helen waited and waited. As it got dark, Mary came out to the curb at the front of the school where she sat and put her arm around her. When the rain was threatening, Mary carried her to a cot waiting in the gym, her eleven-year-old, lanky frame sobbing and limp over Mary's body.

Three days after Will and Hannah Taft disappeared, everything at the school changed. Mary was returning to the gym from the adjacent classroom carrying a jar of Vaseline. It had rained hard the night before, and Mary skipped around several puddles that formed on the sidewalks under the covered walkways.

"Breakfast in fifteen minutes. Make sure you're ready and your beds are made," Mary said as she entered the gymnasium through the double doors. The gym hummed with the noise of children milling about and speaking to each other. Some sat on their cots or dressed themselves.

Mary took a seat next to Helen on her cot and said, "Here, pull your hair back away from your ear." Mary took a small dollop of Vaseline and wiped it gently on the scabs behind Helen's right ear. Helen winced at the cold jelly.

"You have to stop touching it."

"I know. It itches so bad though." Helen looked across the gym. "Do you think my parents are coming back today?"

"I hope so." Mary could see Helen trying to read her face. "We'll see. Here, you can keep this Vaseline. I'd like you to put a little behind your ear every couple of hours or whenever you feel like you have to itch it. Okay?"

"Okay. Thank you, Miss McElroy."

"We'll be fine, Helen. I bet they'll be back anytime now."

"Who are they?" Helen asked, pointing to five men in light blue uniforms standing at the gymnasium doorway.

Mary faced the soldiers.

"Ma'am, are you in charge here?" asked one of the men in a booming voice that silenced the children.

"I am."

"Can we speak with you outside?"

The soft thud of Mary's footfall on the maple gym floor was audible in the dead silence as she walked between cots toward the door.

"Ma'am, I'm Captain Wilson," one of the soldiers said when they were out on the sidewalk in front of the gym, the doors closed behind them.

Mary was struck by how wide he seemed. He was wearing some kind of padding under his uniform, his chest curved into his shoulders in one large, amorphous mass. He differed from the other soldiers and stood a few feet from them. He had no helmet nor gloves, while the others, who were clearly younger than he, were heavily armed. He had a freckled face and thick red hair that sat in tight curls against his head.

The other soldiers, all teenagers, seemed almost jolly, clueless, and ready to follow orders. Each of them proudly held a rifle in a black-gloved hand, wore a helmet with goggles strapped to the front, and black flack vests hung with several tools. Mary figured these were soldiers from the border zone, which she had never seen before. This was what some of her previous students had become.

"I'm Mary McElroy. The teacher here," Mary said, studying them.

None but the green-eyed leader spoke, and he did so sternly, slowly, and with his brow furrowed.

"Miss McElroy, we're here under orders to watch over these children."

"Watch over them?"

"Yes," the captain said, glancing down at his watch. "We'll be here for the next few days."

"Why? What's this about?"

"We have our orders. Is there a dry room we can occupy during the rain? Somewhere away from the children?"

"Yes, you can have a classroom."

Captain Wilson removed a small note pad and pen from the front pocket of his light blue jacket. Looking down on Mary, he asked, "How many children are here in the school?"

"Twenty-two," Mary said. "No, twenty-three."

"Twenty-three," he said, repeating her answer while writing it down.

"And the oldest child? How old is he or she?"

"Fourteen." Mary eyed him while he wrote. "What's this about? What's going on?"

"Is he the tallest child here at the school?" he asked, ignoring her questions.

"I guess," Mary responded, confused.

"About how tall is he?"

"About my height." The captain looked up from his notepad and regarded Mary.

"Okay."

He put the note pad away and turned to the others. "Follow Miss McElroy to the classroom, collect the gear and set up there. We'll need to start immediately." Turning back to Mary, he said, "Ma'am, can you show these men to the room?"

Mary looked at him and didn't move. Since she'd never seen a soldier as apparently high ranking as Captain Wilson, she took the opportunity to question him. "Do you know the whereabouts of any of these children's parents? Where have the people of Gonzales been taken?" Mary stood tall and tried to look strong, but fear was burgeoning inside her. Her heart bounced up into her throat.

Captain Wilson stared down on her blankly. He seemed almost incapable of reading any of her emotions. Mary followed with another question. "Are you planning to reunite any of these children with their parents?"

Apparently realizing he wasn't going to be able to ignore her, he said, "I don't know, Ma'am. We're only here to watch over the children." Clearly becoming irritated, he continued, "I have no more information for you. We have our orders. Can you please show these men to the room?"

Mary looked all five over, then said, "Come with me."

CHAPTER ELEVEN

The sun was setting on Will and Zach as they moved through the gunpowder fallow fields outside the abandoned town of Soledad. Will stopped several times to scan the horizon behind them.

"What are you looking for?" Zach asked.

"I have a feeling we're being followed." Turning to look downvalley, he said, "We'll need shelter in the next hour or so."

At dusk, on the edge of a field of lettuce that spread in straight rows that faded into the heavy night sky, they found an old cinderblock pump house with a dilapidated pump in the center of the small room. They sat opposite each other on the concrete floor, legs stretched out in front of them, leaning on their packs as the first raindrops began to fall. Will drifted off to sleep.

Sometime later, the rain intensified, and he awoke. He sat and listened to the distant rumble, the hissing sounds of a running river from all directions, and drips of different sizes pinging off the metal roof. The building whispered all around him. He looked across the tangle of rusted metal pipes to see that Zach was gone. The pump house door was ajar, and Will could smell sulfur and garlic blowing in on the air. Each breath was heavy and uncomfortable to take in.

He rose and looked out into the darkness. Zach's pack hung from a bolt on the pump head. The rain had brought on colder temperatures, so he pulled the door closed and sat back down. He crossed his arms over his lower chest and drifted off to sleep again. Just before sleep came, Will had a vision of a tall chain-link fence, with the fingers of children gripping tightly to the wire. The chain link expanded and enclosed a complex of low buildings where skulls lined the inside of the fence. It expanded once more and Will saw a fence around the whole Valley, and it was burning. Crimson flames belched out sparks that rose on a plume of black smoke into the night sky. He opened his eyes to the darkness of the pump house and the flames from his vision still streaked his field of view. As his vision faded, he drifted off to sleep once again.

Will had no idea how long he'd been asleep when Zach pulled open the door. He was soaked, and his hair laid in thick blond lines stuck to his forehead. He stood like a statue in the darkness, where Will could hear drips of water falling off him onto the dry concrete. Zach took off his jacket and hung it on the pump.

"I always think the next time I get wet is the time that's going to kill me, but it never does."

"Can you smell the sulfur?"

"Sure. It smells like garlic cooking to me. It's more intense when you get out into it. I don't mind it. It's always stunk like that."

"When was your first time?"

"I was young. Nine. On my way back from the barn and I found a salamander at the creek crossing. Can you imagine? I'd never seen anything like it. Had seen no actual wild animals at all, for that matter. It had a beautiful orange belly. It didn't move, so I picked it up right out of the creek. I held it and played with it. Amazing. I was distracted, and before I knew it, it was raining on me. I ran in the rain back to the barn, thinking I was going to die, but I didn't. Didn't even feel anything. When I got back to the barn I was soaked. I dried off there and told nobody."

"Your parents never found out?"

"No, not then. A few weeks later my younger brother and I were making hay forts in the barn when a downpour started. I told him I could go out into the rain and it didn't hurt me. He wouldn't believe me, so I walked out into it. He was seven at the time."

Zach sat silently for a long moment. Will waited. His voice was a hollow whisper when it returned. "I didn't think I was the only one, that I was special. I thought when I survived that first rain that, that, that it was just all stories." After another long silence, Zach continued, "I wanted to show everyone that it was just stories. I encouraged him to come out and see for himself."

Will heard the soft thud of Zach's fist hitting the concrete.

"It was pouring, and he barely made it out to me before he went down. By the time I had drug him back to the barn, he wasn't breathing."

"I'm so sorry," Will said into the darkness across the room. His voice wasn't much more than a whisper. He was only four feet away, but Zach was a shapeless figure in the dark, a formless voice drifting toward him.

"I was just a kid. I didn't know."

"I understand."

"When it rains hard like it did tonight, I've opened my mouth and let the rainwater fill me up. Nothing. I've let it soak me for hours, until my skin is wrinkled, and still nothing. Yet he was gone in seconds."

Will sat silently and listened to the words, not knowing what to say. He could hear Zach shivering. After a long silence Will said, "We do dumb things when we're kids."

"How old is your daughter?"

"She's eleven."

"Eleven," Zach repeated.

"You'll meet her in three days, maybe two if we get good weather." As he said it, he hoped what he'd just said was true. Will let his palms rest on the concrete floor below him. It felt cold and damp. "I've been gone from her for too many days now. I'm sure she's so scared without me and Hannah there."

"Is that your wife?"

"Yeah." Will was silent for a long time, staring into the darkness. Shapes twirled and morphed on the inside of the dark pump house wall. He continued, "It was just a few days ago, but if I think about her now, I can't remember her face. I have to hold on to her memory, but the harder I try to think of her, the more she seems to disappear."

Will stroked the cold concrete with the tips of his fingers. Zach was silent. The rain subsided.

The weak light from a diffuse moon shrouded by dense clouds was completely gone and the darkness in the pump house was now complete. It made him feel hidden and safe. At that moment he felt like he could say all the loving things that were in his heart, something he always had difficulty doing. Now it was all he wanted to do, but she wasn't there to hear them. His wife was gone, her cold body in the sands above the Salinas.

It was an image he couldn't exile from his brain, yet as hard as he tried, he couldn't remember her face. He wanted to tell her how much he loved her and how much he appreciated her, that she was his source of purpose. As the thoughts came to him, he realized he may never say them.

They had fought the night before they escaped from the camp, him trying to convince her to stay and let him go alone, her refusing to separate. He went over each word of the conversation, asking himself what he could have said differently.

Will pulled a slow breath into his lungs, and the rank stench of the rain made him cough.

"Did you see anything else out there?" Will finally asked. "An easy way around or through Soledad for us when it stops raining in the morning?"

"I scouted along the edge of the longvalley highway. It was raining hard, and I couldn't see much. Two cars passed on the highway, going slow. There was one thing at the longvalley ramp. Some kind of truck parked at the top of the ramp. Not a typical loader."

"What do you mean?"

"I saw it in the lights of the passing trucks. I didn't get a great view of it, but it looked like a modified army vehicle."

"A jeep with a silver corrugated roof?"

"Maybe. Like I said, it was dark and raining pretty hard."

"Are you sure that's what you saw?"

"No. I didn't want passing cars to see me, so I didn't go any closer. Maybe it's nothing."

"Maybe," Will said, but he had an idea whose jeep it was. In the complete darkness of the pump house, he no longer felt safe.

CHAPTER TWELVE

Salinas City was unusually cold and bright on the morning that Science Minister Ben Harrison stepped out of a car onto the sidewalk behind the Valley Administration Building. Normally a thick shroud blanketed the city with pestilent low clouds. A smell that fluctuated between burnt gunpowder, sulfur, and cooked garlic had hung in the city air for so long that Ben could no longer smell it, but this morning was different. It was clear and crisp. A smell redolent of exhaust and the rotting sweetness from the overflowing marshes that surrounded the city blew over the skyline through the tall buildings on a cold northerly breeze. All the buildings, sidewalks, and streets seemed washed clean by the previous night's torrential rain.

The copper morning sun amplified and reflected in a million droplets that shined on the large windows of the Administration building as Ben looked up before entering. While the UP guard waited, Ben turned slowly in a full circle, looking at the other buildings and the low mountains barely visible in the distance. His breath raised a white cloud around him.

As he peered upward, a droplet of water from a ghost cloud landed on the lens of his glasses and ran down his cheek. Ben could feel the skin go briefly numb where the droplet had touched him. He removed his glasses and quickly wiped the water from his cheek. Upon returning his glasses to his head, he felt a brief wave of nausea come over him. He studied the sky, trying to discover the origin of the raindrop, but nothing in the unblemished blue above him remotely resembled a cloud. He breathed deeply and entered the building.

His assistant was waiting for him in the hallway beyond the revolving doors.

"Morning, sir."

"It's a beautiful one. I haven't felt the urge to stay outside in a long time. I'm feeling it this morning, though. Have you been outside?"

"Why?"

"The sun is shining."

"I'll have to go out later," he said skeptically, peering out the glass front of the building. He turned back to Ben and said, "There are more, sir."

"More what?"

"More survivors. Children."

"Here?"

"Yes, Colonel Adams's men brought them in last night."

"How many are there?"

"Two. A girl and a younger boy."

Ben shivered, thinking about what those children had been through.

"Have you talked to them?" Ben asked.

"No. There's a guard outside the door."

"Is Colonel Adams here?"

"I haven't seen him."

"Alright, get ready to run the same tests on these two. Check vitals, draw blood, and make sure they've eaten. Be comforting."

"Of course."

"I'll be there shortly," Ben said, turning down the hallway.

In the elevator, Ben rubbed the skin on his cheek, and the feeling had not yet fully recovered. He wondered if in the seconds before dying in the rain a person felt pain or numbness. He thought of the children again and hoped for the latter. He removed his coat and hung it on the rack next to the lab door. As he turned, he was startled by the Valley Manager who was standing right behind him.

"Sorry to sneak up on you like that."

The Valley Manager's perennial halitosis filled the space between them. Ben tried not to recoil.

"Valley Manager."

"You've heard we found two more?"

"Just now."

"Can you believe it?" the Manager said with excitement.

Ben shook his head.

"I wonder how many more there are. I wonder if you're one."

Ben rubbed his numb cheek. "Not likely."

"A much greater portion of our population than we know of could actually be able to survive it."

"I hope we don't have to find out."

"If we weren't being overrun at the borders, we could screen the soldiers. One soldier who can operate in the rain is worth fifty who can't."

"Screen?" Ben felt himself getting angry. "You're talking about killing people? Our people. Our Valley's children."

The Valley Manager ignored his comments. "Finding soldiers who could survive the rain is what we need, but we can't afford to screen them. The children are the answer."

Ben tried to calm himself, realizing that arguing would do no good.

The Manager continued, "I've heard reports of escalating resistance activity here in the city. With the heavier rains, we haven't been able to counter." The Valley Manager looked over Ben's shoulder to the windows. "This sunshine should help."

Both men turned to look out the window. The morning sky reflected off the black lab bench countertops.

"Is this the result of yesterday's seeding flight?" the Valley Manager asked, nodding to the windows.

"It's too early to tell. The bacteria we released were meant to compete with those causing the rain, but I'm not sure how it could work so quickly."

"Well, I hope you're on to something. Our men need sun, and a lot more of it."

"We'll know more when we do the sampling flight later this afternoon," Ben said.

"Do more sampling, make another seeding flight. Do whatever you need to do. If these rains don't stop, the whole Valley, our way of life, is in jeopardy."

"I'm doing everything I can," Ben said. He could feel himself starting to sweat. Something about the way the Manager watched him while he spoke made him nervous. He couldn't help but feel that the screening of children was partly due to his failure to improve the weather. He made his face blank, as he knew the Manager would take advantage of his guilt.

"In the meantime, keep working with the children. Figure out how they survive and if we can replicate it."

Ben nodded.

The Manager stared at him and looked disappointed. Ben averted his eyes, lowering his gaze to the ground. "Don't fail here. We found them for you; now figure out if we can make more. I'm also discussing with Colonel Adams and other UP command ways we can use them at the border."

"Do you ever think about your parents?" Ben asked, trying to change the subject. "Do you remember when you were their age?"

"Why?" The Valley Manager stared at him indifferently. "They're gone. They were from a bygone and weak generation. One that tried to create peace and failed."

"What if we weren't taken from them when we were so young?" Ben asked.

"We weren't taken; they gave us up." The Manager eyed Ben, trying to read his face. "It was best for the Valley."

Ben looked down at his feet again. "I suppose," he said. "I think it would help if we found these children's parents."

"Why?" the Manager asked.

"I'd like to test their parents, see if the resistance is hereditary."

"I'll ask Colonel Adams to have them found."

Ben watched the Valley Manager closely, realizing at that moment he was probably lying. No such effort to find the children's parents would be made.

The Valley Manager nodded at Ben.

"For the Valley," he said.

"For the Valley," Ben repeated.

The Manager spun around and left the lab. Ben leaned against the bench, thinking about the rain and what to do next. There were too many problems, too many variables. He felt overwhelmed. *One thing at a time,* he told himself.

A short time later, the door opened, and his lab assistant walked in.

"Sir, I did the exam and drew blood from the two children who just arrived. You need to come see something immediately."

CHAPTER THIRTEEN

When the rain stopped in the early morning hours, the pump house grew cold and silent. Will awoke with pangs of hunger and discomfort from the damp concrete below him. He looked across at Zach, who was hunched over his pack, sleeping. The light of the seasick dawn snuck under the pump house door. Will rose, tiptoed over Zach, and pulled it open. A sheet of silver light came over the eastern Gabilans, and heavy clouds still hung in the downvalley sky.

"Zach." Will toed his thigh with the tip of his boot. "Zach. Wake up. It's clear, and we have to get going before the sun is up."

Zach's blond hair was stuck to his forehead where it had dried from the night before. The rest of his hair was a mess of bleached streaks and yellow hay. A peach fuzz of white hairs crossed his upper lip, faded on his cheekbones, and became thicker once again above his eyes. Longer white hairs projected randomly from his freckled chin, and it occurred to Will that Zach may have never shaved. He opened his eyes slowly and looked up at Will, not yet distinguishing the real world from his dreams. He blinked rapidly. His eyes were bloodshot on the inside corners with visible red veins that ran from the sapphire blue irises around the inside of the eyeball. He stared up at Will, his pupils contracting in the line of blue light coming through the open door.

In an attempt to say something, Zach just grunted.

A minute later they were both outside the pump house, Zach rubbing his eyes with the heel of his palm, peering into the distance.

"Soledad," Will said. "Looks like it's still raining there."

"I heard rumors about Soledad growing up. What happened?"

"I'm not sure. I think it was destroyed and abandoned in the early wars. There hasn't been a loading ramp down to it from the longvalley in many years."

Across the patchwork plane of agricultural fields, they could see buildings rising in a tight cluster. A white-water tower on a cross-braced metal tripod stood above the town and leaned as if it would fall at any minute. Beyond the water tower were purple stands of weedy eucalyptus, a jagged forest planted by the wind.

"Should we go around?" Zach asked.

"We don't have time. We're exposed out here. We need to move quickly, stay alongside the highway, out of sight. Past Soledad, we can get back down into the riverbed. Hopefully, the rain holds off for the rest of the day."

"It doesn't look good," Zach said, nodding to the clouds above Soledad. "I'm hungry."

"Take this," Will said, tearing the last heel of bread from the old man in half. "We'll get more food soon."

They went out across the muddy plane toward the town as the morning warmed. Water puddled between black furrows in the fields, and the heavy clay stuck to their boots with each step. In a field of unharvested broccoli, Zach bent to snap the green heads from the plants. The first rays of sun fell onto the Valley floor.

"Don't eat too much of that," Will said, nibbling on a head himself. "You'll just get sick."

"I'm so hungry," Zach said with green partially chewed broccoli in his teeth.

"I know. Me, too."

They entered the town along an abandoned road whose pavement had long ago been destroyed. Mustard weed and horehound had taken advantage of cracks in the tarmac, making the road barely recognizable for long stretches. Some houses still stood with entire walls missing, their insides exposed and streaked with mud. At other lots along the road, all that remained was a concrete foundation or a stack of bricks, once a chimney, slowly being melted by the rain.

They came through a neighborhood in which the roofs of each house were collapsed, as if some giant had carelessly pushed over each house, smashing some and tearing others apart. Splintered wood was strewn about, wrecked, rusted, and stripped cars, everything covered with a thin layer of brown mud. They came to the front of a house where they looked over a low picket fence into a deep, wide hole in the ground. The facade of the house seemed undamaged, but there was nothing left of it beyond the front wall.

"This place looks like it got bombed long ago," Zach said.

"Yeah," Will said, looking around nervously. "Do you get the sense we're being watched?"

Zach looked around. "No. Everything seems abandoned."

"I don't think it is. Stay alert and keep that rifle in your hands."

They came out of the old residential neighborhoods, past an empty school, and into the downtown where the destruction was much greater. Not a single pane of glass remained unbroken. Many of the buildings looked like they had blown out from the inside, spewing their guts onto the street in front of them. Street trees, long dead, were cracked, splintered, and torn in half in front of the buildings.

A sign that read Soledad Hotel hung cockeyed from a wire and swayed slightly. They crouched at the corner of an old brick building and surveyed the street and destroyed buildings beyond. A slight breeze blew on the morning sun, and a loud truck passed on the longvalley highway above them. Zach picked up a glass block that had fallen out of the wall below the hotel sign.

"You think one of these places has anything to eat?" he asked.

"I'm sure people have gone through them hundreds of times and got everything valuable."

"There," Will said, pointing along the sidewalk. "Let's move around these buildings and keep going."

They hustled along the sidewalk, coming out into the street to go around piles of rubble. On the far side of downtown, they crossed in front of a deserted gas station and convenience store with its windows and glass front door completely gone.

"There has to be something to eat in there," Zach said, limping behind Will.

"I doubt it."

"Come on, we should at least check."

Will looked around. "Alright, quickly."

Pebbles of safety glass crunched underfoot as they stepped through the broken windows into the store. Metal shelving units were bare and knocked over. They moved around the store purposefully, driven by their hunger, looking at each shelf, then behind the counter on which sat the open and empty register.

"Here," Zach said, pulling a brown cardboard box from a lower shelf behind the counter.

Behind the box was a smaller white box with bold red and green lettering on the side that said Hostess Fruit Pie. Zach tore the box open, and inside were four oblong pillows, individually wrapped in blue, green, and red plastic. *Apple Fruit Pie with Real Fruit Filling.* Zach set the rifle down on the counter, threw a fruit pie to Will, and pulled open another.

When Will opened the wrapping, the smell of caramel and cinnamon came to his nose. He slipped the folded pastry out of the bag, looked it over carefully, then bit down on the orange, blistered crust with its layer of hardened, opaque, sugar glaze. The crust was firm but yielded a soft gelatinous apple jelly from the inside. His senses were invaded, and he instantly felt ravenous. Each bite was better than the previous. Everything he'd eaten in his life to that point was a mild version of the apple pie. Hints of the pie were in the apple orchard whose fruit he'd picked as a youth. Each bite contained the best parts of the apple, the orchard, and the golden afternoon sun from those happy days long gone.

No caramel, nor cinnamon essence, flavors from a world long ago gone, had ever dissolved on Will's palette. He breathed deeply, and aromatic flavors, not natural, but created by man for man, coated his nasal passage. For all its vague familiarity, he couldn't remember having tasted anything like it before. For a moment, and Will didn't recognize it, there was no pain in his cheek, no dead wife and missing daughter, just hunger being satisfied.

He looked at Zach, whose eyes were closed, and he was chewing intently with one hand on his lips. Zach opened his eye and saw Will looking at him.

"What is this?" he asked with a full mouth.

"I don't know."

"So good."

Will stopped chewing. He was looking out of the darkness of the convenience store in the bright light of the parking lot. Four men stood there, three of whom had rifles pointed in their direction. A shudder went through him. Two more men stepped around the front edge of the building, each with a gun aimed at them.

"Don't move," one of the men yelled.

Will put the last bite of pie into his mouth, and he could see Zach do the same.

"Hands up," came a second command.

They both lifted their hands, Zach, with an apple pie in each.

"Turn around and face the back wall. Keep your hands where we can see them."

Will was grabbed from behind, the handgun removed from his belt, and patted down the length of his body.

"Alright, outside. Walk slowly or you'll get shot."

Will squinted as the bright morning light reflected off the old pavement in the gas station parking lot, blinding him briefly before his eyes adjusted. With their hands still raised, they were marched into the middle of the lot where the four men awaited them. The two men standing on the edge of the group fanned out and formed a wide circle, one with his gun on Will, the other on Zach.

Will knew these men were seasoned, clearly not UP soldiers. Each man was focused and careful, and they were in their late thirties or forties, much too old for the UP.

"What did you find in there?" the man in the middle of the group of four asked, looking at the wrapped pastries in Zach's hands.

Zach made no effort to answer. His white hair was ablaze in the morning sun, and he looked down on the leader, a Hispanic man who was much shorter than he.

"Let's see. Hand those over."

Zach handed him one of the pies.

"Both of them."

He reluctantly relinquished the second pie to the leader's outstretched and waiting hand. He took the pies and handed them to the man standing next to him and turned to Will.

"What are you two doing here?"

"We're headed to Gonzales," Will answered.

"For what reason?"

"I live there. My daughter is there."

"Willie Taft?" The leader took a step back to get a better view of Will. The men turned to watch the surprise on their leader's face. Will squinted at him and turned his head slightly to the side. "Willie. It's me, Jose."

"Jose Alvarez?" Will looked the man up and down.

Jose spoke to the other men. "I know this man. We served together."

Jose smiled, and wrinkles formed in the dark skin around his eyes. He was a thin, muscular man, maybe Will's age, but could have been ten years older. His leathery skin exposed the fact that he'd spent most of his adult life in the sun. His face was darkly peppered with a five-o'clock shadow. Despite his rugged appearance, he had undeniable warmth in his large brown eyes.

Will couldn't help but smile when he saw Jose's grin. "I thought you were dead," Will said. "You never made it back."

Jose approached Will with his arms open. They hugged, each pounding the other on the upper back.

"I thought I'd never see you again," Will said.

"Well, here I am. Not everyone who didn't come back from the border is dead."

Confusion crossed Will's face. "Yeah, but the explosion. I was there."

"I survived. Barely." Jose lifted his flannel and exposed a large scar that went across his stomach and ended at what looked like a hole in his skin that never filled in. The scar was much lighter than the dark skin surrounding it. "It took a long time to recover. It didn't take long to escape though."

"And now you're here in Soledad?"

Jose jerked his head and looked around. "Were you followed?"

Will looked back into the upvalley distance. "I don't think so," he said, but he wasn't sure.

Everyone looked but saw nothing moving.

"We're too exposed here," Jose said, no longer smiling. "Let's get out of the open."

Jose nodded to his men, then turned back to Will and said, "Follow us. We'll talk more in the prison."

CHAPTER FOURTEEN

Mary McElroy watched while the soldiers toiled in the grass field behind the school. They began work early in the morning the day after they arrived. As Mary crossed from the cafeteria to the gym, she heard the repetitive high metallic ping of a fence post pounder. From their two trucks, the soldiers had unloaded fencing material, posts, wire, and tools. By lunch on the first day they had methodically erected an L-shaped run of tall fence.

At lunch, Mary stepped out of the cafeteria and sat on a concrete bench watching them from a distance. The soldiers were eating on the grass. Their leader seemed sullen and sat by himself facing the distant fields while the four younger men ate, smiled, and laughed at each other.

After lunch, Mary checked their progress from the gym, where she had told the children to stay inside. In the mid-afternoon, the soldiers stopped work abruptly, set their tools and unused fencing material in a pile under a covered walkway, put on their helmets, gloves, and rifles, and marched out toward the Salinas River. When the soldiers had disappeared beyond a long field adjacent to the school, Mary let the children into the play yard. Mary distractedly pushed a little girl on the swing while other children played, some of whom inspected the work of the soldiers.

"What are they building, Ms. McElroy?" the girl asked.

"I don't know."

"Are they done building it?"

"I don't know."

"Are they coming back?"

"Probably."

Just then, where the Salinas cut a depressed scar through the Valley floor and a line of cottonwoods rose above the flatlands, the sound of gunshots came to Mary and the children. A moment later, more gunshots. Each distant explosion poked at Mary's nerves.

"Alright, everyone, they're just training. It's time to go back inside," Mary said loudly as the children were gathering around her. "Jason, collect your brother and go around the school and make sure everyone knows it's time to come back into the gym."

That night it barely rained, and Mary had difficulty sleeping. The faint smell of garlic and the sound of rain on the flat asphalt roof of the classroom had grown to comfort her. She thought of one of her older students whose parents had disappeared from Gonzales early on. Two weeks ago, a UP guard came to the school from the ramp guardhouse to look at the children. The guard asked the boy, who was fifteen, to come with him, and he never returned.

As she laid awake, Mary wondered about the fate of all her children. Were they to be collected by the UP, at younger and younger ages, to defend the Valley at its edges and never return? What would become of Gonzales when there were no more children? What would become of her? There were already few adults left. How could this be happening to her town, to her Valley? The recent arrival of the soldiers was unsettling. They weren't interested in collecting the children, and not knowing why they were at the school made her nervous.

Mary didn't sleep for most of the night. Drizzle from a sky that refused to fully rain coated the buildings and water ran in thin sheets at the bottom of the gutters. A loud drip rhythmically pounded the metal drain box outside the classroom. She fought the urge to let in the dismal hope that her disappeared husband would someday return. It was a thought she could no longer entertain. His faded image in her mind made it too difficult to go on with her daily work of running the school, keeping the children healthy, acquiring enough food for everyone, and in the short time that remained, teaching them to read and write. She kept her only remaining photograph of him, of their wedding party, between the pages of a bound notebook on the shelf, which she hadn't opened in months.

In the night, Mary rose from her mattress to get herself a drink of water. She carefully moved to the sink in the low light. After drinking, Mary spread the blinds on the window above the sink and peeked out into the wet schoolyard.

A shock went through her, and fear spiked in her chest. Mary didn't know if what she was seeing was real. On the other side of the yard, Captain Wilson was standing like a statue looking directly at her classroom. The drizzling rain was coming down all around him, and he was completely soaked. Mary quickly let go of the blinds, and they snapped shut. Her heart pounded, her knees felt weak, and she hadn't taken a breath. When she opened the blinds again, Captain Wilson was nowhere to be seen. Mary went to the classroom door and with shaky hands confirmed that it was locked.

Just before dawn the next morning, after lying awake for the rest of the night, Mary sipped her tea and tried to read. She had stared at the same page for ten minutes. Far to the east, an apricot-colored string of light came over the Valley wall and laid across the soft back of the Gabilans as the sun began to rise. Mary was relieved by the light it brought to the school. At that moment a familiar sound came to her, that of a fence post pounder driving a metal post into the sod in the yard. Mary went to the window and looked out to see that the night's drizzle had ended, and the sky was clearing. Each ping of metal on metal drove her attention outside.

At the sink in the corner of the room, Mary looked into the small mirror that hung on the wall behind it. She would be twenty-six in three weeks. She pulled the skin on her upper cheekbones to the side, making the significant bags under her eyes disappear. She quickly washed her face and brushed her teeth as another post was pounded. She left the empty tea mug in the sink, finished dressing, slipped on a pair of shoes, and went out the door and down the ramp of the classroom.

She was on her way to the gym when she decided to stop and look at the soldiers. The four younger men worked on a post in the enclosure's corner while Captain Wilson looked on. He turned to see Mary watching them. He nodded to her with a strange smirk, and all the fear from the previous night came rushing back. She hurried off to wake the children.

That afternoon Mary sat on a bench in the schoolyard. It was cold, and in the moments when clouds cleared, the sun warmed her slender hands as she shuffled through papers, reading paragraphs written with large pencils by small, awkward, untrained hands. She made comments on the papers and drew the occasional smiley face while watching the soldiers working on their fence.

It was now three-sided. Horizontal bars connected each post, and they were rolling out the chain link between the posts. At the corner, they cut the chain-link from the roll and returned the roll with all the other fencing supplies to the adjacent area under the covered walkway. Each soldier put on his jacket and flack vest, and within minutes Mary was watching as they marched off into the fields, with Captain Wilson trailing them.

On that second day, no gunshots rang out from the river. Mary oversaw the children on the play yard, watching the weather carefully until it was nearly dark when she corralled them into the cafeteria for a dinner of baked beans, carrots, and cornbread. During dinner, the sky opened up with a boom and pounded the cafeteria roof with sheets of rain. Mary half hoped that the soldiers had been caught out in it and would never return. As soon as she had the thought, she felt guilty for having it. Either way, such was not the case. After her evening reading with students, during which she had to speak louder than usual because of the noise of the rain on the arched gymnasium roof, Mary looked out to see the light on in the soldiers' classroom.

The hard rain subsided to a drizzle during the middle of the night. Mary slept poorly, with a desk propped up against the classroom door, eventually waking as morning light filtered in through the classroom windows from the clearing clouds. While making her bed, she heard the familiar sound of the fence post pounder.

Twenty minutes later she was down the ramp and under the walkway on her way to the gym. She stood for a moment to watch the soldiers closing the gap on their three-sided fence. The water from the night before had darkened the galvanized steel of the chain-link, beads collected in the wire joints of all the fencing diamonds and reflected the sun.

"How are you feeling?" Mary asked Helen Taft in the gym after shouting her regular morning commands. Helen sat on the edge of her made bed, looking down at her shoes with her head in her hands. Mary sat next to her and put her arm around her. Helen felt cold, and Mary pulled her in tight.

"When are my parents coming back?"

"I don't know, sweetheart. Hopefully soon."

"I miss them. I couldn't sleep last night."

"How is your ear?" Mary asked, pulling Helen's hair back. "Have you been using the ointment I gave you?"

"Yes. It's not bothering me."

"Alright. Well, it's time to eat breakfast. Do you want to help me get the apples from the refrigerator and cut them?"

Helen looked up at Mary, tears blooming in her soft eyes. "I want them to come get me so bad. I don't like living here."

"I know, sweetheart, but we have to get on with the day and hopefully they'll be coming back to get you soon. There's work to be done. And, besides, right now I need your help."

Helen nodded and blotted her tears with the back of her hand.

That afternoon the soldiers worked in the trampled grass coiling the top of their fence with a loose spiral of razor wire. One of them had gone to the truck and returned with a gate that connected the last two posts. Like a stretched slinky, they pulled the last bit of razor wire over the top of the gate after securing a heavy, locking latch to the adjacent pole. When the gate was attached and the chain-link fencing wired securely to each post, the soldiers were finished with their square enclosure, six feet high all around and thirty feet wide on each side.

It was late morning on the third day when the soldiers lingered proudly by their newly erected fence after returning the remaining materials to their truck. Mary watched them from her bench wondering what they were so adamant about keeping out of their little square patch on the grass. A chill ran through her when it occurred to her that maybe the fence wasn't meant for keeping something out, but for caging something in.

CHAPTER FIFTEEN

Will and Zach hustled behind Jose Alvarez and his band of armed men on a well-worn path through fallow fields. Unsown tomatoes spreading wildly into the barrens crowded the edge of the path and clung to their old fruit like oversized flesh-toned raisins. A humid sweet rot and the smell of manure rose in the midday heat from under the feet of the men in front of them.

In the downvalley distance, the guard towers were the first to come into view, followed by the high wire fence. Beyond the fence was a complex of cream-colored low buildings that seemed to rise unnaturally from the unbroken plane of dark brown agricultural fields surrounding them. As they approached, Will could see that the fence was breached in several places, and one of the guard towers was almost entirely burnt. They went down into a paved ditch, squinting against the hot reflection of the white pavement, then up onto an area of sparse grass and red dirt at the base of the tall fence.

"What is this place?" Zach asked.

"The old Salinas Valley State Prison," Will said as they passed under an arch cut in the fencing. "How's your leg? You seem to be limping more than usual."

"I'm fine. Just a lot of walking. It'll be nice to sit down for a minute."

Jose stopped and made a loud whistle into the prison yard, then turned to Will and Zach. "Soledad was destroyed during the wars of the regional breakup. Long before we occupied this place. We've been here several years, completely empty when we found it."

Jose pointed to what looked like a stack of bleached sticks piled against the inside wall of one of the guard towers. "See that?"

"What is it?" Zach asked.

"That's a pile of bones. Skeletons were lying undisturbed all over the yard when we got here. Thousands of them. Everything but the bones had rotted away."

"What happened?"

"When the wars came, the prison guards locked the inmates in the yard to die in the rain."

Zach stared at the pile of bones and grimaced.

Jose continued, "It must have been terrible. Thousands of caged men screaming, fighting each other as they died. The place was like an aboveground graveyard when we found it." Jose studied Zach. "Why aren't you with the UP fighting at the border?"

"My leg is hurt."

Jose looked down at Zach's leg. "You sure? You're not working for the UP?"

Zach looked indignant and slightly worried. "No," he said loudly, then looked at Will.

"Can he be trusted, Will?" Jose asked, turning to Will.

"He's good. Stop messing with him," Will said, and the look he gave Jose ended the conversation.

Jose smiled at the other men. "Come on, let's go inside. Lunch is being prepared," he said, then he whistled a second time.

Will could see that two of the guard towers were occupied, each by two men with rifles, who watched them as they walked. They came through a narrow corridor between adjacent buildings into an internal courtyard surrounded on all sides by two-story buildings. The courtyard had a small patch of overgrown grass and a wide blacktop surface with a basketball court and a line of handball walls. One of the handball courts was occupied by four children who stopped their game to turn and watch the two new visitors. The courtyard smelled of something cooking.

They followed Jose and the other men into a cinderblock building on the far end of the courtyard whose metals doors had all been removed. Stepping inside, Will was nearly overwhelmed by the smell. Several women were around a long table preparing food, and a stew pot boiled over an open fire, filling the room with a hearty sweetness that made Will's mouth water. The old fume hood, once used in the kitchen when gas and electricity were available, now served as an open chimney for the fire pit. The stove was replaced by a blackened steel rack on which sat a large silver pot. Down the wall from the open fire was another fume hood, this one attached to a crudely built brick oven. The women looked up and smiled disinterestedly at Will and Zach as they entered, then went back to the preparation.

Jose put the two confiscated apple pies on the table. "We have dessert," he announced. The women laughed. Hearing their laughter, Will realized he hadn't heard laughter since before he and Hannah had been collected.

Other people from the prison complex filed into the modified mess hall.

"Please, sit," Jose said with a hand outstretched to the front of the long table. Will and Zach sat while Jose brought them two mugs and poured a thick green fluid into them. Will sipped it, then drank the rest in one gulp.

"What's that?" Will asked.

"Nopal juice. At least the rain doesn't kill the cacti."

"Or any crops for that matter," Will added.

"If it did, that would be the end of all of us." Jose studied the green drink. "It's the crops that the outsiders want. Our fertile soils." Jose spoke directly to Zach. "They have nothing outside this Valley. The San Benicians are not our enemy. They're as desperate as we are. What land they have is dry and poisoned, yet we battle them while our rich soils lie fallow."

"Wouldn't they take everything from us? Our Valley?" Zach asked.

"Oh, my friend, the lies you've been told. The right questions aren't even asked anymore."

"What are those?" Zach asked.

"Is there a better way? How do we stop this endless warring? How should we be treating our neighbors? What do they want from us, and is there enough for everyone?"

Will looked around the room. People stopped to listen to Jose.

"For the Valley! Right?" Jose said loudly. "There is a better way. We can make an overabundance of food in this Valley." Jose waved his hands around the kitchen. "We have nobody to grow it. Imagine if all those soldiers, all those wasted lives, could return to the fields."

Jose continued, projecting his voice throughout the room. "Instead, the Administration has become blind with power. Corrupted by their own short-sighted vision. They no longer care for the people of this great Valley. The Administration and the UP must be stopped."

Will watched Jose closely. It occurred to him that Jose had become a different man in the years since he'd last seen him, with new and altered loyalties and convictions. Until that moment, Jose had never struck Will as a leader. He caught Jose's eye as he stopped talking and felt momentarily self-conscious. Jose sat next to them to drink from his own cup.

More women and children came into the room, then other men behind them, removing their hats as they entered. They washed in two deeps sinks at the side of the room, then each stood waiting while a bowl of stew was ladled for them. Steaming pans of cornbread, fresh from the brick oven, smoky and caramelized, sat at the center of each communal table.

A small towheaded boy with eyes a pale metallic shade of blue left his mother's side and walked cautiously toward Will and Zach. He pointed at Zach. "You have hair and eyes like me."

"I do," Zach said, looking down at the boy, smiling.

"Why are your eyes so red?" the boy asked.

"Come back over here," his mother called.

A woman carefully set two bowls in front of Will and Zach, each with a healthy cube of cornbread balanced on the rim.

"Thank you," they said in unison.

Both looked up, waiting like hungry dogs for the command that it was alright to eat.

Once the room was filled with people seated in front of their food, Jose said in a loud voice, "Everyone, we have two special guests today. My old friend and war mate, Willie Taft, and his traveling companion Zach Taylor. Here's to them, for making it out from under the oppressive control of the Valley Management to be with us."

Everyone drank and someone yelled, "For the Valley" from the back of the room, and "For the Valley" was repeated.

Will and Zach looked at Jose. "Eat, my friends."

An hour later Will and Jose stood in the courtyard watching from a distance while Zach played handball with the children.

"I'm so sorry, my friend. It sounds like Hannah was wonderful." Jose put his hand on Will's shoulder. "What happened to your cheek?"

Will touched the dried Steri-strips with the pads of his fingers. The pain had subsided, and for the first time in days, his jaw wasn't aching.

"I killed a man. The one who wounded Hannah as we were escaping the camp." Will stroked his wound, lost in thought. "I couldn't talk her out of going with me. He cut me, too, before I got to him. Once we were out, I, I couldn't stop her bleeding."

"Terrible," Jose said, returning his hand to Will's shoulder.

As his old friend looked away, Will closed his eyes. Tears squeezed out of their corners, spilled down across his tan cheeks, and sat on the stubble of his beard. The telling of the previous day's events was surprisingly difficult.

A ball rolled in their direction, and Jose picked it up and threw it back at the children. "What's your plan now?" he asked.

"I have to get back to Gonzales. Back to Helen."

"And the kid?" Jose asked, nodding toward Zach. "He'll go with me, I guess."

"We could use him."

Will considered what Jose was asking. "We can ask if he wants to stay, leave it up to him."

"Okay," Jose said.

"I should be asking you what your plan is," Will said, wiping his face. "What are you doing out here?"

"We're surviving. Trying to rebuild some semblance of community."

"Do you think it can last?"

"We're well defended," Jose said, gesturing to the guard towers. "If they wanted to take us, they probably could. For now, Soledad seems to be written off by the Valley Management."

They sat in silence watching Zach and the children. The courtyard was warm, and Will felt like lying back on the grass and falling asleep.

"There are agents of the resistance in all parts of the Valley," Jose finally said. "It's a dangerous time. Everything is changing, and we have big plans. A way to get our Valley back."

"What do you mean?"

"The Management has become desperate. Valley residents don't have the loyalty they always did. The border zone is being attacked more and more successfully, the wall is being breached from the outside. Eventually, the Valley will be overrun."

"Is that a good thing?"

"If the resistance leadership is correctly allied, I think we can get peace back to the Valley."

"Seems like a long shot."

"It's all we have. We can go on living this way. The collections, separating families, people dying in the upvalley labor camps, disappearances. How long could we go on letting our lives be overrun? We had none of the everyday pleasures we once enjoyed. At least here in the prison, we control our own destiny."

"You're fighting against a well-outfitted army." Will looked around the prison yard. "You keep fighting and some or most of these people will die."

"What choice do we have? There's nothing to go back to. They'll die even if they don't fight," Jose said. "We do what we have to."

"What about the rain?"

"What about it? There's nothing that can be done. We live with it. We all do."

"How many people are here at the prison?"

"We have nearly fifty, and we're smuggling new people from the midvalley towns and Salinas City areas all the time."

Will and Jose watched Zach hobble around on one leg, laughing. He had a small child on his shoulders.

Will tugged carefully on a blade of grass until, with an inaudible click, the tube slid forth from its sheath, white and tender. He chewed on the soft part.

"Do you ever think about what happened?" Will asked.

"What do you mean?"

Will looked at Jose as if he couldn't believe he had to explain. "You know what I mean. When we were over the border."

"Every day." Jose caught Will's eyes. "We were kids. We should never have been there or been required to do what we did. Are you surprised they want to attack the Valley? It's not just our fertile ground they want. They want revenge for what we did."

"I thought you were dead. I would've looked for you."

"I know. You wouldn't have found anything, though," Jose said.

Will looked back down at the grass, and they sat in silence for another minute, then finally he asked, "And what about Millie?"

"What about him? I know nothing about him."

"I heard he survived. I met a man in the San Ardo camp who said he knew him."

"I don't believe it. Of all of us who deserved to die out there." Jose shook his head. "The things he did."

Will said, "I tried to stop him."

"Well, I hope the rumors are wrong. I hope he's gone."

"Me, too."

Will looked around. He was no longer tired. He felt like a caged animal in the courtyard. The buildings and fencing all seemed closer than before. "We need to get going. We have several hours before the rain. We have to keep moving downvalley."

"Okay, you talk to the kid, see if he wants to go on with you or stay, and I'll get some food loaded up for you."

"We'll need our guns back as well."

"Sure," Jose said as he got up and headed back toward the mess hall.

Will rose and watched Zach. He seemed so young, barely older than the children he played with.

"Zach," Will called to him.

Zach came over, out of breath and sweating, his golden hair in wild clumps. When he smiled, Will realized that it may have been the first time he'd seen him do so.

"We're leaving?" he asked.

"Right away."

"Okay, let me grab my stuff and say goodbye to the kids."

As Zach turned back to the yard, Will said, "Hey, let me ask you something."

"What?"

"Do you want to stay here with Jose and these people? They could use your help."

Zach hesitated, thinking about the question. He glanced down at his leg.

"They need all the able-bodied people they can get," Will continued.

"But don't you need my help?" Zach asked, disappointed.

Will hadn't anticipated the question or the look of abandonment on Zach's face. "I want what's best for you. I told Jose I'd ask."

"You saved my life and probably my grandma's life, too. I'm staying with you until you get your daughter. I can always come back here after that."

They nodded at each other, and Zach walked away to the handball court to retrieve his pack.

When he returned, Jose was approaching with two paper bags.

"You decide to stay, my friend?" he asked Zach.

"I'm going with Will."

"I figured. Here's some food. Should last you a day or two if you stretch it." He handed a bag to each of them. It was heavier than Will expected.

They followed Jose back out of the inner courtyard to the edge of the guard tower. They stood where the arch of clipped wire led to the ditch and the dark quilt of Valley fields beyond. Jose whistled, and two men emerged from behind the wall of a distant guard tower carrying Zach's rifle. One man handed it to Jose and the other retrieved Will's handgun from his belt, placing it in Jose's outstretched hand. They nodded and retreated without a word. Jose handed the gun to Zach, who tucked it behind the strap of his pack, then he turned to Will.

"Willie Taft. I can't believe it. I hope I see you back here soon," Jose said, handing him the gun. Will stuffed it into the back of his belt and hugged Jose. "I want to meet that daughter of yours."

"You will."

"Be careful out there. Stay hidden. Move by the river when possible and stay away from the towns. You get caught out here in the midvalley, they'll shoot you on sight."

Jose walked away, then without turning back said, "Oh, and enjoy the apple pies."

Will and Zach each opened their food bag and there, carefully placed on top of the other items, was a Hostess apple pie, still in its wrapper.

In the distance, Millard Fillmore laid at the base of a tall bluegum tree, patiently watching through the scope of his rifle. The sun was high in the sky behind him, and he steadied the crosshairs on Will as he and Zach emerged from the ditch along the edge of the old prison.

CHAPTER SIXTEEN

After an hour of walking, Will and Zach stood above the riverbank and could no longer see the prison behind them. Will scanned the horizon, yet still couldn't shake the feeling of being watched. He was relieved to be heading into the cover of the willows along the Salinas. Between where they stood and their destination of Gonzales, the river ran chocolate and silent in a deep channel, with well-worn paths skirting its edges on both sides.

"How far are we from the school?" Zach asked, savoring his last sip of prison cactus juice.

Will looked at the sky, then down the river and back at Zach. "A short distance now. In good weather, we'd be there tomorrow morning. I've been along these paths before."

They hustled along a footpath through low muddy areas, stepping over the twisted willow trunks. Each old stem was covered with dead lichen, ancient remnants from a time before the rains.

Farther along the footpath, they climbed back to the top of the bank where Will crouched and peered into the darkening downvalley haze. The leaves fluttered around him, and a cold and stinking breeze washed over them. Will felt a tingling in the pit of his stomach, an inkling of panic as he scanned the fields for an old rain hut.

"We'll need shelter soon," he said to Zach, nodding downvalley and rubbing his wounded cheek.

Zach nodded.

"We're close. Look there."

He pointed into the thick haze where the fields were interrupted by what looked like a wide clump of trees barely raised above the plane. A spherical water tower was visible, and the clouds above the town were black.

"Gonzales?"

Will nodded. "Already starting to rain there."

Fields fell off and stretched out from the raised bank of the river on both sides. A short distance ahead a dirt road led away from the river, back toward the longvalley highway.

Will said, "We need to follow that to some kind of shelter."

"There, maybe?" Zach asked, pointing to a distant structure surrounded by fields on all sides.

"We'll see."

They jogged down the bank and into a field of sugar beets, leaping over each row on their way to the dirt road. Like fat, sunburnt, Caucasian necks with purple and green hair, the beets emerged from the dark soil, gorging on the sun, rolled and disfigured by their unnatural daily sugar accumulation.

"These are past due for harvest," Zach said as they reached the road. "We used to grow beets."

"Those are, too," Will said, pointing to the field on the far side of the road. Artichokes were as high as their chests, candelabras of prickly gray-green crowns projecting skyward from each plant. Some were so far gone that their thistly spirals had opened to expose iridescent blue furry flowers.

"Jose was right," Zach called out. "The Valley's filled with unharvested crops."

They left the river behind them, jogging eastward along the edge of the artichoke field. Although it wasn't much, Will was happy for the cover of the unharvested plants. A dilapidated convoy of transport trucks glided silently along the raised longvalley freeway ahead.

They came to a ruined shed at the edge of the field. It looked like a weary ship marooned in a sea of soil, twisted and lopsided, its tin and plywood slumped and barely standing. Breathing hard, Will pushed the door open and the hinges clicked and creaked with rust. Inside, everything was dark and without definition. Will's pupils dilated enough to accept the low light from the small double hung window in the far wall.

The single room was mostly empty, a packing shed that at one time was partly converted to house farm workers. A table and two knocked over chairs sat at one end of the room. Two broken down bunk beds, missing mattresses, and slats of wood falling off them sat beyond the table. The room smelled of mold, and Will instinctively drew short breaths.

"This will work to keep us dry," Zach said, still holding the rifle he'd drawn when they entered.

"Maybe. Look at that." Will pointed to an area where the wood floorboards were darkened, water-stained, and rotted away. Open dirt, wet and dark, sat below the wide hole in the floor. "Water leaks in through the roof."

"Should we look for something different?"

"We might not have time."

Will stepped back outside and looked up at the sky, condensed and growing dark. The smell of sulfur was in the air and the tin roof rattled in the wind. He scanned the horizon, the fields, the longvalley highway, then back toward the river.

"We don't have other options. Those clouds are coming on fast," Will said.

"What about under the highway?"

"Too dangerous. If the wind blows the rain sideways, I'll be done."

"What's that?" Zach asked, pointing to the highway.

Beyond the fields, a vehicle was parked on the top of a produce loading ramp on the highway.

"A transport truck pulled over maybe."

Zach squinted. "Looks smaller than that. Some kind of jeep."

Will looked at the sky, then back at the wrecked shed. "I don't think I have any options. If water comes in through the roof, hopefully, there's a dry spot inside," Will said.

Fear and sickness were creeping into him with each burning breath.

Will said, "If I start to get sick or pass out, get me to the driest area you can." He felt a knot in his stomach, and his mouth grew dry.

They could see the rain coming only a short distance away.

"Of course."

"And if I don't make it through the night, get to the school in Gonzales. Just leave and go straight there. Don't stop, rain or shine, until you get there. Helen's teacher's name is Mary McElroy. Tell her I sent you for Helen."

"You'll be fine," Zach said, trying to be reassuring.

"Repeat the name."

"Mary McElroy."

Will looked at Zach and nodded. "You keep her safe. Understand?"

"Of course."

"She can't stay at that school. She's not safe there."

"Get her back to Jose at the prison. You two can stay there."

"It'll be dry enough in there."

"We're about to find out."

Will stared up at the stinking darkness, then took one last look at Gonzales. He stepped inside as the first drops pinged off the tin roof. He thought of Helen, a short distance away on the other side of the clouds. She was so close. He breathed in the sickening incense and felt nauseous as his eyes began to sting. They'd be together again soon, he told himself, if only he could survive the night.

CHAPTER SEVENTEEN

Captain Wilson darkened the double doors of the Gonzales school gym where Mary McElroy stood with her back to him, helping students at one of several wide round tables.

"Miss McElroy," Captain Wilson said loudly.

All the children fell silent.

"Yes?" Mary's voice was hollow as she slowly rotated to face him.

"I need to speak with you."

Mary was leaned over a low table helping a young boy with his writing. She stood straight and turned to face Captain Wilson. He scared her, but she tried to conceal it. His disingenuous tone of mock civility bothered her, and she could sense that his intentions were far from good. Since seeing the captain in the rain, the previous night, she had an unshakable feeling of dread. She could feel her heart beating in her throat as she faced him.

Realizing that the children were listening, Mary left the gym through the double doors into the covered walkway, and Captain Wilson followed.

"I'd like you to let the children out in the yard this afternoon. We can watch over them."

Mary considered what he was asking. Her eyes squinted. "You'll watch over them? What are you talking about? Where will I be?"

"You'll be here as well. Same as always." The Captain mustered a fake smile. "It's a nice afternoon. Let the children out to play. You've apparently been avoiding that while we worked."

"They've never needed to be watched over before. What has changed?"

The captain didn't answer, and his face grew stiff and cold.

"Those are your orders, Ms. McElroy. Don't test my patience. Let the children out when you're done with the lesson, or we'll do it for you." He stared straight at her with a cold and vacant look. His pale blue bloodshot eyes were piercing, and a shot of panic went through her. Mary looked at the other soldiers lingering a short distance away. None of them met her gaze.

Back inside the gym, Mary said loudly, "You all can finish up what you're working on and go outside for the rest of the day. Don't wander too far from the yard, and make sure you can hear my voice when I call you back in."

Papers rustled, chairs squeaked, and children went pouring out into the afternoon sun. Mary trailed them into the yard where the afternoon was still and pale. The morning breeze had abated, and Mary could feel the reflected heat off the blacktop as she took a seat at her play yard bench.

From that very bench, through the seasons, Mary had learned the Valley weather and its nuanced transitions throughout the year. Despite the year-round evening rains, she knew the differences in seasons as well as any Valley inhabitant. Wispy hints of backlit fog dissipating over the dark edges of the Santa Lucias signified the end of summer. The Valley seemed to hunker down under a blanket of thick, brown, morning haze as fall ended. She knew that the cold blue winter sunshine after the new year would come without a breath of wind. By then the plowshares had ripped linear gashes in the fallow fields and the morning frost sat on the black corrugations like crystalline dust.

The longer days of early spring followed. It was a season of the steady upvalley wind and the great greening of the brown Gabilan hills. When the flowers on the hills beyond Gonzales were in full riot, the weather always changed again, to its unpredictable early summer party when subtle floral scents mixed with the sting of heated eucalyptus floating in on the evening breeze with the sickening sulfuric garlic.

That afternoon was in the time when the seasons were the hardest for Mary to predict, after the chill of early spring but before the Gabilan's wildflowers had begun to bloom. *When do I start calling the children in?* She wanted to leave a safe amount of time before the evening rain yet maximize their time outside. Some late spring days were warm and dry, and Mary knew the rain wouldn't come until long after dark, but on others, like that afternoon, the sunshine was strangely paler, precarious, as if it were fighting through high clouds that no human could perceive.

When it was raining downvalley, Mary's calculations were easy. She could smell the sulfur in the air and would have the children in at the right time, but on that day, she got no sense of rain elsewhere in the Valley. From her bench, she looked up at the thin blue sky and briefly entertained the idea of it fading to a black and clear night.

She had only seen such a night twice, both when she was a child. She remembered clearly how light came from beyond the darkness, from the countless connected stars unfurling in a brilliant swath across the Valley sky. The land was so black at its corners and the light so clear, their meeting at the Valley's edge seemed to set the whole world in motion. On those two nights, the Valley sky swung open like a gigantic door, and the entire universe paraded by overhead. She wanted so badly to share that same experience with the children some night.

While Mary sat, the soldiers circled the school, their light blue helmets looking silver in the golden afternoon. She watched each soldier make a counterclockwise progression around the yard, looking out to the fields and hills beyond. Each soldier waited at his post for fifteen minutes, then after being relieved by a second light blue helmet would move onto the next post. *What are they guarding us against?* Mary wondered.

Four boys, mimicking the soldiers, circled the chain-link enclosure. The children held sticks like guns and joined each other at outside corners, moving from post to post. *It'll be real for them sooner than they think*, Mary thought. Finally, one of them got up the courage to try the gate. He pulled on the latch but couldn't get it open.

"Come away from there," Mary yelled from her bench. The boy put his hands down and joined the others, pretending like he hadn't heard her.

When the children had been outside for several hours and she was done with all her papers, Mary saw the first hints of the coming rain. The flowering pear in the schoolhouse yard had lost all its ephemeral blossoms in one of the previous week's downpours. Mary had paused in the early morning light, marveling at the circular pattern of white blossoms carpeting the blacktop. Now the trees' new leaves were fiberless, supple, and many barely held themselves horizontal on the branches. Some, in fact, did not, and those leaves hung downward, quaking like an aspen in the slightest breeze. It was these leaves that Mary noticed first. They started the slightest flutter, even before she could perceive any change in wind direction. She studied the Valley's edge, looking for a second sign, and it wasn't long before it came.

Mary rose and walked to the edge of the play yard where she could have a better vantage point of the downvalley distance. A darkness had accumulated there, and the strong delineation between earth and sky was disappearing. She knew the weather would be changing fast now. The late spring rains were unpredictable, but Mary now knew what was coming. Even though she couldn't yet smell it, a strong upvalley wind was bringing serious showers within the hour.

She circled the yard, visually accounting for all the children. If she could see all of them, she could give them another fifteen minutes with no danger of exposure. The smell finally came to her, like someone roasting garlic, pleasant at first, but then quickly overwhelming. She watched the soldiers, still on their beat, and wondered if they knew what was coming.

"Ms. McElroy." Mary turned to see Captain Wilson in full uniform, flack vest, and a holstered firearm on his side. He was coming from the gate of the fence enclosure.

"Yes?"

"Are all the children accounted for?"

"Yes."

"How many?" the captain asked.

"How many what?"

"How many children are outside?"

"All of them. Twenty-three."

Captain Wilson turned toward another soldier at the edge of the play yard and signaled to him. He raised his arm, held up two fingers, made a fist, then held up three fingers. The soldier nodded in the distance.

"Ms. McElroy, can I have a word with you inside?"

"Sure, but it's time to get the children back inside. Can we speak after that?"

"No, there'll be time to get the children in. I need to ask you some questions," Captain Wilson said.

Mary's confusion began to yield to fear as Captain Wilson took a step closer. She wanted to back away but didn't move.

"Can't we talk here?"

"Inside," the Captain scolded, holding his arm out in the gym's direction.

"I have to start dinner soon," Mary said, almost pleading, suddenly not wanting to leave the children.

"Now," the Captain said, his arm still pointing to the gym.

Mary walked toward the gym, and Captain Wilson followed her without another word.

As they came through the open double doors of the gym, Mary began to turn around to look at him when she felt him grab her shoulders from behind. A wave of terror went through her when she felt how strong he was. She let out a scream as he pushed her down onto the wooden floor. He forcefully pulled her arms behind her back, and an internal pop and excruciating pain came to her right shoulder. She couldn't breathe. With his knee on her back and both her wrists in one of his hands, he retrieved a black zip tie from his vest.

"Don't fight me," the captain yelled.

She continued to struggle against his weight as he slipped the zip tie over her wrists, and with a sound like something tearing, bound them together cruciform. Mary tried to roll under his weight, but he pushed down harder on her back. Panic was stalking her from all sides.

"Calm down," he said, letting up on her a bit. "Don't make me hurt you."

She wiggled and tried to roll again, and he hit her hard on the back of the head so that her forehead and face slammed the gym floor. Mary saw white light and momentarily lost control of her limbs. Adrenaline surged through her. The captain gathered her legs and put a second zip tie around her ankles. He rose, reached down, and rolled her over onto her side.

Mary took a deep breath, looked up, and saw Helen Taft sitting on her cot a few feet away, mouth ajar, aghast. The captain saw Helen at the same time. As he moved in her direction Helen let out an involuntary scream and darted off the cot away from him. Within a few steps, he grabbed her from behind and picked her up off the ground.

"Helen, run," Mary screamed at her, but it was too late. He'd already grabbed her.

Helen shrieked and kicked into the air while he held her securely from behind.

"Let her go," Mary screamed, her mouth was red with blood from where she'd hit the floor.

"Calm down," the captain said, his voice icy, gritting his teeth, gripping Helen firmly.

With Helen still kicking and screaming, the captain carried her out of the gym.

Mary tried to catch her breath. She'd never been so scared. She could taste the metallic blood in her mouth. She tried rolling toward the gym doors but screamed when she rotated onto her dislocated shoulder. Flopping onto her back, she slid across the floor. At the threshold, she rolled on her good shoulder where she could see through the covered walkway to the play yard and fence enclosure beyond. The sound of her own rapid short breaths scared her even more.

All the golden light of the afternoon had left the day, replaced by something gloomy and dark. She watched Captain Wilson carry Helen toward another soldier, who was waiting at the fence enclosure gate. She was kicking and struggling the whole way. He set her down and shoved her into the cage. Like a confused wild animal, Helen ran to the distant corner and turned in a defensive position, eyes wide and terrified, her face frozen in horror.

Mary saw the other soldiers arrive with children, both small and large, pushing them into the cage. Most went in without a fight, puzzled by what was going on. Others were scared and screaming and had to be carried inside the fence. Mary lay on the floor of the gym, helplessly watching the scene. From somewhere out of her viewpoint she heard the loud crack of a gun being fired, then a second shot came.

"You'll be okay. It's okay. It's okay. It's okay," she said under her breath to the children. She tried to muster the strength to scream, but only a breathy howl came forward, and none of the children heard her.

In the minutes that followed, as the sky darkened and the smell of sulfur descended on the school, the remaining children were brought to the cage. The largest boy, apparently unconscious, was drug by a soldier onto the grass into the center of the enclosure where he laid motionless. A small boy kneeled next to him and rubbed his head. One of the soldiers entered the cage, and with his gun waving, he yelled at the children to stop moving. Captain Wilson made a count. The soldiers exited the cage, and the captain strapped a lock around the gate, then the soldiers were gone from Mary's view.

The children circled inside the cage looking up at the sky and into the distance for help. Some pulled on the chain-link with both hands, small fingers wrapped around the wires. Another boy sat in the corner with his knees pulled up to his chest, rocking back and forth. Helen Taft hovered over him, trying to comfort him. A dark-eyed girl kept yelling, "Help. Ms. McElroy. Help. Ms. McElroy? Ms. McElroy?"

From where she laid, Mary heard the echoes of footfalls outside, then the two doors in front of her were slammed shut. Stinking acidic air from the crack under the doors blew on her face. She heard more footsteps, then nothing. A dark line of scurrying ants crossed the gym floor just inside the door.

The silence was broken by the first barely-audible thuds of raindrops on the sidewalk outside the gym. Mary held her breath and listened carefully. *Maybe it will hardly rain tonight, maybe they will survive*, she thought, but as she thought it, she knew it was unrealistic. She screamed again as a wave of dread and terror came over her for what was about to happen to her children. She had to get to them somehow. She tried to roll against the door and screamed again as a lightning shot of pain ran through her shoulder.

Mary quieted the rasping sound of her panting to listen for the children. Her whole body trembled. No sound came from beyond the closed doors. The line of ants had grown thicker and was now crawling over her. She heard the occasional soft tick of a droplet from the toxic sky exploding on concrete outside the door. She couldn't distinguish the sound from the subtle clicks of the gym's floorboards settling and held out hope that the rain would miraculously not fall on that night.

Like a thousand slender sticks all being broken at once, the rain came down all around her. Her whole body shuddered, and she screamed, "No."

The wind picked up, and the air from under the door whistled. Mary felt nauseous. The pain in her shoulder was unbearable, and she wanted nothing more than to be able to move her arms. She thought she heard a muffled scream, then the rain gathered into a steady hiss, like a river running over the school. Water was everywhere. Sickness consumed her. Mary rolled back and forth in utter horror, taking shallow panicky breaths, screaming the names of her children into the hollow silence of the gym.

CHAPTER EIGHTEEN

By the time the rain was falling steadily on the roof of the old shed, Will and Zach had pulled the two chairs and table to the driest corner of the room. They set their guns on the table and packs on the floor.

"Here it comes," Zach said, his eyes rolled up to the ceiling.

They could hear the roar of water moving their way. The wind picked up, and the old shed creaked. Will held onto the table as if the whole building would be blown out from under them. Will's eyes darted back and forth between the ceiling and the small window. Water ran in long streaks down the glass. Zach took a small candle from his bag, lit it, and put it on the table between them. The rain grew to a roar, and Will felt as if they were floating away in a river. The sickening air permeated the shed, and his throat burned unbearably.

The first drips started to come through the ceiling above the rotted floor. A few drips became a trickle, then water was running as if from a faucet. The stream of water fell through the room and splattered onto the floor and the dirt below it. Thin puddles formed with water dripping into them, raising small bubbles that skated across the surface and vanished at the edge.

Will's eyes started to sting and tear, and he raised his hand to his throat. A drop of water came from the ceiling above them and landed on the table. Zach's candle went out and the room was dark. Both rose quickly and pulled the table out of the way of the drip. Zach relit the candle. Will was blinking, trying to catch his breath.

"You okay?" Zach asked, watching Will closely.

"Yeah. My eyes are stinging. It's hard to breathe."

The rain intensified, and both men rose again from the table, listening. The shack reverberated under the frequency of the water, the tin a tight drumhead. Another trickle came through the ceiling boards nearer to where they stood, and water ran down the far wall and over the inside of the window.

As Will retreated to the opposite wall, more drips came through the ceiling, this time from all parts. Through watery eyes he looked at Zach, water was coming down on his shoulder, darkening his shirt.

Will felt lightheaded and leaned hard against the wall. At that moment it occurred to Will that he might die here. He looked at Zach in desperation.

"Get under the table," Zach said, pushing the table closer to the wall.

The pain and swelling in Will's throat grew, and his mouth and lungs burned. He sucked in short quick breaths. He kneeled under the table while Zach crossed the room and pulled the damp broken boards from the bunk beds and stacked them on the table.

Will's vision began to blur and draw in from the edges. His legs felt heavy, and he laid on his side in the fetal position trying to draw breath. He felt the flame in his lungs entering his bloodstream. The tired old boards lining the wall behind him began to blacken and soak through.

"You're alright. You'll stay dry under there," was the last thing Will heard Zach say.

Will's nightmare lasted until the predawn hours when the clouds finally cleared. He couldn't recollect if he was awake or asleep for the endless hours during the incessant rainfall. He had vague memories of dry heaving at some point and crying out for his daughter. Always the table was there above him. He stared at the underside, with its scratch marks and drips of hardened brown lacquer. Zach was also there, talking to him, occasionally silent, but always drying Will's face with his shirt.

It was still dark when everything changed. The roar of water faded to a trickle, a gentle patter, then long before the sun came up, the rain stopped altogether, leaving nothing but blackness and silence, then both Zach and Will slept. Eventually orange light faded in over the black mass to the east, and clouds were pulled upward from the Valley floor. Orange and brown wisps of condensed water and disease glided away to the south and dissipated. While they slept, the Valley around them seemed to breathe a sigh of relief, and in a matter of moments, everything was less troubled.

Out across the dripping sugar beets and artichokes, the flood-stained trees on the banks of the Salinas held tight to the shifting sand. Their black limbs folded into the mud and were covered with brown water as it seethed downvalley. Neither insect nor beast crawled below, and all was still except for the water. The sulfuric stink left on a new wind.

The shack creaked loudly, waking Will, though he was still exhausted. The door was open to the outside, and Zach leaned against the doorjamb, shirtless, watching the sunrise. He was eating a piece of thick tortilla out of the paper bag from the prison. Light came from the nascent sun to the east, setting his white hair aglow. He turned to Will with bloodshot eyes.

"Morning."

Will didn't answer. The table had been moved off him, and Zach had laid his shirt and coat over him. He looked in Zach's direction, still disoriented.

"You don't look so good, my friend," Zach continued with his mouth full. "You should eat something. Here, take this."

Will looked out the window, then at Zach. He lifted a shaky hand to receive the tortilla.

"What happened?" Will asked.

"You barely made it through the night. Kept most of the water off you, but you were sick."

"How about you?"

"Me? Nothing. Same as always. Couldn't get sick if I wanted to. I was awake most of the night. Tired now, but ready to go when you are."

Will put the piece of tortilla into his mouth and chewed. He stretched his arms and rubbed his cheek, then pushed himself up from the floor. The dried bandage was half peeling off his wound.

"Here, have a drink."

The sweet cactus juice washed away the pain and swelling in Will's throat. They stood silently at the door and watched the sun come up.

"You saved my life," Will finally said after collecting his thoughts. He put his hand on Zach's bare shoulder.

Zach's bright red eyes squinted at the corners as he smiled. "I just kept you dry."

"Thank you."

Will was filled with gratitude. The possibility, no the probability, of seeing his daughter in a few short hours hit him like a revelation. He'd survived the night and now was on the cusp of reuniting with her. He looked back at Zach with a wide grin.

CHAPTER NINETEEN

The sun was just above the eastern horizon when Will and Zach got on their way. One hundred paces out, Will turned to look at the half-fallen shed that had nearly become his coffin.

"Zach," Will yelled ahead to him. "Look."

On the roof of the shack with its wings outstretched in the morning sun sat a red-tailed hawk.

"Wow. What is it?"

"A hawk," Will whispered. Both men watched while the hawk's head rotated like a nob on its shoulders, halting its swivel to stare at them.

"I've seen one before," Will said. "A long time ago."

"I never have. Saw a dead blackbird when I was a kid."

"I've heard birds end up in the Valley sometimes. They get off course, or they come here to die."

"Beautiful."

Will stared at the bird, made eye contact, and nodded to it as if it would understand the gesture. They walked on, leaving the bird and the broken-down shack to steam in the morning heat.

They approached the longvalley highway, backlit to the east. It sat like half of a suture, concrete pillars disappearing into the soil, pulling the ends of the Valley together. Turning downvalley, they skirted along its western edge, Zach limping in front of Will. The highway loomed high above them and cast the stretched shadow of its steel railing on the ground in front of them. Will paused to look up at the highway and listen for traffic but could hear none.

"It's still there." Zach pointed ahead of them to the edge of the highway at the same vehicle they saw at dusk the night before.

"It's not a UP transport truck," Will said, looking up.

"Some type of jeep."

"We need to head back toward the river immediately," Will said, scanning around them.

"Why?"

"That jeep."

As they turned toward a path through the fields back to the river, Will heard someone yell.

"Hey. Hey, hold it right there."

Millard Fillmore stepped out from behind one of the longvalley highway pillars with a rifle held firmly to his shoulder, the dark brown barrel pointed at Will. He was backlit, and his long coat almost reached the ground.

Will and Zach froze, then another yelled command came. "Take off your packs and set them on the ground. Real slow like."

Will squinted into the morning sun.

"Do it now. The gun in your belt, take it out and toss it onto the ground in front of you. Slowly, or you get a bullet through the chest."

They did as they were told, Zach first, then Will. When Will's gun had hit the soil in front of them, Millard approached cautiously, pointing his rifle back and forth between them.

"Step back away from the packs."

When he was within ten feet Millard stopped.

"Millie," Will said under his breath, confirming his fears. Seeing his face again was like replaying an old nightmare, a monster he'd long hoped was dead, arisen from his past.

"Willie Taft," Millard said in a mocking tone.

"Mill, goddammit. What do you want with us?" Will asked but knew there would be no reasoning with this man.

"We're headed back to the labor camp. A lot of folks are waitin' for you back there."

Will shook his head. "I'm not going with you."

Millard looked at his gun, then at Will. "Far as I can tell, you don't have much choice."

"I'm not going back. Not now," Will said quietly, with resolution. His teeth were clenched, and his pulse was speeding. He could feel his frustration being replaced with anger.

Millard looked at Zach. "What about you, son? Shouldn't you be with the UP?"

Zach didn't answer.

"Too gimpy to fight, huh? They'll be happy to see you in the labor camp with all the women and old folks. Each of you put these on." Millard reached around to a clip on his belt, and with a one-handed toss landed a pair of handcuffs in front of each of them.

Zach bent to pick up the handcuffs, but Will stayed standing, staring at Millard.

"I'm not putting those on, and I'm not going back with you." Will looked over Millard's shoulder toward Gonzales, then back at Millard. He clenched his fists.

Millard took a step back and lifted his gun toward Will.

"I've got permission to bring you back dead or alive."

"Mill, what are you doing?" Will yelled in disgust. "You work for the UP labor camp now? You know that's not right. After all we had to do for them."

"I should've killed you long ago when I had the chance," Millard said, the smug look returning to his face.

"Maybe you should've, but you didn't. The UP isn't what it used to be. The Valley administration is broken."

"I don't know nothin' about all that," Millard said, looking down at the handcuffs still on the soil. "They still pay me regularly."

"We saw UP soldiers who killed children in Greenfield," Will said.

"Oh, shut up with all that, Willie. My job's to bring you back. I don't want to drag your dead bodies to the truck, but I will. Now put on them handcuffs."

Will rubbed his hand over the wound on his cheek. The skin around it felt numb and cold. The stubbly hair from his beard was softening with length. He looked at Zach, then at the handcuffs, then back to Millard. He bent slowly, making eye contact with Millard the entire time, and picked up the handcuffs.

Millard took another cautious step away from Will and aimed the rifle barrel toward his head. "Don't you try anything stupid. Just put them cuffs on slowly."

Will slipped his wrists through each side of the loose rings of metal and tightened them with a ratcheting sound. Zach did the same.

"Alright, now turn around and start walking. Let's go. Toward the ramp."

Millard bent to pick up the guns and packs while Zach and Will continued in the downvalley direction along the highway. Will could see the old spherical Gonzales water tower in the distance. He clenched his fist in the handcuffs. He felt strangled, overheated. He seethed with anger.

Once they were up the ramp and next to the jeep, Millard said, pointing to Zach, "You ride in the front. Willie, you're gonna drive."

He set his rifle and the confiscated weaponry on the back seat, then took out a handgun from beneath his coat. He lifted it toward Zach and said, "Come over here. Hold out your hands." He unlocked Zach's cuffs with one hand while holding the handgun on him with the other, always watching Will, cautious of what he might do. "Handcuff him to the driver's side door," he commanded Zach, "and Willie, you try anything I'll shoot you both. I oughta just shoot you both right now anyway, so you don't cause me any more trouble."

Once Will was behind the wheel of the jeep, one hand cuffed to the door, Millard had Zach secure himself to the passenger door. Millard rolled a toothpick between his teeth as he handed the keys to Zach.

"Lean over and start it up," he commanded.

Will pulled onto the longvalley highway, leaving the Gonzales skyline to dwindle in the side mirror.

The knobby tires hummed loudly on the smooth highway surface as they rode in silence. Will drove slowly, thinking of ways to escape their situation. Crash the jeep? Get shot. Speed up? Get shot. He could kill all three of them, but what would be the point? How would that help Helen or get him any closer to her?

Zach, who'd apparently never been up on the highway, watched the Valley pass, his mouth hanging open. The sun was nearing the peak of its daily arch, and the sky was pure blue in front of them.

Millard spoke to Zach. "Did you know this guy is a fully decorated war hero?"

Zach looked at Will, who continued to stare straight ahead, one hand on the wheel.

Millard went on, "Yup, came back from the border zone a real hero. Nobody knows what happened out there, how he survived, how he made it back." Millard was silent for some time, then said, "I know, though, 'cause I was there with him. I know what we did."

"You mean what *you* did?" Will said.

"Mr. War Hero here doesn't want to take credit for what we did out there."

After more silence Millard addressed Zach. "Killin' folks is easier for some than others. Some people just don't like to admit how easy it is for them."

They rode in silence with the windows down. The warm air fluttered through the jeep. They drove over endless crops, fallow patches, and myriad shades of green, and Will could smell the familiar sweetness of the fields below. All his time in the fields surrounding Gonzales had trained him to recognize the time of year and what was being grown by the odor alone.

Will heard Millard going through their packs in the back seat.

Millard said with his mouth full, "Damn, this is good. I hit the jackpot with you two."

Neither Zach nor Will spoke.

"This food must have come from that broke down prison in Soledad."

Zach turned his head to look at Millard.

"That's right. I watched you. I watched you the whole way. Limpin' along, thinkin' you were free. And you know what, Willie? I saw Jose, too. Trained my scope right on him. Took a lot of control not to squeeze that trigger. He was probably talkin' some bullshit to you about them livin' free in that prison."

Millard scoffed. "I'm looking forward to going back there for him someday. Tell you what, the Administration's gonna love knowin' about that resistance stronghold in that prison. Thank you for leading me to them."

Millard nudged Zach's shoulder with the barrel of the handgun. "Willie tell you about how that half-breed piece of shit was with us out past the border zone? Everyone thought he died out there. Guess not." Will glanced at Millard in the rearview mirror. He was leaned back against the seat with a look of satisfaction and the remains of an apple pie in his hand.

"Willie here and Jose and I were all part of the same unit. This is back when the Valley was expanding. We got separated from the rest of the unit in San Benician territory. We were way behind SB lines. What a mess. Ain't that right, Willie?" Millard asked, poking him with the gun.

Will didn't respond. He stared forward at the oncoming road trying not to betray any sign of interest in what Millard was saying.

"The three of us had to cross Hollister to get back into the Valley. Benito soldiers were everywhere. A whole battalion between us and the border. Our unit was supposed to be sneaking out past the Gabilans, then we were going to make our way north to raid the SB Hollister weapons factory. When they found us, they came down hard. It was a suicide mission from the start. As far as we knew, the whole unit was gone except for us."

Millard trailed off and looked out the window for a while.

"Anyway, we were hidin' out trying to make it back, and we lucked upon that factory. Had what we needed to blow it up, too, destroy the whole thing, but Willie refused. They had women and a bunch of children workin' in there. Hundreds of them. Far as I was concerned, you help produce weapons for the enemy, you can die like everyone else, child or not. Once we blew half that building apart, I started killing everything in it. Like a good soldier ought to. Mr. War Hero here tried to stop me." Millard stared at Will. "You were weak back then, just like you are now. Always too nice to do the proper job of a soldier."

Will continued to stare blankly at the road ahead. His jaw was clenched.

"How's that shoulder of yours anyway?" Millard asked, then turning to Zach said, "This coward nearly got me killed. Had to neutralize him. Jose never made it out of the building after setting the explosives. I still don't know how either of you made it back. Suppose you got friendly with the SB soldiers or somethin'. You a traitor now, Willie?"

Finally, Will broke his silence. "You shouldn't have done what you did out there. It was unnecessary," Will said. Everything about Millard disgusted him.

"They were enemy combatants, and your weakness put us all in danger." Millard's voice was rising and coming forth as an angry croak. "You're no hero. I was the damn hero. I'm the one who killed our enemies."

"They were unarmed children," Will said, suppressing his anger.

"We were children, goddammit," Millard yelled, letting his rage get the best of him. He lifted his handgun to the back of Will's head. Will could feel the barrel shaking against his skull as he let his foot off the gas pedal. Millard pushed the barrel hard into Will's head and said, "Keep driving," then retracted the gun to the back seat.

They rode in silence, Millard picking his teeth and occasionally making a hissing sound as he pulled air through them.

A UP transport truck appeared in Will's rearview mirror. It was moving fast and bearing down on them. Millard turned to see what Will was looking at.

"What's this?" Millard asked.

When the truck was just behind them a hollow voice came across the truck's loudspeaker. "Pull your vehicle to the side."

CHAPTER TWENTY

Mary laid awake on the gym floor, hoarse from screaming, rancid air stinging on the back of her throat. Sometime during the night, the rain found its pace of endless whispers, and heavy clouds belched out their blood boiling sickness onto the darkness below. She panted and struggled against her restraints as the rain drummed a cold and steady murmur on the walkway outside the gym. At some point, she thought she heard screaming, but it was muffled and distorted by the sound of water running everywhere and the ringing in her ears. She kept yelling the names of her lost children as the dark hours passed, clinging to the futile hope that they would somehow hear her and be comforted by her voice.

She passed out, only to be repeatedly jolted awake by the pain in her shoulder. She oscillated in and out of a partial dream state throughout the dark early morning hours, repulsed by the stink wafting across her face from under the door. She finally awoke in the silence after the rain had stopped. A barely perceptible sliver light stretched underneath the gym doors, and Mary knew that the sun would soon rise over the Gabilans. She waited. If she could maintain stillness, her shoulder would stop its incessant burning. All she wanted was to hear the joyful morning voices of the school's children, but silence prevailed.

The light under the door had grown bright when Mary once again heard boots on the sidewalk. The gym doors opened. She struggled to look up to see Captain Wilson.

"Alright, Miss McElroy, time to get up," the captain said with an almost triumphant tone in his voice.

Mary laid on the floor silently, unresponsive. There was only the burning pain in her shoulder and the horror of what had happened to the children.

He spoke in a low and cold tone. "We had our orders. This is for the good of the Valley."

Mary squinted into the distance beyond Captain Wilson's boots, through the open gym doors where the tan covered walkways of the school were soaked dark with rain. She saw the fence and beyond it, a soldier was lifting a limp child from the grass.

"No, no, no, no," Mary cried in a hollow whisper.

"I'm going to cut the restraints off your legs. Don't fight me or I'll have to hurt you," Captain Wilson said as he leaned over to roll Mary onto her stomach.

Mary screamed at the pain in her shoulder.

"My shoulder. Please don't move me," she said.

Captain Wilson ran a hand along Mary's back and across the outside of her right shoulder.

"Damn it," he said under his breath, then more loudly, "your shoulder's dislocated. I told you to stay calm. What did you do?" He cut the zip tie, and her arms fell to her side. Mary screamed again.

He lifted Mary and rolled her onto her back. While Mary screamed, he pulled her arm up and away from her. She heard a deep thud and felt a hit of intense pain in her shoulder as the joint pulled back into place. The pain subsided almost instantly, and Mary looked up at the captain, who was leaning over her, staring down at her, still holding her arm.

He smiled a wicked smile. "There, I bet you feel better now." He gripped her arm and continued to stare.

She was wide-eyed with naked fear, completely still, until he set her arm down on her side and stepped away. Mary peered out the gym doors toward the fence enclosure again.

"Why?" she yelled and began to cry.

Captain Wilson didn't respond.

Outside the gym, the schoolyard, the grass, and the fields beyond laid calmly in the pewter morning light. Each blade of grass shimmered with droplets of spent water, soon to be evaporated, clinging to the margins of everything. As the sun crested the low rim of the eastern hills, thousands of clear prisms took in its light, scrambled and reflected it in all directions. Within minutes the day was yellow and bright.

Captain Wilson stood by the doors with his back to Mary looking out into the schoolyard as Mary struggled to her feet. Over his shoulders, she saw the children, supine and motionless forms on the lawn, some on top of each other. Mary held a hand to her mouth and thought for a moment she might throw up. The air around her grew heavy and hard to breathe. She looked on as two soldiers carefully lifted a child and carried her out of the fence enclosure. The child's clothes were soaked and hanging off her awkwardly. Mary rolled her shoulders back and gulped in air, her fists clenched, and her nostrils flared.

"Why?" she screamed at him from behind, her voice shaking. "Why?"

Momentarily her rage outweighed her fear, and she pounded his upper back with both her fists. He turned around, grabbed her wrists, and slapped her to the ground.

He looked down on her as she recovered from the blow. He kicked her on the side where she laid on the gym floor and said, "Don't ever touch me again. Now get up and follow me outside."

Mary limped out into the morning sun following at a safe distance behind Captain Wilson. She squinted and held her shoulder with her other hand. The smell of sulfur had dissipated, replaced with the old smells of the Valley, fresh soil, diesel fuel, and wet straw.

Mary walked in a daze toward the fence. The gate was wide open, and the small bodies of children laid haphazardly about the inside, some facing the sky, others face-down in the grass, some still in a cold wet embrace.

CHAPTER TWENTY-ONE

As the UP military truck came up close behind them, Will slowed Millard Fillmore's jeep.

"You two don't move. Stay seated," Millard said as Will pulled the jeep to the side of the highway. In the rearview mirror, he could see the light blue uniforms of UP soldiers riding in the truck's front.

Millard pushed open the back door. The voice came again over the loudspeaker. "Stay in the vehicle." Four UP soldiers exited the truck with their rifles out and waited a short distance behind the jeep.

"Throw any weapons out of the vehicle," said the voice through the speaker.

"What is this?" Millard asked. "You have something to do with this?" poking Will's shoulder again with the handgun.

"Throw your weapons out or you'll be shot."

Millard studied his handgun for a moment, then tossed it gently out the open door onto the concrete edge of the highway.

"Stay in the vehicle and lift your hands where they can be seen."

Millard put both hands up, and Will and Zach each lifted their non-handcuffed hand.

A fifth soldier set down the microphone in the front of the UP transport truck, stepped down out of the truck, and approached the jeep. He studied the vehicle for a moment. "Proceed," he said to the other four soldiers, who approached the jeep cautiously.

"Keep your hands where they can be seen, and slowly exit the vehicle."

Millard scooted along the back seat with his hands in the air and stepped out onto the highway. "The two men in the front seat are my prisoners. They're each handcuffed to the door," he said.

"What's your name?"

"Millard Fillmore. I'm under orders from the San Ardo Camp Director to return these two."

"State your names," the soldier yelled into the front of the car.

"Will Taft."

"Zach Taylor."

"Handcuff key," the soldier said, holding out his black-gloved hand to Millard.

"These two are my prisoners," Millard said, his voice low and irritated. "I work for the Valley Administration."

"Give me the key," the soldier repeated.

One of the other soldiers turned his rifle on Millard.

"Alright," Millard said, pulling back his coat.

The soldier took a step back and lifted his rifle to Millard's head.

"Slowly," yelled the soldier.

Millard put both his hand's palm up, then slowly went to his front pocket. "Calm down, just keys," he said.

"What's this about?" Millard asked.

"We have orders to take these two men to UP headquarters."

"I have a job to do, and I've been told to take them back to the labor camp in San Ardo."

"I don't care about your job," the soldier said, taking the key from Millard. "We have orders," he said, handing the key to another soldier. "Unlock them. Collect any weapons from the vehicle."

"Whose orders are these?"

The soldier ignored Millard's question.

After being unlocked, Will stood on the highway and squinted in the midday sun.

"You own this vehicle?" the soldier asked Millard.

"Yes."

"You can proceed back to San Ardo now. We'll inform the camp of the change," then, turning to another soldier, said, "Load the prisoners in the back of the truck."

"These are my prisoners."

"Not any longer."

Will and Millard made brief eye contact, and Will couldn't help but smile as the soldier pushed him from behind in the direction of the UP transport truck.

"I'll find you again," was the last thing Will heard Millard Fillmore say.

Will and Zach were each led by a soldier behind the transport truck up steps into a holding area. The rear of the truck was a metal-walled room with two built-in benches along each side, a place for carrying soldiers or prisoners. At the back of the chamber, another small door led to the driving cabin in the front of the truck.

"Sit there," a soldier said, pointing to the benches, then closed and latched the door behind them. Will and Zach sat across from each other in total darkness except for a white line of sunlight raking across the metal floor from under the back door, each rivet on the floor casting a long shadow.

Will heard doors slam shut, and the UP truck engine roared to life. Some short turns were made as the truck reversed its direction on the highway, gears ground, and they both leaned sideways as the truck accelerated back onto the highway in the direction from where they had come.

"What's going on?" Zach asked Will.

"I have no idea," Will grumbled. "Better than the situation we were in."

"I hope so."

They rode in silence. The engine of the truck hummed, and the darkness was comforting to Will. He had a great sense of relief to be headed away from Millard. He was exhausted from the sickness and lack of sleep during the previous night. He closed his eyes and an image of Hannah came to him. She was tucked under the canopy of a low shrub, lying in the sand. Rain was dripping on her face through the leaves. She smiled at him.

The light on the ceiling fluttered, then came on. Will squinted as he opened his eyes. The inside walls of the truck were white under the surgical light, and Zach's hair looked almost blue. There was a pounding on the metal door that led to the driving cabin, the sound of the door being unlatched, then it slid open.

Jose Alvarez, in a blue UP soldier's uniform, ducked under the small door and sat on the bench next to Zach.

He slapped Zach's knee and said, "Surprise," with a wide smile.

"Jose?" Will asked, a grin stretching his lips.

"You didn't think we were just going to let the two of you wander off and not keep tabs on you?"

Will was dumbfounded.

"If we did that, you'd be arriving back at the labor camp in an hour or so."

"But this truck? The uniforms?"

"We hijacked a convoy a few months back. The uniforms and transport truck come in handy."

"You knew where we were since leaving the prison?"

"I had someone watch you. They lost track of you until this morning when you got caught by the highway." Jose smiled and said, "I told you to stick to the river basin."

"Well. Thank you."

Jose nodded. "We still have to get you to Gonzales. You never know what could happen on this highway."

Will looked at Jose in the cold metallic light. The smile left his face. "That was Millard Fillmore who picked us up."

"I know. I saw from the truck," Jose said, shaking his head. "Apparently he's tracking and collecting people for the UP now."

"He won't stop until he finds us again."

"Well, that shouldn't be too easy for him. We left him with no weapons, and he seemed convinced that we were UP soldiers."

"He knows about the prison."

Jose nodded. "I figured."

Will looked at Zach, who was silently watching both of them. "I don't think we've seen the last of him."

Jose patted Zach's knee again. "We'll be in Gonzales in less than an hour, my friend. Have you eaten?"

"Not really," Zach said.

"Hold on."

Jose reached into the driving cabin and pulled out two thick rolls in brown paper. Zach and Will unwrapped the sandwiches and devoured them.

"I have to watch out up front. I'll let you know when we're about to arrive."

Less than an hour later Jose yelled to Will from the front, "We'll be in Gonzales in five minutes. We'll drop you two at the top of the access ramp, then head back to Soledad. We can't blow our cover with this truck. We need to use it and the uniforms in the future."

"Sounds good."

"They'll come and pull you out of the back. The ramp guardhouse might be occupied, so we'll let the UP guards know that you're supposed to return to the town."

The door to the front of the transport truck was open, and Will squatted and peered through the front window as they approached the Gonzales ramp and guard station.

"Alright, here we go," said Jose. "Get ready to come out the back of the truck, like you're returned, prisoners."

"It looks empty," Will said.

"Pull up right on the guardhouse," Jose said to the driver. "It looks empty. Alright, get ready. We'll move on, just in case we're being watched." Jose turned to Will and took a long look at him. "Good luck, my friend. This place could be crawling with UP. You need to be careful."

"We will be."

"We can't watch out for you anymore. You're on your own down here."

"I understand."

Jose paused and seemed to consider his words carefully. "Something is about to happen, and I'd recommend you get in and out of Gonzales as soon as possible. Don't stay here. This part of the Valley is no longer safe and will get worse soon."

"Why is that?" Will yelled over the roar of the engine as the truck slowed.

"Never mind. Once you get your daughter, head back upvalley as soon as possible. You understand?"

"Yes."

"Alright. Get going then and be careful."

"Thank you," Will replied.

"See you again soon, hopefully, but not too soon." Jose smiled and turned back to the driver.

The brakes screeched and hissed as the truck came to a stop. Will and Zach went to the back to be let out. One of Jose's men unlatched the back and lifted them down onto the asphalt and into the white midday sun. He set their bags down, then returned to the front. The truck's engine raced as it made a three-point turn, then roared off back in the upvalley direction.

CHAPTER TWENTY-TWO

Will squinted and surveyed the top of the ramp, allowing his eyes to adjust. The rough hum of the transport truck faded in the distance. He picked up his pack, opened it, and retrieved his handgun, which Jose's men had left inside. He opened the barrel to see that each chamber was full, spun it, clicked it closed, and put the gun under his shirt in the back of his belt.

"No more rifle."

"Yeah, we'll have to get that back later. Either Jose has it or it got left in Mill's jeep."

"What now?" Zach asked.

The guardhouse at the top of the ramp was empty, and the metal ramp gate was wide open.

"We have to get to the school," Will said, rushing in the direction of the town. "Down the ramp. Let's go."

They hustled down the same concrete and metal ramp that Will had worked on for many years, loading produce into trailers to be pulled up its steep incline and moved off toward Salinas City or the upvalley camps.

"Where is everybody?" Will asked at the bottom of the ramp. "They must have collected everyone after Hannah, and I were taken."

The thirteen streets that made up Gonzales were laid out long before the wars of Valley independence and hadn't been repaved or maintained in any way in Will's lifetime. Although he was born in Gonzales, on the ninth of its thirteen streets, he'd never seen a car drive along them, and plants had long ago reclaimed most areas of concrete. There were well-worn paths on both sides of the streets, where once sidewalks had run. Now whole areas of road were vegetated, and in some spots, particularly along Fifth Avenue, which led to the school, people had planted corn, flowers, and tomatoes in areas where once cars had supposedly driven.

The idea that each family or even individual people had once owned and operated a vehicle seemed preposterous to Will, and he barely believed the old time stories, yet there they were, abandoned strips in each Valley town, curbs, gutters, parking lots, cracked sidewalks, broken pavement, vast stretches of impermeable material, all returning to the earth.

Will remembered the day he'd spent with the digging bar in the middle of the road in front of his parents' house, pulling up heavy chunks of concrete. He was amazed by the quality of soil under each section, as if the streets were laid down not for cars but put there by forward-thinking Valley residents from a bygone era to preserve the best agricultural soils, lying in wait for hundreds of years undisturbed below a skin of asphalt.

As they moved through the empty streets, Will experienced all the familiarity of his hometown. So recently they'd been in the back of Millard's jeep with no hope of getting to Helen, and now here he was, on the leafy streets, soon to reunite with his daughter. A weight seemed to lift from his chest as he drew a breath. A sense of relief came over him, one he hadn't felt since he and Hannah were forced from Gonzales at gunpoint.

The afternoon sun was bright and beautiful on the rundown houses of Gonzales. Where once there had been front lawns, a diversity of vegetation littered the yards and spread unbroken into the streets. Elms, ornamental pears, and palm trees originally planted as street trees had long ago reseeded and their progeny were mature and made stands in the old streets, doing their part to break up and dissolve the concrete.

"We have to be careful," Will said. The town was quieter than he'd ever heard it. "It's like everyone's been collected. There could be UP soldiers still here."

"Where's the school?"

"A short distance that way, but we're going to make a quick stop on the way."

"Where?"

"We'll go by our house."

At a corner house in what was at one time an old Gonzales neighborhood, but now looked like an overgrown ghost town, Will came off the dirt path, slipped through a break in the privet hedge, and entered his front yard.

"This is your place?" Zach asked.

Will looked around, and a sadness came over him. "It doesn't seem like it so much anymore."

"Well, it looks like a nice old house."

"We tried to keep it up. We were happy to have it. Always working on it."

"I haven't ever been this far downvalley," Zach said. "The houses are much older here."

Will grabbed the worn brass knob on the front door. "It's locked. We'll have to go around back for the key. Hannah probably locked the front door the morning we were collected as she left with Helen. I was already in the fields and I never had a key," Will said proudly. "There was never any need nor reason to lock the house anyway."

Around back was a small yard surrounded by tall hedges. Four tidy square beds of open soil were cut out of the grass that surrounded them. One was fallow, one had a stand of snap peas tied up on twine between two old wood stakes, a third had young tomato plants, and the fourth was over-planted with a riot of roses in several stages of blooming.

Will paused and surveyed the small garden. He could feel Zach watching him, wanting an explanation.

"Hannah loved her roses. And the snap peas were for Helen. She grew them herself and waited every day for the first peas to arrive."

Will went to the pea patch. Each plant wore a garland of newly opened bright white flowers. He searched the plants for the delicate fruit and pulled the only three he could find off and put them carefully into his pocket.

On the back porch, Will wiped his shoes on the mat, and Zach did the same. They opened the door and stepped into the kitchen. The linoleum floor shined, the room was bright and cheery, neat, yet well lived in. The air was stale and smelled of overripe fruit. A small kitchen table sat empty except for a clear vase surrounded by fallen rose petals that had turned from yellow to orange as they dried.

"I'll be right back. Check the refrigerator. Collect everything that's edible into that bag," Will said. "There may be something that's still good in there for us to eat."

Zach opened the refrigerator, and a warm, moldy smell emerged.

"The fridge isn't cold," he yelled into the next room.

"The electricity has been on and off for months now," Will yelled back. "When I was at the upvalley work camp I saw the diesel generators at the San Ardo power station."

Will returned to the kitchen from the back room. "Nobody in Gonzales depended on there being electricity. At one point we stopped using the refrigerator all together. Hannah must have left some stuff in there assuming we'd get back to it that night. Load up what's in that cupboard."

"What's that?"

"It's Helen's favorite doll. She loves this little thing. It's the only one she ever wanted. It's been bothering me, her sleeping at the school without it. I also got this."

Will held a handgun in his other hand. "Guns weren't allowed in the town, and it would be bad if you were found with one, but I kept this hidden. My father gave it to me when I turned fifteen. We used to walk out into the arroyos to the east early in the morning, and he taught me how to shoot it." He retrieved the other gun from his belt and handed it to Zach. "Here, keep this one. It's loaded."

Will looked around his house and thought of what else they may need while Zach carefully tucked the gun into his belt.

"I think we've got everything. After we get Helen, we can't come back here. It's too risky staying in Gonzales now that it's been cleared out. We'll have to head back to the prison."

"Alright."

"The school could be well guarded. If something happens to me, get Helen back to Jose and the people at the prison. Alright?"

"Of course."

"Let's go then."

CHAPTER TWENTY-THREE

Back on the street, they set off toward the Gonzales school with Zach limping after Will at a strenuous pace. Each step reminded Will of better times, and it occurred to him that they hadn't just taken his wife and child, but his hometown, his way of life, and his memories.

They hurried along a raised path where railroad tracks had once born their abundant cargo, but all that remained were coarse pieces of granite on which the tracks had once sat. The metal in the tracks that at one time traversed the Valley floor had long ago been collected, melted, and refashioned for more useful purposes.

They raced down off the raised path onto another disintegrating sidewalk that led along the edge of old Fifth Avenue toward the school. Will paused looking around carefully. Everything was quiet. A slight breeze ruffled the leaves of the old camphor trees that arched overhead in the deep cobalt sky. He felt uneasy. *What if Helen was gone, too?*

"Something doesn't seem right. I've never heard it this quiet here," Will said.

"Nobody's here. Every house looks empty," Zach replied.

They came to the end of Fifth Avenue to the entrance of the school. The play yard and blacktop were bright in the midday sun. Will was running as he came around the entrance where the gym joined the other buildings. He ran along the covered walkways, stood silently listening to himself breathing, then started to open classroom doors. He pulled open the gym doors, and there were cots everywhere and tables with papers. It was as if the children had just gotten up from their seats.

A deep dread crept into his mind as Will ran to the cafeteria. Out of the corner of his eye, he saw a square fenced in area on the schoolyard lawn. He slammed the cafeteria door open and there was nothing but the hollow echo off the back wall. He ran back out onto the sidewalk in front of the gym where he met Zach.

"Nobody's here. It doesn't make sense. Children don't get collected."

Zach looked around, breathing heavily, and didn't reply.

"These children, they were all too young to be collected. Maybe they've been moved to the fields for harvesting," Will said, scanning the horizon.

They ran across the schoolyard blacktop and peered out into the fields in the distance. A sea of green and brown stretched to the east in front of them. They could see as far as the Gabilans, and no moving figures disrupted the horizon.

"Where could they be?" Will asked.

His eyes followed the rows of the great fields back from the distant horizon to an area just in front of where he and Zach stood. There, off the edge of the yard, where the school ended and agricultural fields began, he saw black soil heaped into a line of small mounds. The fresh clods of dirt were still wet from the previous night's rain. A wave of fear came over Will as he thought back to the scene they had seen at the school in Greenfield.

"What is this? No, no, no," Will said as he ran off the blacktop down onto the soil where the mounds were.

He fell onto his knees beside one of the piles and pulled the dirt away from the top onto his lap. He clawed frantically at the loose soil until with one hard pull, he scraped along something more solid and freed the bluish white hand of a child. As he uncovered the pale dirty hand, he felt a shock run through his system, like some piece of machinery just seized up in his chest, the gears grinding to a halt. All the muscles in his body seemed to contract simultaneously, and he kept crying, "No, no, no, no."

In horror, Will pushed back away from the grave. He looked at the other mounds, at the small dirty hand, and to Helen's doll that laid face-down on the dirt next to him.

CHAPTER TWENTY-FOUR

Ben Harrison approached the lab bench where his assistant sat with his back to him, studying something intently in a microscope. Ben didn't want to startle him, so he coughed quietly.

"What was it you wanted me to see?" Ben asked.

"I still can't believe it. You need to look at this." He rose from the stool to make room for Ben, took a slide down from the shelf above the microscope, and mounted it on the stage.

Ben slid his glasses up onto his forehead, peered through the lenses, and focused the microscope. Inside the droplet of rainwater, millions of the same artificial bacteria Ben had studied his whole career vibrated and budded, forming new cells. Tiny stinking bubbles grew and formed a haze around each cell. "They're expanding. Looks like the same increased rate we've been seeing."

"Yes, but now watch this." He leaned over and put a drop of pink fluid on the edge of the microscope slide. The fluid quickly wicked in between the slide and coverslip.

Ben looked up, blinked, then bent his head over the scope again. Each bacterial cell in the microscope's field of view slowed in its movements, grew fuzzy, then peeled apart.

"What?" he finally asked. "Unbelievable."

He was silent, and his mouth hung open as he focused on the slide.

"Show me another one," Ben said.

The assistant handed another slide to Ben, who mounted in on the scope. They repeated the procedure with the same result.

"There's no alcohol in that?"

"No, just blood and water."

"Does it happen every time?" Ben asked.

"I've checked it twelve times," he said, pointing to the mess of slides on the bench beside him.

He looked down at the vial of pink fluid. "Is it the same for all of the children?"

"I'm about to find out."

Helen Taft sat cross-legged on the couch in the white-walled room inside the Valley Administration building. Ben Harrison knocked gently on the door and pulled it open. She looked up at him with interest, then looked past him to see if anyone else was coming through the door. Her disappointment was obvious.

"Hello, Helen, I'm Ben."

She looked up at him but didn't answer. A small boy with bed-head straw hair rocked on the chair next to the couch.

"Hello, Jimmy, how are you?" Ben asked.

"Fine," the boy responded, blankly staring at the wall on the opposite side of the room.

"Are you two hungry?" Ben asked.

"Yes," they both said in unison.

"Alright, come on, let's go down the hallway and get breakfast."

Neither of the children moved, then Ben extended his hand out to each of them and waited, doing his best to be non-threatening. Jimmy studied him, then came off the chair and stood next to him, looking at Helen. She reluctantly took Ben's hand, using it to pull herself off the couch, and they all turned to the door.

"Sir, I can't let you leave with the children," said the teenage UP soldier at the door as Ben opened it.

"We're just headed to the cafeteria down the hallway."

"Sorry, sir. My orders are to make sure the children stay here until Colonel Adams arrives."

"Do you know who I am?" Ben asked.

"Yes, sir," the soldier said, becoming uncomfortable. "The Valley Science Minister."

"I don't care what your orders are, these children are hungry. You can guard them while we go to the cafeteria, or you can stay here."

The boy's eyes darted down the hallway and back to Ben, who stared at him unwaveringly.

"I'll follow you and the children, sir."

"Alright, then," Ben said, leading the children out of the room. "Come on, Helen, Jimmy. What do you want to eat?"

"What can we have?" Jimmy asked.

"We'll see. It's a big cafeteria."

In the cafeteria, with the soldier standing behind their table, Jimmy ate pancakes with his hands, while Helen picked at her oatmeal with a spoon, taking small bites.

"Helen, do you know why you're here?"

She stopped eating and looked up at him. "Because we're not dead, like all the other children." Her eyes became glassy with tears.

Ben was taken aback by her honesty and clarity. "Yes, that's right."

"Are my parents here?" Helen asked Ben. "They were collected about two weeks ago."

"Our parents are here?" asked the boy, looking up from his pancakes, suddenly interested in their conversation.

"They aren't here, but we're looking for them and hopefully they'll be coming soon."

Ben watched them eat, then said, "I'd like to ask you some questions about what happened at your school in Gonzales. Would that be alright?"

Helen looked down at her oatmeal, then briefly made eye contact with Ben. She nodded.

"What did you feel when it started to rain?"

"I was scared, but I felt nothing."

"Did you know you'd be fine?"

"Yes."

"Yes?" Ben asked, surprised. "How did you know?

"I just knew. I wasn't ever afraid of it. I'd never been out in it like I was that night, but it never bothered me. I just knew."

"How about you, Jimmy? Did you know the rain wouldn't hurt you?"

"When is my mommy coming?"

"Soon, Jimmy," Ben said. The boy looked up at him with sad, distant eyes, trying to read the face of this unfamiliar adult. Ben's heart ached for the boy, and he reached out and patted him on the shoulder. "How are your pancakes?"

"They're okay," Jimmy said with a blank stare.

"Helen," Ben said, turning to her. "After breakfast, we're going to run some tests. Is that alright with you?"

"What kind of tests?"

"Nothing that will hurt, just asking you some questions, listening to your heart. Have you ever been to a doctor before?" Ben asked.

Helen thought. "I don't know. I don't think so."

"Well, it won't hurt," Ben said.

"Alright." Helen took a bite of oatmeal while Ben waited patiently.

"Can you smell the rain before it comes?" he asked.

"Can't you?"

"I can. What does it smell like to you?"

"It smells like someone is cooking, but something stinky."

"Did the smell change when you were out in the rain?" Ben asked.

"No. It got worse and worse. Really stinky."

"Then what?"

"Then, that's all. Nothing. It went away when the rain stopped."

Ben eyed Helen as she went back to her oatmeal. She was the oldest person who could survive the rain whom he'd ever had a chance to talk to. He had so many questions but didn't want to overwhelm her.

"Are you a scientist?" Helen asked after finishing her bite.

"I am."

"I've heard about scientists at the school. Like Einstein."

"Yes, like Einstein." Ben smiled.

"Why does the rain hurt people?" Helen asked.

"There are small invisible organisms in the clouds called bacteria. The bacteria make chemicals that make people sick."

"How did they get there?"

"A long time ago some people were trying to make the weather better in the Valley, so they made the bacteria and put them in the clouds, hoping they would make it rain more."

"Did it work?"

"It did. It started to rain a lot more. The Valley was hot and dry for a long time, so the rain was a blessing at first. We could produce everything all the people in the Valley needed. The Valley used to be part of a larger country, long before you and I were born, but after the rains came it made no sense for the Valley to stay a part of that country anymore."

"But why was rain a good thing if it made people sick?"

"It didn't make people sick at first. Something happened in the clouds. The bacteria mutated and made poisons. And it rained more and more often."

"My teacher could tell every afternoon when the rains would come. She would always make sure everyone was in on time. She was good at it."

"Sounds like a good skill."

"Ms. McElroy was the best," Helen said, looking around as if Mary McElroy was going to be sitting somewhere in the cafeteria. "Do you know where she is?"

"I'm not sure, but I'll find out," Ben said. "Did you ever see either of your parents out in the rain?"

"No. They were always careful to keep us out of it. Mom hates the smell."

"Does the rainwater taste different to you?"

"I don't think so."

"Did you taste it when you were out in it?" Ben asked.

"I guess so. It was raining so hard, some of it got into my mouth. It didn't bother me or taste like anything."

Ben looked at Jimmy, who was staring across the cafeteria, then back at Helen, who watched him closely.

"Are your eyes stinging?"

"No."

"Did they sting in the rain?"

"What's going on here?" a loud voice asked from the other side of the room.

Ben saw a stout redheaded officer coming quickly through the door of the cafeteria. He was angry. The soldier guarding their table turned toward the officer.

"The children were hungry," the soldier stuttered.

"You were told to keep these children in the room."

"Yes, sir, but—"

The officer looked past the soldier, glaring sharply at Ben. Ben rose from his seat next to the children and stepped toward the officer. He could see Helen gripping the table in fear.

Ben held out his hand to the officer. "I'm Ben Harrison. Valley Science Minister."

"I know who you are," the officer said coldly, not extending his hand to Ben. "We're under orders to keep these children in the room until we hear otherwise by Colonel Adams."

Helen and Jimmy had risen from the table and were cowering behind Ben.

"The children needed to be fed."

Although the soldier was much heavier than Ben, he was still shorter. Ben looked down on him, growing angry.

"What's your name?" Ben asked.

"I'm Captain Wilson."

"Who's your commanding officer?" Ben asked with clear irritation in his voice.

Captain Wilson looked up at him with contempt. "I report directly to the Colonel Adams and the Valley Manager. Now let's get these children back to the room."

"I'll take them back when they're done eating," Ben said, holding his ground in front of Wilson.

Captain Wilson stared up at Ben, then looked down at the children hiding behind him. He shook his head slightly, then a slight smile came over his face. "Alright, then. Five minutes. Have them back in the room."

He turned away from Ben to the wide-eyed soldier. "You come with me," he said, then stormed out of the cafeteria.

After the soldiers had gone, Ben turned around to the children. "It's alright. They're just trying to make sure you're safe."

Helen was shaking her head, looking terrified. "He was the one," she whispered.

"What do you mean?" Ben asked.

"At the school. He was the one who locked us out in the rain."

CHAPTER TWENTY-FIVE

Will sat on the ground with black soil mounded on his lap, tears falling down his grimy beard. He stared for a long time feeling broken and numb. He knew he'd have to exhume each one until he found her, and the thought of pulling her cold body out of a mound of soil was unbearable. He was barely conscious of the world around him, staring down at Helen's doll.

"Willie," someone yelled from the school.

Will and Zach turned to see Mary McElroy running in their direction.

"Mary," Will yelled back, rising to meet her.

Will held his arms open and embraced her. She was crying, her lip swollen and cracked, and both eyes were black. Will held her against his chest for a long time. Eventually, he let her go and asked, "What happened here? Are you okay?"

"Soldiers came. A few days ago." She began to cry again. "Oh, Willie, they forced them all out into the rain."

"Why?"

Mary grabbed Will by the shoulders and looked straight into his eyes. Her jaw was tense and rigid. She was fighting to hold herself together. She tried to speak slowly and clearly. "She's alive. Helen is alive."

At the mention of his daughter's name, Will's vision narrowed, then blurred with more tears. His lip began to shake, and although he wanted to ask more questions, he couldn't. He had to wait for the knot in his throat to loosen.

"What do you mean, she's alive?"

"She's alive." Mary's eyes were wild. "She survived the night in the rain. Her and Jimmy, the Buchanan's little boy."

"Where is she now?" Will asked, gripping Mary firmly by both shoulders.

"They took them from me. I tried to stay with them, but they're gone. They wouldn't let me go with them." Mary sobbed and mumbled something unintelligible.

"How long ago, Mary? How long ago did the soldiers leave with Helen?" Will asked, unintentionally shaking her.

"They left this morning. They left me here with three soldiers. They stayed all day to dig the graves." Mary quickly glanced past Will at the fresh mounds on the edge of the yard. "There's nothing I could do. I'm so sorry, Will. I tried to protect them."

Will held Mary again. "Are the soldiers still here?"

"I don't know. I fell asleep for a while and haven't seen anyone since I woke up."

Zach took a step away from them and began to nervously scan the school.

"Are there any other children alive? Is there anyone in town?"

"No, not that I know of. They're all gone. All my children—" Mary started to cry and shake again.

Pressed against Will's chest, she said in a muffled voice, "The whole town. Everyone was taken. Willie, what's happening?"

"I'm not sure, but we have to go right now. We aren't safe here."

While he held Mary, Will watched the clouds accumulating in the downvalley sky.

"Mary, this is my friend Zach," Will said, letting her go.

Mary turned her head and seemed to see Zach for the first time. They nodded to each other.

Mary looked past Zach at the churning of murky condensation in the sky beyond. "It'll rain soon."

"How long?" Will asked, looking up.

Mary wiped her eyes with the sleeve of her shirt and studied the sky. "We have about fifteen or twenty minutes, maybe less."

"Come on then. We need to make it back to my house." Will turned back from looking at the sky and asked Mary, "Do you need anything from the school before we go? We may not be coming back."

Mary looked around at the schoolyard, the gym in the distance, then at the mounds of disturbed soil. She went to the grave nearest them, kneeled, and mounded soil up over the exposed child's hand. She gently patted the soil down over the covered hand and turned to Will and Zach.

"I have nothing here anymore."

CHAPTER TWENTY-SIX

As they ran through the streets of his hometown, through the over-grown mid-road gardens of Fifth Avenue, onto the old railroad track, and along the back of the neighborhoods, Will was struck by the vacancy of it all. Helen was no longer there. Neither was Hannah. No friends nor family remained. A town with no people was no longer a town at all. As he ran, Will understood that he would soon say goodbye to Gonzales forever.

The trees shuddered around them in the wind of the swelling storm, and the smell of garlic was overwhelming. Moments after they made it under the covering of Will's porch, the sky opened above them and heavy drops clobbered the roof. In seconds it was pouring, and Will could feel a burning in his throat. He instinctively moved away from the edge of the porch where water splattered on the painted boards. Mary held her shoulder and looked winded and dazed, her blackened eyes red and watery.

"The front door's still locked," Will yelled at Zach over the roar of the rain. "Can you go around back? We can't be out here much longer; there's too much water in the air." Will held his throat and felt light-headed.

Zach nodded, then looked at Mary, then back at Will.

"It's fine. Go," Will yelled.

Zach stepped out from under the porch covering and into the rain. Water instantly darkened his shirt. Mary let out a scream and raised her hand in Zach's direction, but Will held her back.

"He'll be okay. It doesn't hurt him."

Moments later Zach opened the front door from the inside, and Mary and Will rushed in.

"How are you feeling?" Will asked Mary

"I'm fine. I just need to sit down."

"What happened to your shoulder?"

"Nothing. I'll be fine," Mary replied.

"Here," Will said, pointing to the couch. "I'll bring you a glass of water."

Will stood at the kitchen sink rubbing his eyes. He turned the water on and drank from the faucet, then poured a glass for Mary. After handing her the glass he sat opposite her on a chair in the living room.

"Should we build a fire?" Zach asked, nodding to the fireplace.

"That may be a bad idea since we seem to be the only ones in town. It may draw attention."

"But the rain. Nobody would be out, even if they were here," Zach said.

"Okay. There's wood on the back porch to the left of the door. If you'll go out and get some, I'll start the fire," Will said.

As Zach left to collect wood, Will watched Mary as she stared into the distance. He'd known Mary for many years, through the death of her husband and the collection of her students for UP service, and always considered her to be one of the most resilient people he'd ever met, but now she seemed changed.

Her eyes met his. Her broken face was pale and tired, and she stared at him, unblinking, for a long moment.

"Had you not shown up, I would have walked out into the rain tonight." Her cracked lip began to quiver, and she lifted a hand to steady it. "I was all alone, the only person left in Gonzales. I have nothing anymore. My children." She couldn't go on and covered both her watery eyes with her hands.

Will moved next to her on the couch, putting his arm around her. "Mary, I'm so sorry," he said.

"It's coming down pretty hard out there," Zach said as he returned with an armload of wood.

"It never used to be this bad when it rained. It seems like even the air is poisonous now," Will said.

Mary looked up. "I've noticed that, too. It's gotten worse, just in the last month."

The kindling smoked and crackled as it was engulfed in thin blue flames. Will felt himself breathe deeply for the first time in several hours. The warmth and dryness of the flames reminded him of the few nights without rain or clouds when his father lit large fires in their back yard. He sat for hours in his mother's lap, staring at the flames as they died down to coals. Even then he knew it was a rare and special thing to sit with his relatives around a fire under the stars of the Valley sky. It was an event that humans had shared in that same spot for millennia, yet in his lifetime he'd experienced fewer than ten cloudless nights.

Mary and Zach pulled up chairs behind Will and raised their hands toward the warmth of the fire as it jumped against the sooty surface of the firebricks. For a long time, nobody spoke. Their faces glowed, and the warm reflection of the flame danced in their watery eyes. The fire heated the skin of Will's face, and he scratched carefully around the dried wound under his beard.

Zach rose and removed his wet shirt to hang it near the fire. Mary eyed him closely.

"How many of you are there?" Mary asked. She couldn't hide the suspicion in her voice.

Zach looked at her, confused at first, then replied, "There's just one of me."

"You know what I mean," Mary said.

"I don't know. I've never met anyone else like me, at least that I knew about." Zach turned to Will and asked, "Did you know?"

"Know what?"

"About your daughter?"

Will looked at Mary, who had turned to see his response. "No. I never suspected it. She always seemed afraid of the rain."

"Maybe she didn't even know," Mary said.

"I doubt that," Zach said. "I knew since I was a boy. It's a feeling you get when it rains, or maybe a feeling you don't get."

"Do you have any idea where they may have been taking her?" Will asked Mary.

"No. I was so upset. I can't even remember what was said. I know that the lead soldier, a redheaded captain, drove away with her, Jimmy, and another soldier in a transport jeep. I watched them go."

"What was his name?"

"I only got his last name, Wilson," Mary answered.

Captain Wilson. Will mouthed the words but barely any sound left him.

"The three other soldiers who stayed wouldn't say anything to me. They just worked away digging their holes while I screamed at them." Mary faced the fire in silence.

"Now that I think of it," she continued, "they had a truck in front of the school. It wasn't there when we left the school. They must have gone once they finished burying the—" Mary's voice trailed off and she began to cry. Will put his hand on her back.

Will's living room was dark except for the slow dancing of orange light on the plaster walls. He looked around at his meager possessions, a simple history told in objects, mostly accumulated by his wife and daughter. All else was lost, and now, none of it mattered.

Mary looked up at Will and asked the question he knew she'd been waiting to ask. All it took was one word.

"Hannah?"

Will shook his head and choked out the truth. "She didn't make it. During the escape from the camp."

Mary's face stiffened, and her body swayed ever so slightly in reaction to his words. "I'm so sorry, Will," she said in a shaky whisper.

He stared at the floor and didn't speak.

"We'll find Helen," Mary said, trying to be reassuring.

Still looking down, Will said, "I know we will. Thank you."

Turning to Zach, he said, "Tomorrow my plan is to head toward UP headquarters."

"You think that's where they've taken her?"

"We have nothing else to go on. I'll find this Captain Wilson." Will paused and stared at the flames. "I should go on by myself and you and Mary head back toward the prison."

"It's up to her, but if it's all the same to you, I'd rather continue downvalley. We've come this far. I'll see this through with you."

Mary sat up and looked at them both. She nodded and said, "I'm staying with you, Will."

Will looked at them both. "The farther downvalley we go, the more dangerous it gets. More rain, more UP, more war. You both realize that?"

Mary and Zach both nodded.

"Alright." Will continued, "We'll leave as soon as the rain stops. Meanwhile, we should get some rest. You two lie down and I'll stay up for a bit and keep watch. Mary, you can use the bedroom, Zach the couch."

"Let me take the first watch," Zach said. "I'd like to go for a little walk."

Will looked at him carefully, wondering where his loyalty came from and how far he would test it.

"Just make sure you aren't seen, if there is anyone left out there. Give me a couple hours of sleep, then wake me so you can rest."

"Okay."

"Would you mind if I slept out here by the fire, on the couch next to you?" Mary asked Will.

"No problem. I'll sleep on the rug," Will replied.

Early the next morning, the rain stopped, and Will was sitting on the front porch. Light was yawning across the eastern Valley, the sun hadn't yet risen, and the Valley was still blanketed in clouds.

Will knew the time to leave his house and Gonzales, likely for the last time, was drawing near. For years his heart was tethered to this home. This town had been his redemption, his chance at another life. He thought of Hannah and how she'd loved this house. All the upkeep was work done out of love. He sat on the porch, whose boards they had sanded on their hands and knees each night for a week after returning from the fields.

He thought of Helen and how much she looked like her mother. His heart came up into his throat. This house was the location of all her first times. The day she was born, right there in that bedroom. How nervous he'd been, worried about Hannah, then after Helen came screaming into the world, everything seemed right. The worries that plagued Will about his past, about the future of the Valley, melted away on the day Hannah gave birth. That baby girl was his antidote for the world that had shown him so much darkness and pain.

Her first word was formed right there on the front porch. Heywilly. Something she'd picked up from her mother, a quickly slurred version of "Hey, Willie." Heywilly. Heywilly. She said it over and over as she crawled from her mother in the kitchen to where he worked on the front porch railing. The first time she took any steps in his direction was in the living room, stumbling like a drunken sailor into his open arms. He thought of the first time she called him Daddy. There was also the night not so long ago when they had to explain to her about the collections, how it may happen to him and Hannah. How adult she was, taking it all in stride, saying, "It's okay, Daddy. For the Valley."

He felt like so much of the good fortune he received after returning from the war wasn't meant for him. A wife, a child, a comfortable house; these were all things never meant for him, but there he was, being comforted by his daughter as he explained the cruelties of the world to her. He had done such terrible things and was good at doing them, like a tool being used for its right purpose. In a strange way, the soldier and ruthless killer version of himself were truer than the husband and father.

This house meant nothing without them. Neither did Gonzales nor the great Valley that cradled them. His love of the Valley, which at one time he was willing to carry out the unthinkable for, was only love for the Valley's people, and now that was gone, too.

Will's chest felt tight. He rose and focused on the parting clouds in the sky above Gonzales. *Captain Wilson.* He mouthed the vile name. He turned to go inside and wake Zach when a massive explosion shook the entire house.

CHAPTER TWENTY-SEVEN

Will saw the shock wave as it moved from the house out into the trees. Their leaves all fluttered at once from the intense wind blowing over them.

Within seconds Zach was on the porch with Mary following him. "What was that?" he yelled.

"I don't know," Will replied, coming down off the front steps into the humid morning air.

All three were standing on the sidewalk in front of Will's house when the second explosion hit. A flash of white light sparked across the pewter dawn sky. Milliseconds after the light had passed, a concussion wave hit, followed by the sound. The second eruption was much larger than the first, and all three ducked and cowered involuntarily where they stood on the sidewalk.

"Look," Will yelled, pointing in the distance, beyond the water tank, toward the longvalley highway. He ran down the street for a better look. Zach and Mary followed. The highway was backlit by the weak light of the not yet risen sun, and they could see a pillar of smoke rising from a section of the longvalley freeway.

"Quickly, back to the house," Will said, looking around.

They ran back to the front porch and into the living room, where Will gathered up necessary possessions into his backpack.

"Mary, on the floor in the closet in the bedroom there's another pack. Look through Hannah's clothes for something warm." Will turned to Zach. "Was there any food left in the kitchen?"

"I have it all."

"Get everything packed up then. We need to leave here immediately. This place will be crawling with UP in no time."

"What's going on out there?" Zach asked.

Will just shook his head and shrugged.

While packing his jacket into the backpack, Will saw Helen's doll in the bottom. He pulled it out and studied it. A bit of mud was smeared on the felt material on the doll's back. Will took a moment to clean the soil from the material and carefully placed the doll back into the bag.

When they made it back out onto the street, the sun was closer to rising, and mercury light had overtaken the entire sky from the east. Will turned to look at his house one last time. Black tree canopies were outlined in the sky beyond. A soft breeze was blowing, and the smell of sulfur was dissipating. A cloud of thick white smoke was forming over the longvalley freeway.

They moved quickly under the trees on the neighborhood streets and up onto the trackless railroad levee. From there they had a clear view of the longvalley highway. The clean unbroken line of concrete pillars was destroyed in a wide section, and the tarmac had crumbled and fallen to the Valley floor.

Within a half hour, they were down among the willows on the banks of the Salinas. The river ran silently downvalley through the black stems. All the water from the previous night's rain ran its cyclic course, oozing in the dark silence from the depths of the mud.

It was only there, hidden in the river's path along the Valley floor, that Will felt safe enough to take a moment to rest and think. The three of them sat, breathing hard, on a downed log in the sand.

Mary watched Zach rub his thigh and asked, "Are you okay? You're limping."

"I'm fine. It's an old injury."

Since the previous night, when she'd seen him step carelessly out into the rain, Mary watched Zach intently. Zach scanned the river basin. "I need to pee. I'll be back in a minute," he said to Will, who nodded his response.

After Zach had walked away, Mary turned to Will. "What happened back there?" she asked.

Will shook his head. "The resistance, I think."

"Who is this boy with you?"

"I met him upvalley, after escaping from the camp. He was injured and his parents were gone. I agreed to let him travel with me. He saved my life. Kept me dry when I was sick in the rain."

"But, Will, he—" Mary said, pausing halfway through her statement.

"I know. The rumors were true." Will looked down and toed the sand with his boot, shaking his head. "And Helen's one, too. Unbelievable. Either way, he's a good kid."

"How far are we from Salinas City?" Zach asked loudly, coming out from behind the willows down river.

"Not far off. We can stay along the river almost all the way into Spreckels. If it's clear, we're less than a day's walk from Salinas," Will said while standing.

"Have either of you been to Salinas City before?" Zach asked.

"When I was a girl my dad took me there once." As they started walking again, Mary pulled on her hair and tied it into a loop at the back of her head. "He was a teacher in Gonzales for many years, and we rode on the produce truck into the city for him to get a shipment of textbooks. It only took about forty minutes on the back of that truck, but it seemed like a completely different world. I can still remember it. The buildings were so tall, crowded with people. On the way to the book repository, my dad stopped at a small shop where they had coffee. It was the first time I'd seen it, and I haven't since, but I can still remember the smell of that shop, like burnt paper and spices."

Mary paused, and they walked in silence. She finished by saying, "After that one trip, we never had the opportunity to return."

"How about you, Will?" Zach asked.

"Yeah, I've been there." Will hated the idea of returning to that revolting city, which he'd hoped to never see again. "It's not as impressive as you think. Mostly crowded and dirty."

"Well, I've heard it's huge," Zach said.

"Yes, it's huge," Will responded, following Mary. "I served with a guy who lives in Salinas City and works for the Administration. I've been to his apartment before, and I think I can still find it. Hopefully, he still lives there."

Will followed Mary and Zach along the river, watching it flow over its sandy banks. The Salinas had run by him all his life, and memories floated past on the cold muddy waters. He looked down at the dark sand and thought of Hannah's body buried just upstream.

He thought of that first perfect afternoon nearly fifteen years ago. They were only a short distance from where they now walked. It was an autumn afternoon, and the sun was mellow and warm. No breeze moved the leaves. Everything save the river was still, and they were alone at last.

The river ran near the tomato field where the late season plants were tall enough to hide their brief escape. Their hands were stained green from pruning and staking. He was recently back from the border, clumsy and slow in the work, whereas she was skilled and dexterous. She led him to a hidden spot where the willows bent and formed a tunnel. Freed from their boots, straw hats laying on the sand, they dipped their feet into the cold water. Hannah's legs, tan to the ankles, braced against the black trunks that crisscrossed the bank. Inside their tunnel, they were hidden beneath the tangle of wild cucumber vines in a riprap of twisted branches and downed leaves, softened with time and rot. His rough hand met her stomach. She smiled, and the vegetation muffled their laughter.

Will studied the chocolate water as it slithered across his frame of view and disappeared in front of them. Without realizing it, his cheeks were hot with tears, and he wiped them while following Zach and Mary along the river's edge. Those misshapen trees, this discolored sand, and that predictable river was braided through his entire life. He wondered if their tree tunnel bed was still there. Maybe the scent of her skin still hung in the air, the sound of her laughter in the leaves. He raised his nose, but nothing came to him but the astringent smells of willow and mud on the cold breeze.

He stared straight ahead, keeping one foot in front of the other, following his river downstream. Downvalley. Toward Salinas City. Toward Helen.

CHAPTER TWENTY-EIGHT

"A section of the longvalley freeway has been destroyed," the Valley Manager said, looking panicked as Ben came into his office. His eyes bulged, and he worked vigorously on a bloody hangnail.

"Where?" Ben asked, stunned.

"Near Gonzales. We're cut off from the oil fields."

"What do we do now?" Ben asked.

Colonel Adams sat next to the Manager's wide metal desk. His eyes looked sunken and tired.

The colonel looked up at Ben and said, "I just gave the order to send troops upvalley to begin immediate repairs. But we could be several days without new reinforcements, and we'll be using up fuel reserves until trucks can get through again."

The Manager studied a bloody fingertip. "The timing on this couldn't be worse."

Ben didn't know why, but he thought he heard a slightly accusatory tone in the Manager's voice.

"Who do you think is responsible?" Ben asked.

"We don't know, but we need to retaliate. These so-called resistance fighters are among us. They're deep in the Valley, and at the same time they operate for our enemies at the border." The Valley Manager pounded a half-tightened fist onto the desk. His wrists were so thin they looked as if they may break. He stared for a moment at Ben. "Who knows, they could even be operating from inside the Administration."

Ben glanced at the colonel, then back to the Manager and asked, "This is a military issue. Why did you call me here?"

"We have troops behind enemy lines," the colonel said. "We don't know their status, but their mission is crucial. We need to contact them, to breach the enemy's ranks, but the border is too fortified."

Ben looked at the colonel, confused, then at the Valley Manager.

The colonel continued. "It's likely that the explosives used to destroy the longvalley highway came in through the Prunedale border at night, during the rain. We believe the Benicians have men." The colonel paused and looked at the Valley Manager. "Actually, we don't know if they're men, women, or children, but people who can survive in the rain."

The Manager looked at Ben and said, "We need the same type of people. And we have them now."

"Do you mean the children?" Ben asked.

"Yes."

"The oldest is a girl. Barely eleven," Ben said in disbelief.

"She can be trained," the Manager said. "They all can. If they can move over the border in the rain, they can gather information and carry munitions to target locations."

Ben watched the colonel for a moment. He was stone-faced. Turning back to the Manager, he asked: "Are you serious?" He was beginning to sweat. "This is what you've come up with?"

The Valley Manager stared at him blankly.

"Do you know how dangerous what you're talking about is? Children at the border, carrying explosives?"

The colonel watched them in silence, shifting slightly in his chair.

The Manager, trying to control his emotions, whispered, "This is our best option, Ben. This is why we looked for them. We have to use them, or the search was in vain." Ben had known the Manager a long time and could recognize slight changes in his impassive face, minute wrinkles around the eyes, exposing cracks in the facade.

"This is insanity," Ben said, looking to the colonel to agree with him.

The Valley Manager finally erupted, pounding his desk again in anger.

"Colonel, will you give us a moment," the Manager said loudly.

The colonel didn't respond. He got up, stood straight, pulled down the front of his uniform, and walked stiffly out of the office, slamming the door behind him.

"Sit down," the Valley Manager said, pointing to the chair the colonel had just vacated. Once Ben was seated, the Manager tried to calm himself with a deep breath and said, "What choice do we have here?"

"You're talking about sending our only hope of a solution on a suicide mission," Ben said, his voice involuntarily rising as his anger began to overtake him.

"We're running out of options. The resistance is deep in our Valley." The Manager's voice was also getting louder. "I won't sit by and let them destroy us."

"This isn't the Valley we grew up in. Not the Valley we've always fought for." Ben felt disgusted.

Neither said anything.

Finally, in a calm and cold voice, the Manager said, "We can't let our enemies get the better of us. They've destroyed part of the longvalley freeway, which weakens us greatly. Now it's us or them. The children will be used, and they'll be used how and when I say."

"I need more time with them."

"I'll ensure that their preparation happens here, so you still have access to them. Finish your experiments." The Manager gave Ben a strange look, akin to pity. "Make something work."

The two men stared at each other.

"For the Valley," the Manager said, almost taunting Ben.

Ben hesitated, then repeated, "For the Valley," through his teeth.

With a weary wave of his hand, the Valley Manager said, "Send the colonel back in on your way out."

Ben stepped outside the Manager's office and the door closed behind him. Colonel Adams waited down the hallway, watching the shrouded city below from a tall window.

"He's ready to see you again," Ben said, approaching the colonel. In the perilous world just beyond the thick glass, high clouds spewed a toxic drizzle onto the tall buildings.

Without turning to Ben, Colonel Adams said, "We caused all this. The suffering and the endless warring. It's almost like we've gotten what we deserved with this rain."

The colonel turned toward him and watched Ben carefully. The two men made eye contact, trying to read each other's faces.

The colonel nodded slightly and looked both ways down the hallway. In a low whisper, he said, "I want to stop this, the same as you. There may be something that can be done. We'll talk later."

Without another word, he walked stiffly back toward the Manager's office.

In the elevator back down to his lab, Ben's mind raced. What did the colonel mean? He needed more time with the children. From the beginning we've been the architects of our own demise, he thought. If bloodthirsty Benician marauders overrunning our borders laid waste to the Valley from the outside, would it be worse than what we have now?

The elevator dinged and the doors slid open, but Ben didn't move. He saw it all so clearly at that moment. Foreign armies weren't to be feared. His Valley was being destroyed from the inside.

CHAPTER TWENTY-NINE

Will Taft, Mary McElroy, and Zach Taylor walked the river path downstream all day toward Salinas City. Along the way, in a riparian tangle, water curled and eddied into muddy pools, each raising a brown foam. Closer to the river's outlet, flood damage in the basin became increasingly obvious. They stepped over trees laid haphazardly down by recently swelling storm waters.

The day got colder and darker as they went, and the sun never broke through the clouds. Nearer to the city, the sun moved somewhere out of sight, beyond the murkiness above and without ceremony, the afternoon began to fade. The reek of garlic became more intense as they moved downstream, yet still Will pushed onward, watching the unpredictable downvalley sky closely as he walked. He slowed to wait for Zach and Mary, and as they approached, both looked tired and worried.

A slight breeze came up, cooling the sweat on Will's forehead. Mary was standing next to him, breathing heavily and peering up at the sky.

"What do you think?" Will asked.

"It's close," she said.

Will studied their surroundings. There was no real shelter, and the sky beyond the river was dark and agitated.

"It's time for us to look for shelter," he said. "The weather's changing fast."

As he spoke, a rumbling sound rode on the wind. With a low drumming, it began to rain a short distance downriver.

"That's coming our way. Right now," Mary screamed in panic.

"Come on," Will yelled, and all three set off upriver at a dead run as the rain approached them from behind. Their footsteps hammered the ground and sweat ran down Will's face. Will's eyes watered, and the trail ahead of them began to blur. There was no time to outrun the rain, but there was nothing to keep them dry. No rain shelter, no man-made structure, just the bank of low willows.

"There, quickly," Will said, pointing to a twisted thicket of stems at the river's edge.

He followed Mary into the semi-darkness of a short tunnel in the vegetation that they knew had little chance of protecting them. They kneeled in the dappled light listening to the approaching rain, gasping for breath.

"Pull off your jacket and keep it over Mary," Will yelled to Zach. "Try to keep her as dry as possible." Will took off his own jacket and handed it to Zach. "Use this one, too. Do your best to keep her dry. Stay close to the tree trunks. The leaves will shed some of the water."

The rain was a short distance down river now. With every breath, Will's lungs filled with acrid garlic, and the tears in his stinging eyes blurred his vision.

"Will," Mary said, grabbing him. "I can't breathe."

"Stay calm. Take short, slow breaths. Stay down. Here, push your way under that trunk as much as possible. Zach will keep you dry."

Seconds passed and the rain drew closer, pounding the ground a short distance away. Mary was lying on the ground, mumbling, almost delirious.

I'm going to die here, maybe right now, Will thought.

The river roared as the rain swept across it, and water splashed all around. Will took strained breaths as he helped Zach tuck his jacket over Mary.

"Will?" Zach asked, looking at him with concern.

"You get to Helen. Do whatever you can. Keep her with Mary."

Will crouched next to Mary, spreading the jacket over her. The surface of the river just beyond their willow shelter came to a boil, and the sky rumbled above them. Water drops thumped on the sandy bank just beyond the brown water.

Wind shook their shelter. Will felt nauseous and shivered uncontrollably. His vision blackened around the edges, and he became lightheaded. He felt his knees liquify. What strength he had left was giving way. He looked at Zach one last time as he melted onto the ground. The rain grew louder and more intense. Will tried to breathe, but couldn't, bracing himself against the sand and leaves. His vision narrowed to a pin, and all he could sense was the roar and coming wetness. His eyes closed.

Will saw Hannah's beautiful face in the golden afternoon glow of the Gonzales tomato fields. She was laughing and drawing him toward the river, but he didn't want to go. She kept pulling harder and harder on his arm as he resisted. Her face morphed into Millard Fillmore's. Millard laughed sadistically and said, "Let's get wet!"

Will jolted awake. He was still looking at Zach, whose mouth was moving. He was saying something, but Will couldn't make out any sound. The roar of the rain was distant and much quieter.

"It turned. It turned," Zach was saying.

Will took shallow, burning breaths and blinked to clear his eyes.

"What?" His voice came forth as a harsh croak.

"The rain. It went off into the fields."

Will blinked hard and sat up. His lungs continued to ache and burn with each breath. He looked out at the river. Its surface was calm.

"It rained for a few minutes, just right there. Then it went off in the other direction."

Will looked down at his lap and moved his hands across his thighs in surprise. "We didn't get wet?"

"Not at all."

Will stood, bracing himself on a branch. His knees felt weak and shaky. He looked down at Mary, who was in the fetal position in the sand, under the jackets, still unconscious. Will kneeled back down, peeled the jackets off her, and saw her chest rising and falling.

"How long were we out?"

"Only a minute or so," Zach said.

"Help me pick her up."

Together, they lifted her limp body and moved out from under the thicket onto the sandy bank. A breeze was coming down the river, and the acidic air was clearing. Somewhere beyond the willows, Will could hear the distant and terrifying trundle of falling rain.

"Help me lift her onto my back. We have to keep moving."

With Mary on his back and Zach limping behind, Will struggled along the river trail as fast as his burning muscles would allow.

Mercifully, the breeze thinned the clouds, and the late afternoon sun showed brighter through the ceiling of haze than it had all day. Farther downriver, the reluctant sky nearly cast Will's shadow onto the trail's edge as he felt Mary's limp weight stiffen on his back.

"Will?" she asked softly.

He stopped and carefully kneeled so that she could come off his back.

"You're okay. We survived it."

"How?" Mary asked.

"The rain turned before it got to us."

"I was suffocating," Mary said. "I thought I was going to die." Her voice cracked, and tears fell over her pale skin and blotchy red cheeks.

They sat in a patch of wild periwinkle on the edge of the trail, Mary with her head down between her arms.

"Thank you," she said, looking up at Zach, her eyes still full of tears, holding her shoulder. "Thank you."

Zach nodded.

"Are you okay to walk for a bit?" Will asked her. "We're not that far from the city."

"Help me up," Mary said, offering her hand to Zach.

She stood and closed her eyes. Will steadied her. She shook her head and drew a deep breath. "I can walk."

Will and Zach followed closely as Mary took her first few slow and unsteady steps down the path and into a small clearing. She stopped in her tracks, let out a scream, and stumbled backward into Will.

CHAPTER THIRTY

Just ahead was a body sprawled face-down, motionless on the path. Will pulled Mary back behind him.

"Take your gun out," Will said to Zach, who scrambled to pull the handgun from his belt.

"Cover me while I look. This may be a trap."

Will came around the body slowly. The man was wearing a dark blue backpack that had flopped up on top of his head when he fell. Will gently kicked his boot and no response came. He crouched and lifted the pack off his head. It was soaked through along with all his clothes. Will rolled him onto his back.

He was a young man, about the same age as Zach. His eyes were clear and wide open, as if he were awake, staring at Will and about to say something. The boy's cheeks were clean-shaven, rosy, and blotched. Will pulled a leaf out of his matted, wet hair. His pink lips were covered partly with sand. Will felt for a pulse first on his wrist, then feeling none, reached for his neck, which was warm to the touch. Will put his ear to the boy's open mouth. No breath came.

Mary turned her head sideways to get a better look at the boy.

"Oh no. Billy. Billy. I know him." Mary came to her knees next to Will. "Is he breathing?"

Will shook his head.

"Quickly, hold his head up," Mary said, wiping the sand off his lips.

She leaned over and blew into his lungs, then felt the boy's chest for the right location, and holding her palms out, one stacked on top of the other, pushed down rhythmically. She leaned over and blew another full breath into him and continued to pump.

"Here, push here," she said to Will, moving his hands onto the boy's chest.

Will pushed down and felt the boy's rib cage flex below his wet shirt.

"Keep pumping," Mary said, then breathed again into his mouth.

For a whole minute, Mary and Will worked on the boy with no result. Mary leaned over him to listen again for any breath. Will put his ear to his chest, and no sounds came from within.

Will looked up at Mary and shook his head. "I'm sorry."

Mary's mouth hung open and she didn't respond. With the tips of her slender fingers, she combed the hair straight on the dead boy's forehead.

"Billy," she said under her breath.

"He must have got caught out in the same rain that almost got us," Will said. He looked around. Zach was a way off, gun in hand, watching the trail behind them. Will beckoned to Zach, then looked down at the dead boy, whose eyes were growing milky while the color left his cheeks.

"He was a student of mine. Collected by the UP several years ago. When he was still so young." Mary paused and put her hand to her mouth. "He was such a smart and kind boy. His parents went missing early, and he was with me at the school for a long time. He helped me with all the younger children."

Tears streamed down Mary's cheeks.

"They just came and took him one day, and he never came back."

Mary wept, while Will came around the body and held her to his chest. He could feel her small frame shaking uncontrollably against him. Will looked up at Zach, then to the sky beyond him. The evening was coming on, and clouds were accumulating again.

Will waited until her shaking subsided. "Mary, we have to keep moving."

"What will we do with him?" Mary asked, her voice still muffled by Will's chest.

"We can't do anything for him now."

Mary pulled away from Will and looked up at him. "You just want to leave him here?"

"Look," Will said, pointing to the sky beyond Zach. "We don't have much time," then to Zach, he said, "Check his backpack."

Mary started to cry again. Her sobs were muffled against Will's jacket.

"I can't do this anymore. I can't live like this. What has happened to our Valley?"

She pushed away from Will and looked down at the boy's body. A hard and cold look came over her face. She kneeled next to the dead boy and removed bits of sand and leaves from his hair. She swept her hands down over his bluing face, pulling the boy's eyelids closed, then mumbled something imperceptible.

Will glanced at Zach, who had opened the main pocket of the boy's backpack and was extracting a cube wrapped tightly in thick gray plastic.

"Stop," Will yelled. "Don't move."

Zach froze. "What is it?"

Will approached Zach cautiously.

"Careful. Hand that to me slowly."

Zach cautiously set the cube onto Will's hand.

"What is it?" Zach asked again.

"It's an explosive. We used them when I was in the UP. This cube could kill all three of us."

Will looked into the open backpack where several more gray cubes were stacked. He placed the cube on the ground, then opened the pack wider and went through the smaller pockets.

He removed half a loaf of bread and a clear plastic container of water and handed them to Zach.

"There it is," he said while pulling out a small black box attached to two wires. Handing the small box to Zach he said, "Hold this. It's the detonator. It has to be separated from the explosives." He zipped all the pockets closed again and looked at Mary, who still had one hand on the boy's forehead.

"Mary, we don't have a choice but to leave him out here. There's nothing we can do for him."

Mary pounded her fist in the sand next to the body. Finally, she rose and squinted into the weather with a numb and expressionless face.

"It's just not right," she said, then without another word she walked off down the trail.

"Put that into your bag or a pocket, in a dry place," Will said to Zach, pointing to the detonator. He carefully lifted the boy's pack and put it over his shoulder.

"Let's go," he said as they hustled off to catch Mary.

The sky grew darker as they rushed along the gravel path. Farther downriver they came to more and more concrete until the river was entirely channeled in a deep culvert.

At the outskirts of the Spreckels Sector of Salinas City, Will crawled cautiously up the concrete bank onto a tall levee. The sound of distant thunder rolled across the sky at the far reaches of the Valley.

"Wow, look at that," Zach said, crawling up behind him.

Salinas City sprawled chaotically in front of them. A hundred rundown skyscrapers, maybe more, spread across the indiscernible horizon. The longvalley highway branched into the city at many places with raised concrete bridges that swept around buildings and down onto the unseen streets.

Will hadn't seen Salinas City in several years and wasn't happy to be seeing it again. The deep boom of thunder, which he could feel in his chest, trundled again across the Valley floor somewhere beyond the city.

They rose, looked at the dark clouds churning unpredictably overhead, and hurried down off the concrete embankment into the city streets.

CHAPTER THIRTY-ONE

The three travelers headed toward the tall buildings at the center of Salinas City. They stalked along abandoned streets, each with a palpable hopelessness hanging in the dank air. Dark buildings stood like ruins, long past their prime, biding their time before returning to the mud. They moved under covered sidewalks built of wood and tin, partially consumed by foul rot and mildew. A few people walked hurriedly by them on the opposite side of the road.

As they got closer to the city center, the streets grew more crowded. Lights were on in some of the buildings, but there was no electricity for the street lamps. Strings of unlit bare light bulbs were hastily tacked overhead in the covered sidewalks. They passed countless old buildings with their concrete bases blackened with the wicked sheen of age and neglect. Clouds hung over the buildings like a mirror covered in soap scum, refusing to reflect. Nobody seemed to notice them, nor care.

Will hadn't been as close to so many people since the labor camp, and he grew increasingly nervous as they walked. He palmed his lower back, confirming quick access to his pistol while watching Zach and Mary, who remained distracted by their surroundings.

It was growing dark, and the air was thick with garlic and diesel exhaust from the city's power generators. The night sky covered the city like a rotting wet blanket, and each breath was burning in the back of Will's throat. They came off the street into the lobby of a four-story apartment building. Zach and Mary followed Will up the stairs to the third floor. At the top of the steps, Will was struck by an uneasy feeling. The image of himself lying on a concrete floor, screaming in pain, flashed through his mind. He froze in his path and looked around.

"Everything okay?" Mary asked.

Even though something felt terribly off, Will answered, "Fine," and came off the wooden steps onto a carpeted hallway. The old floor creaked and smelled fermented and sour.

Will knocked loudly on an old door on which the number three was turned sideways and faced the floor. They looked at each other, waiting for an answer. Will knocked again, and they heard someone moving just inside the door. Will instinctively took a step back, pushing Zach and Mary away from the door.

"Who is it?" yelled a gruff voice from inside, the three words blurted in a long slurred single sound.

"Dick, it's Willie Taft."

"Who?"

"Willie Taft. Let us in." Will's voice was loud in the hallway.

Like a drumhead, the door amplified the sound of two chains being pulled from their slots, then a deadbolt unlocking, then another. The door came open just a crack at first. They waited. As Will reached out to push it, the door came open the rest of the way and a rotund, bearded man leaned his head out into the hallway and looked in both directions.

"Get in here. Hurry up."

They stood on the worn parquet floor of the apartment vestibule, their eyes adjusting to the dim yellow light. The man standing in front of them was a few years older than Will, swollen and hairy. His full beard hung loose and the hair on his head was cut short and even, giving his head the appearance of a rounded ball of fur. He wore a black t-shirt and boxer shorts, exposing thick thighs blackened with short curly hair. His shoulders were massive, and the t-shirt strained over his ample belly.

"Willie," the large man said loudly after the door had closed. His arms swung open. "Willie Taft. Come here, little man." He pulled Will into a tight embrace, and Will could smell the alcohol on his breath.

"Dick. Thanks for letting us in," Will said, pulling away from the embrace. "How have you been?"

"Not good," Dick said with a smile. "Not good at all. Come, put your bags down. Sit in the kitchen." Dick's voice was overly warm and hearty.

They took their backpacks off and laid them on the wooden floor. Will's shirt was wet with sweat. He kept the dead boy's pack over his shoulder as they followed Dick down the hallway into the kitchen.

"Who are your friends?" Dick asked while offering the chairs surrounding his table.

"I'm Zach," he said, reaching out his hand, watching their furry host carefully.

"And I'm Mary."

"Charmed," Dick said with a minor bow. "Please sit. Can I get you a drink?"

"Sure," Will replied, setting the pack with the explosives onto the floor behind the kitchen table.

Dusty glasses clinked out of the cupboard in Dick's doughy hands. He set the glasses on the table and left the room, returning moments later with a stool for himself and an unmarked clear bottle of reddish-brown fluid. He poured short glasses for everyone.

"This is the good stuff," he said, carefully pouring the same amount into everyone's glass. "It's not actually," he continued, "but it'll work." He broke out into a booming laugh.

"For the Valley," Dick blurted out.

"For the Valley," they repeated.

The hot alcohol coated Will's throat as he looked across to Zach, who was cringing from the drink. Mary drained the glass in one long gulp and sat stone-faced, pushing her glass toward Dick for another.

"I like her," Dick said to Will, pouring another splash into Mary's glass. "It's been a long time, Willie." Dick looked at him with the soft eyes of someone who'd drunk too much. His smile was warm. "Are you here to take down the empire? Destroy the UP?"

"Not really."

"I always expected you'd be leading us someday. Ruling over this wretched Valley."

"Well, you were wrong about that. Are you still working for the Administration?"

"You two know this man saved my life? Twice," Dick said, tapping the rim of his glass on Will's and smiling widely at Mary. Turning to Will, he said, "I still do. Higher than I probably should admit. They call me Trade Minister now. Trade," he scoffed. He glanced at Zach and said, "I should report this young man right now." His loud laugh returned.

A storm broke somewhere high above them. Rain came down with a loud crack followed by a low rumbling boom. As the water pounded the building, Dick's laughter trailed off. They all looked to the kitchen window where there was only blackness outside and sheets of water running along the outside surface of the glass.

"What does it matter anyway?" Dick asked. "This rain will be the end of all of us." He looked at Zach. "Don't worry, son, I'm just kidding you."

Dick rose, went to the window, and pulled on the latch, making sure it was secure. He ran his hand along the thick rubber weather-stripping at the edge of the window.

"I've heard people have been dying without getting wet. In cars and out on the covered sidewalks," Dick said, turning back to his three guests at the table. "It won't be long until the rain starts killing us in our homes."

Dick returned to his seat, stared at his glass, and was suddenly somber. "So be it," he finally said. He looked up at Will. "Things aren't like they used to be, are they, my friend?"

"No, they aren't." Will felt the effect of the alcohol.

"It's great to see you, though. To what do I owe this unexpected visit?"

"I need your help. I'm looking for my daughter."

Dick sat up and squinted, trying to pay close attention.

"She was taken by UP soldiers from the school in Gonzales," Will continued.

"Why would the UP take a young girl?" Dick asked.

Everyone was silent. Will met Mary's brief glance. Finally, Will said, "They forced the children into the rain, and she survived."

Dick jerked his head back in surprise. "A rainwalker," he exclaimed.

"I had no idea," Will said. "This is my daughter, Dick."

Dick stared at Will for a long moment, blinking. "I can make a call and find out if anyone knows about this."

"I'd appreciate that." Will fidgeted with his glass, then continued, "But I should warn you. I escaped from a labor camp and the UP is after me."

"Where are you staying tonight?"

Will looked around and shook his head. "We don't have a plan."

"You'll stay here then. I insist," Dick said. "I'll make the call now. In the morning, when the rain lets up, we can find out more. There's a UP link line in the lobby. I'll go down and find out what I can."

"Sounds good. Thank you."

Dick drained the last drop of alcohol from his glass and set it down loudly on the table. He left the kitchen and returned wearing a pair of khaki shorts and a jacket.

Standing in the hallway, he said, "I'll be back soon. Make yourselves comfortable. Lock the door behind me, and don't open it until you hear three loud knocks."

Will followed Dick to the door, closed it behind him, and locked the two deadbolts.

Back in the kitchen, he sat at the table across from Mary. "Do you trust him?" she asked in a hushed voice.

Will shrugged. "What choice do we have?" Maybe it was the alcohol, but Will was feeling tired.

"He's the Trade Minister? Who is he?" Mary asked.

"We served together in the UP. He was in my unit. He's a good guy. When my tour ended, I heard that he took a position in the Administration. I visited him here once, many years ago, before returning to Gonzales and meeting Hannah." Will looked around the apartment. "It's barely changed in all these years."

"Hopefully he can help us," Mary said while pouring herself another small shot of the alcohol. "Do either of you want more?"

"Sure," Will replied, hoping that it would help him sleep.

They had finished sipping the burning drink by the time they heard Dick's three loud knocks on the door. Will unlocked the deadbolts and let Dick in.

"What'd you find out?" Will asked as Dick relocked the door.

"The guy I called hadn't heard of any children being collected in Gonzales, but he said he'd ask around and return my call in the morning."

Dick held his throat. "Man, the air burns down there."

"Thanks for calling."

"Are you kidding? It's the least I could do." Dick laid a heavy hand on Will's shoulder. "In the meantime, let's eat something."

Will and Dick returned to the kitchen where Mary and Zach sat quietly looking at their empty glasses.

"Any luck?" Zach asked.

"We'll know more in the morning," Dick replied. "You all look like you've done some hard traveling. I'm going out to get some food. After we eat, you can take a hot shower. Hot water is one of the remaining comforts in this part of the city. The couch folds out into a bed, and one of you can take the floor."

"Thank you," Will said, lifting his hand to Dick's hulking shoulder.

"No problem. Lock the door behind me and wait for three knocks. I should be back within fifteen to twenty minutes."

"Will you be alright out there?" Mary asked, turning to the kitchen window. Driving rain came out of the darkness and hit it sideways.

"I'll be fine. The covered walkways keep you dry, and I'll take this just in case," he said, holding up a gas mask.

The second time Will let Dick out of the apartment, Dick turned back to him from the hallway and said, "It's good to see you, man."

"You, too," Will replied.

"I hope you can find your daughter." Dick stared at him for a moment, then turned.

Will witnessed him carry his heavy frame down the hallway, the carpet slipping and creaking under his weight. As he closed the door and locked the deadbolts, he once again had a vision of himself lying on a cold concrete floor. It was as if he were remembering a forgotten nightmare.

The sound of rain was still thundering outside the building when Will returned to the living room, feeling uneasy. Mary sat on the couch and looked as if she may fall asleep.

Will walked into the kitchen where Zach sat at the table watching the rivulets of rain slide down the outer surface of the window. In the darkness beyond, drops of water could be heard pinging off the metal fire escape.

Will sat next to him.

"This city is so big." Zach continued to stare out the window. "I've never seen anything like it. I feel a long way from home."

Zach looked at the dark blue backpack of explosives on the kitchen floor near the window.

"What are you going to with that?" he asked.

"Hopefully nothing," Will replied.

He took his pistol from the back of his belt and placed it on the table. He rubbed his sore lower back where the gun had sat and stared out the window with Zach, not knowing what to say. Finally, he said, "Hopefully this will all be over soon. Do you still have that detonator?"

"Yeah, right here in my pocket," Zach answered, tapping the front pocket of his jacket.

"We need to keep that dry and away from the explosives."

"I've got it."

"Remember, if we find Helen and anything happens to me, do what you can to get her upvalley, to any place that's safe. That may be at the prison or even back with your grandparents."

"I wonder how they're doing," Zach said.

"I'm sure they're fine. We'll probably be seeing them again soon," Will said, but he worried it wasn't true.

Zach turned back to the window and watched beads of rain rolling down it. For a long time, they sat in silence, then Zach said, "I'm curious."

"About what?"

"This downvalley rain. I wonder if Dick is right, that it's so much worse, killing people who don't even get wet. I'm curious if it affects me."

"Do you feel the burning in your throat?"

"No, nothing."

Zach stood and went to the window. He touched the glass and stared at the water on the other side. He reached up, unlocked the window, and looked back at Will.

Will shook his head. "Not now. Not with Dick coming back."

"The window's low enough. I could just step out onto the fire escape for a second."

"Wait." Will held up his hand. "You'll get your chance. Dick will be back any minute. We shouldn't expose anything to him."

"Why do you want to go out in it?" Mary asked, standing in the kitchen's doorway.

Both Will and Zach turned toward her, neither knowing how long she'd been standing there.

Zach shrugged and said, "To find out how I'd do in it."

"You're not scared?" Mary asked.

Zach shrugged again.

Mary stared at Zach. After a long pause, she said, "The children were so scared." Turning to Will, she asked, "Why would they screen for children if they have soldiers who can survive in the rain?"

Will's mouth fell open. "What do you mean?" he asked.

"When I was at the school, when the soldiers were preparing the cage, one night I saw—"

Just then three loud knocks came on the door, and Mary swung around toward the living room.

Will put out his hand to Zach. "Hold on a minute. Don't open that window." He rose and walked to the front door of the apartment and Mary followed him.

As Will unlocked the deadbolts he said, "That was faster than I thought it'd be."

When he pulled the door open, Dick wasn't standing in the hallway. Instead, it was three armed UP soldiers in light blue uniforms and black gas masks.

CHAPTER THIRTY-TWO

Will tried to swing the door closed, but the lead soldier jammed his boot inside. He pushed with all his weight onto the door while it was kicked from the outside. Abandoning it, he ran toward the living room and was tackled from behind. A second soldier was on Will in seconds, and a third was grabbing Mary. Will struggled to roll the soldiers off him but couldn't move under their weight. Several more soldiers were now in the apartment, one holding Will's legs.

The side of his face was pressed into the carpet, and he could see into the kitchen where his gun was no longer on the table. There was no sign of Zach. Mary screamed in pain as her arms were once again forced behind her.

Will freed an arm and swung it upward just before a soldier's boot hit his temple. A fan of white light spread out in his vision, then narrowed to a dark tunnel. He went limp as a zip tie came around his wrists. He was kicked again, this time on his side then rolled onto his back.

"Get the hood," one of the soldiers said.

Will was on his back, his zip-tied arms below him, eyes wildly moving side to side. There were too many of them, and he had no hope of escaping. He was grabbed from behind, pulled up into the seated position, and a black cloth bag was slipped over his head. Will heard Mary's muffled screams as a bag was placed over her head.

"Weren't there supposed to be three?"

"Check the apartment."

Will heard a scramble of footsteps and doors opening and closing. Mary had stopped screaming, but he could hear her breathing hard somewhere near him.

"You're alright, Mary," he said.

Will was hit with something across the upper back.

"Shut up," said a soldier.

Returning to the room, another soldier said, "Nothing. Nobody else here."

The building rumbled under the pressure of the rain, as if in the middle of a river.

"On your feet," Will was commanded while being lifted to his feet. He grew lightheaded, and white stars stretched out across his dark view of the inside of the black hood.

"You two take him. I'll get the woman."

Will could make out the lights in the hallway outside Dick's apartment through the dark material as he was pushed from behind. He was pushed down through the darkness of the stairwell. As they came into the building's lobby, the air hit him like a fist through the hood. His throat burned instantly, and his face felt numb. He heard Mary let out a brief scream.

Will heard a soldier ask, "Sir, do they need masks?"

"Let them burn," was the beginning of the response, then the rain was too loud for Will to make out any other words.

The main door to the building was open, and Will felt cold air blowing in and heard the rain roaring outside. He took shallow breaths under his hood, and the air was on fire in his lungs. He heard Mary ask from the other side of the room, "Will, are you still there?"

"Mary, I'm right here," he shouted at full volume.

The soldier standing next to Will hit him on the back of the head. "Shut your mouth," he said.

There was the sound of an engine racing outside, screeching tires on wet pavement, then he was being pushed out into the roar. Outside, a soldier yelled at him, "Step up." Will stumbled onto the floor of some type of vehicle, and the door was slammed behind him.

Will laid in the darkness, shivering involuntarily, feeling more nauseous with each breath. "Mary, Mary?" he asked, but no answer came, just the muffled sounds of an engine and tires moving on a wet surface, all just above the thunderous sound of pounding rain.

Will braced himself against the wall as they turned a sharp corner. He tried to lean over to shake the hood off his head, but it wouldn't move. He felt like he might suffocate as he slid along the wall. Despite the burning, he took deep breaths and tried to calm himself. *Survive this*, he told himself. *Survive this.*

"Mary?" he yelled again, but there was only the hollow sound of his own voice fading below the hum of the engine.

Will strained to sit upright as the vehicle raced around corners, coming to an abrupt stop. The door opened, and he was pulled back out into the cold, across a dry surface to the inside of another building. Wet boots squeaked on the floor of a long hallway, and Will could see the glow of fluorescent bulbs passing overhead through the black material. The burning began to subside in his throat, and his breaths came more easily.

"This one here?"

"Yes, put him in there."

He was turned around and patted down before being shoved down onto the concrete floor. The door was closed, and the latch swung home loudly.

"Hello?" Will asked. Again, no response. Only darkness in the hood.

The sharp plastic edges of the zip tie cut into his wrist, and his shoulders ached from sitting back on his arms.

He scooted across the cold concrete floor to the edge of the room, laid back against the wall, and waited for what he knew would come next.

CHAPTER THIRTY-THREE

Outside the Valley Administration, a torrential downpour was falling. A powerful and bitter wind from the western vastness of the Pacific propelled the water sideways, and it danced over the top of the tall building and made it shudder. Ben Harrison could feel the building strain and vibrate against the howl and collision of a million sickening drops as he ducked out of Colonel Adams' office.

Their conversation, which had taken place in hushed voices, left him feeling hopeful for the first time in what seemed like years. These new feelings of hope came with an undercurrent of doubt. Could he trust the colonel, or was Ben falling into an elaborate trap designed by the Valley Manager to expose him as a traitor? Time would tell. After what had been said that morning, it was too late to turn back.

He went down two floors in a cold and stinking stairwell. Back in his lab, he watched the upvalley sky through the tall windows. His hunger reminded him that it was almost lunchtime, a time of day when the rain would usually clear, yet there was no sign of a break. The rain came early the previous evening and hadn't stopped. He couldn't remember a full day at that time of year without relief from the showers, and he wondered if it may never again stop raining in Salinas City.

The Valley Manager knocked on the open lab door, startling Ben.

"Manager," Ben said, turning from the window, instantly uncomfortable in his presence.

The Manager stepped into the lab, and Captain Wilson followed, stopping a short distance from the door.

"Ben, you remember Captain Wilson."

"Yes, hello." Ben nodded to the captain, who stood expressionless.

"What did you want to show me?" the Manager asked.

"We may be on to something," Ben said, wondering why the captain was there. "Sit at that microscope." While the Manager squared himself up to the microscope, Ben reached around and placed the tiny plate of glass on the stage.

"Here's the focus knob," Ben said, pulling the Manager's cold hand to the knob.

"What am I supposed to be seeing?" the Manager asked, looking down into the microscope lenses.

"Do you see thousands of those dots floating around?"

"I do."

"That's rainwater collected outside the building last night. All the tiny dots are the bacteria that make the toxin."

"Okay. Yes. I can see them well now," the Manager said, working the focus knob. "They seem to be vibrating."

"Yes. They're alive, and their numbers are increasing. That's a higher count of bacteria than we've ever seen in that volume of rainwater."

"They're everywhere. So tiny, too."

"Tiny, but toxic. For some reason, they're reproducing more rapidly. I think this increase in numbers explains the increase in toxicity and maybe even the volatilization."

"Volatilization?"

"The fact that people are dying without getting wet. The concentration of bacteria could make that possible."

The Valley Manager looked up from the scope. "This isn't good news. Is this only going to get worse and worse?"

"Their numbers seem to be on the rise." Ben looked down at his bench. "But now, watch this."

Ben took a pipette and plastic tube from the bench. He pulled a small volume of pink fluid out of the tube into the pipette, then set the tip on the edge of the microscope slide. He carefully squeezed a drop onto the slide.

"Now look into the scope." Ben looked over his shoulder at the captain while the Manager looked into the scope. Captain Wilson stared coldly at Ben.

"What's happening?" the Manager asked.

"You tell me," Ben said.

"They've stopped vibrating. They're all stopping."

Ben involuntarily covered his mouth to block the scent of the Manager's breath.

"See how it spreads out across the slide?" Ben asked.

"I do," said the Manager, eye pressed against the microscope. "What is it? What did you add?"

"It's a solution made from Helen Taft's blood. This is probably why she and the others can survive the rain."

"Does the blood from all the children work?"

"Yes, but hers seems to be the most effective."

"What is it? What's in the blood?"

"We're not sure yet. We have more tests to run."

The Valley Manager looked back down at the scope, studied the field of view, then back at Ben. "This is what we've been waiting for. Of course, their blood." He smiled and looked back at Captain Wilson.

"We're trying to replicate it now, but we need more time," Ben said. He stepped away from the Manager and the microscope and said, "I'd like you to wait off on using the children at the border. They're the key to stopping the rain."

The Manager smirked at the recognition of Ben's motives. He stared at him without speaking for a moment, then shook his head. "We'll do no such thing. Their mission must be carried out while the rains are still frequent and intense. Captain Wilson will escort them to the border himself."

Ben and the Manager both looked at the Captain. He stood like a solid mountain of orange flesh. He eyed Ben closely.

The Manager continued, "You'll have to extract as much blood from the children as you can before they're sent."

"And what if they're caught crossing into San Benician territory?" Ben asked.

The Manager shrugged. "We will have won at that point."

"We shouldn't be sending these children to the border," Ben protested, trying to keep his voice calm and not wanting to get emotional in front of the captain. "They are the answer we've been waiting for, and I need more time with them."

"It's a good thing that's not your decision to make. These children are our most powerful weapon, yet you continue to fight against them being used." The Manager shook his head, disappointed.

The Manager looked up past Ben at the sky beyond the lab window and said, "It looks like the rain won't let up today."

Ben twisted his head to the window and looked out at the dark sky. "It's getting worse. This may be the first time that the rain doesn't break."

"Where have you been all morning?" the Manager asked.

Ben tried to be nonchalant. "I've been here in the lab and with the children." Ben's eyes darted to Captain Wilson and back to the Manager. *Was he being interrogated? What did the Manager know about his conversation with Colonel Adams?*

"Checked on the children, huh?"

"Yes."

"Anything else?"

Ben shook his head.

"Have you seen Colonel Adams today?" the Manager asked Ben. He turned to Captain Wilson, who stared at Ben, waiting for his answer.

The captain took a step toward Ben.

Ben's heart raced while he tried to seem calm and casual. He shrugged. "I haven't seen him."

The Manager turned back from Captain Wilson and stared at Ben, then gave him a closed mouth smile. "Hmmm. Okay."

Silence sat in the room, finally broken by the Manager's next comment. "We found the girl's father."

"Taft?" Ben asked, relieved that the subject was changed.

"Yes. He'd come to Salinas City, all the way from the labor camps, to recover her. He's a decorated veteran. Served at the border, commanded missions into San Benician territory."

"Do you know him?"

"No, but Colonel Adams does. Apparently knew him well when he was younger. After his service, he disappeared into the fields of Gonzales. Wanted nothing more to do with the UP."

"Is he here?"

"We're keeping him guarded at a holding facility in the Boronda District."

"I'd like to talk to him, find out if he can survive the rain."

With a mocking smile, the Manager said, "We could find out."

"There'll be no need for that," Ben said.

"He was found in the apartment of one of our people in the city center. He was there with the girl's teacher from Gonzales."

"Where's the teacher now?"

"Also being held in the Boronda."

"It would help me if she was brought here. Some of the children are quite disturbed," Ben said. "And I'd like to examine the father. Can he be brought here, or do I need to go to the Boronda?"

"We can have the father transferred here," the Manager said, turning around to the captain, who shrugged and nodded in approval.

"You should know that he's dangerous," the Manager continued. "He killed a UP guard during his escape from the labor camp and one of Captain Wilson's men in Greenfield."

"Where is the girl's mother?" Ben asked.

"Killed during their escape attempt from the camp."

Ben shook his head in disappointment, then asked, "What's your plan for the father?"

"We'll return him to the labor camp if he makes it back alive."

"What do you mean?"

"He's with my brother now," the Valley Manager said. "Apparently he and Millie served together when they were younger."

"The Benician raids?" Ben asked.

"Yes, the father commanded some of those missions. Millie is waiting for the longvalley repair before he can return the father to the labor camp."

"What's his name?"

"Will Taft."

"And the teacher?"

The Valley Manager turned to Captain Wilson, who said, "Mary McElroy."

"It's important that she's here with the children. They ask about her repeatedly," Ben said, looking at both the Manager and the captain. "Her presence would help the children while they're prepared for the mission."

The Manager considered Ben's argument. "Alright, if you think it's that important and she won't disrupt the training, we'll have her transferred here this afternoon."

"I'll talk to her myself when she arrives," Ben said, then turning to Captain Wilson said, "Have someone let me know when she gets here."

The captain scoffed.

The Manager turned to the captain. "Do as he says. Have the teacher brought here as soon as possible."

The captain nodded and left without a word.

The Manager watched him leave, then turned to contemplate the lab. A skinny finger worked around the edges of his thumb, grinding on a hang-nail. The finger ceased its scratching, and the Manager's calculating eyes came to rest on Ben. Ben felt like the Manager could sense his betrayal, knew everything he had planned and was just waiting for him to slip up.

"Captain Wilson is so helpful," the Manager said almost to himself. "These are dangerous times for our Valley. It's a good thing we have so many strong and loyal subjects."

"I agree."

"Do you?" the Manager asked, pretending to be surprised.

"I do." Ben returned the Manager's stare. "For the Valley."

The Manager rose from the bench, faced Ben, and repeated, "For the Valley," then turned and left the lab.

After he'd gone, Ben pulled the microscope slide from the stage and set it down on the bench top. He lifted the pipette and drew new rainwater into the tube, then held it up to the light. He rolled up the sleeve of his shirt and lifted the pipette tip over the skin on the inside of his forearm. He pushed a few drops of rainwater out onto his smooth white skin and winced as the drops landed. The skin burned at first, then quickly numbed. He set the pipette down on the bench and lifted the tube with the pale pink solution of Helen Taft's blood in it. He carefully pipetted several drips from the tube onto the area of affected skin, then breathed slowly and focused on the feeling of his skin as it changed.

CHAPTER THIRTY-FOUR

For a long time, Will laid on the cold hard floor. He entered a sort of trance, losing track of time, lying still on his back. The black hood became strangely comforting, the world hidden from his eyes. There was only darkness and the sensation of his own moist breath against the heavy material. After several hours, he couldn't remember if he'd slept.

He was thrust back into consciousness by the loud bang of the lock retracting on the outside of the metal door. He quickly came to a seated position. His entire body tensed, bracing himself for impact, but he wasn't hit or grabbed or drug from the cell.

The door slammed shut, and there was only silence. Will felt someone else in the room.

"I'm going to free your arms and take off your hood." The voice was calm, machine-like. "I don't plan to harm you, but if you struggle against me or don't do as I say, I will. Do you understand?"

"Yes," Will answered.

A click and the zip ties were cut. Will pulled his hands around to his lap and rubbed his wrists. The hood was yanked from his head, and for a moment the light was too bright. He closed his eyes, then slowly opened them into a squint.

An imposing redheaded soldier was standing several feet from him, watching him. The soldier was shorter than Will, but not by much. His massive shoulders, thick arms, and hands made him look as if he could yank a tree from the ground. Being tall with a muscular frame of his own, Will rarely doubted his physical superiority, but this man was daunting. Will quickly scanned the room. The door was closed behind the soldier, the room empty except for a sink in the corner and a small metal table with two chairs.

"State your name," the soldier said.

"Will Taft," he said, shifting his weight.

The soldier kept his distance. "Stay seated."

Will studied his uniform. Based on his knowledge of uniforms, this was a higher-ranking member of the UP. He apparently carried no weapon, nothing Will could use to his advantage. Likely, there were many other soldiers just outside the door.

"Where am I?" Will asked. "Is my daughter here?"

"That's enough questions from you. I'm Captain Wilson. I have some things to ask you. If you don't answer them, or answer them accurately, this will go poorly for you. Do you understand me?"

At the mention of the name, the hair rose on the back of Will's neck. He wanted to jump to his feet, cross the room and beat the captain to death with his bare hands.

Captain Wilson seemed to sense a change in Will because he took a step toward him, puffed up his chest, and repeated his question. "Do you understand me?"

"Yes," Will replied, glaring up at the captain.

"How long have you been a member of the resistance?"

"I'm not a member of the resistance."

Captain Wilson hesitated, then went on to his next question.

"Why did you come to Salinas City?"

"I'm looking for my daughter."

"Why did you contact Dick Nixon? Is he also a member of the resistance?"

"I have nothing to do with the resistance," Will said.

"Were you in Gonzales yesterday?"

"Yes. Is my daughter being held here?" Will asked.

"How did you get from Gonzales to Dick Nixon's apartment?"

"On foot."

"Who were you traveling with?"

Will considered his answer. "Mary McElroy. Is she being held here?"

"Who else?" Captain Wilson asked.

"That's all."

"Is Mary McElroy also a member of the resistance?"

Will looked at the captain for a long time. "Look, Wilson, neither Mary, nor I are part of any resistance."

Will put his hands on the concrete next to him, preparing to push himself up.

Captain Wilson stepped back. "Stay seated," he commanded. Continuing his interview, he asked, "Were you aware of a bombing in Gonzales yesterday morning?"

"Yes."

"Were you involved in it?"

"No, I saw it from my house."

Will answered the skepticism in the captain's eyes with a blank stare.

"Why did you come to Salinas City?"

"I came here to get my daughter."

"Other than you and Mary McElroy, can you name other members of the resistance?"

Will shook his head in frustration. "I know you took my daughter from the school in Gonzales. Take me to her now."

Captain Wilson squinted at Will and stood silently for a long time. Will could see the captain's tight control over his frustration beginning to fray. He backed up while continuing to face Will and knocked on the inside of the handleless door. It opened, and he left the room without looking back at Will.

"Take me to my daughter," Will yelled, jumping to his feet and running to the door as it closed again.

Will put his ear to the door but couldn't hear anything outside. He paced the room, went to the sink in the corner, and turned the faucet. It squeaked open, and a trickle of cold water filled his cupped hands, which he splashed onto his face. The feel of his beard was surprising, almost foreign. It had grown significantly, and water stayed in the soft, thick parts on his chin. He felt the wound on his cheek, and the skin was raw and tingling where the cut was growing back together. The other side of his head throbbed where he'd been kicked.

He dried himself with the sleeve of his shirt and went to each wall to see if he could hear anything in adjacent rooms. Was Helen also being held here? He wondered. Was she only one wall away or in some distant building, maybe not even in Salinas City? He thought of her alone in a room with Captain Wilson and instantly started to sweat. He screamed "Helen!" but there was no response. He clenched his teeth as anger burned inside him. He hit the wall. It was cold and unyielding, and his fist ached. He paced the room like a caged animal, kicked the bottom of the door, then kicked it again. The booming sound of his kicks dissipated into silence, and there was nothing. No response from outside.

Will sat at the table and took deep breaths to calm himself. He had to be clear-headed to have any chance of escape. *Stay calm for Helen*, he told himself. He looked methodically around the room. What could he use to his advantage? Where were their weaknesses? The chairs, they could be swung like a weapon. He might also be able to break a leg off the table.

He had no idea what time it was. *Was it day or night? How long had he slept, if at all?* He placed his head on the cold metal table and closed his eyes. Hours went by. He slept, then awoke disoriented. He rose, drank from the sink, then listened again through the walls. Nothing had changed. He was hungry but tried not to think about it.

Time passed. Several hours gone, Will laid on the floor, consumed by hunger, his ear against the cold polished concrete listening to the faint trundle of distant bass sounds from a world he couldn't interpret. He held his breath and weakly pushed himself up to his knees when he heard the rumble of boots in the hallway. The panel at the bottom of the door clanked and hinged open. Without a word from the other side, a food tray was slid across the concrete into the room. The door hinged shut with a bang. Will approached the tray and ate feverishly.

The hum just beyond the ceiling, which Will figured was rain, escalated to a rumble as he wiped his mouth. He laid back down on the concrete and listened. The food churned in his stomach. He thought of Helen and counted the hours since leaving her that morning at the school in Gonzales. A lifetime ago. The things he would say to her now. He recounted each word of his conversations with his wife in the labor camp. In trying to conjure up the faces of the two women for whom he lived, he could only do harm to their images, which were growing distorted and changed in his memory.

Will awoke on the floor some unknown number of hours later, stood, and walked to the sink in the corner of the room. He was stiff and cold. The muffled roar of rain on the roof was still there. He stretched his legs, then sat at the table.

The fluorescent tube momentarily flickered, then went out. The room went completely dark except for a slit of light skirting under the door. He stood as his eyes adjusted, then kneeled next to the entry. He listened intently. Nothing.

The sliver of light from under the door went out, and the darkness became complete. He could no longer see his hands beyond his face. Complete blackness and silence consumed the room. He lifted one of the chairs from the corner and waited in the darkness with only the sound of his steady breathing. Will felt for a moment like he was falling. He set the chair down and sat on it to regain his sense of balance.

A thread of light danced under the door then came the sound of boots in the hallway. Will waited, ready for a fight. The door swung open. A spotlight was pointed at him, and he held up a hand to block it. The dark figures of two men were suddenly on him at each side, then a third and fourth were rushing past the spotlight toward him. Will threw an elbow and hit one of them hard in the head. He heard a grunt and could smell the breath of another trying to grab him around the neck.

"Don't be a hero. Stop struggling," a loud and familiar voice said from behind the light.

Will kicked another soldier, who went flying against the cell wall. As he bent to lift the soldier onto his back, his legs were wrapped up by yet another, and all of them went to the floor. They were now piling on top of him. He bucked and rolled, but their weight was too great. A knee was pressing down hard on his back, and his right arm burned as it was bent up behind him. He panted and grunted as the wounded side of his face was crushed into the concrete floor.

The lights came back on, flooding the room, and Will strained to look up. The bare light tube above him rained down a naked blue illumination. Will saw Millard Fillmore standing at the door. As a sardonic smile came across Millard's face, the black hood was once again pulled down over Will's head.

CHAPTER THIRTY-FIVE

Mary McElroy spent the night alone in a room with a fluorescent light whispering its low buzz overhead. Beyond the light, she could hear rain incessantly beating the roof of the unknown building to which she had been brought. The hood pulled over her head in Dick Nixon's living room was removed only after a nauseous drive through wet streets, at the end of which she was pulled from the vehicle, pushed down a long hallway, and into this room. The zip tie was clipped off her wrists and, as the soldiers in their gas masks turned to leave, she was commanded to sit on the couch, the only piece of furniture in the small room.

As the door's lock clanked shut behind them, Mary was consumed with a sinking feeling. She had nothing now. She no longer knew where she was or where Will or Zach were, and all her children were gone. Even Helen Taft and Jimmy, who had somehow miraculously survived the horrors of the Gonzales school massacre, had been taken from her, but the worst was not knowing what would happen next. She wished she'd walked out into the rain when she had the chance. She collapsed onto the couch, which smelled of mildew and sobbed.

No one came for her, and there was nothing but the muffled barrage of rain on the roof. Eventually, exhaustion overtook her. She pulled the jacket she'd gotten from Will's house up over her head and fell asleep.

Mary awoke to noises outside her door. She jerked up on the couch as the lock clanked. Two young soldiers in gas masks came into Mary's room, their boots and light blue pants wet and stinking with rain. She screamed as they forced her up and led her down the hallway to a bathroom. On her way back to the room, Mary saw a high frosted glass window in the hallway. A pale wash of morning light drew into the hallway, and beads of water grew and spilled along the outside of the glass. She thought she must have slept through the night. After returning Mary to her room, the soldiers handed her a cloth bag with a jar of water and a stale bread roll.

"How long will I be here?" Mary asked the soldier who handed her the bag. His eyes above the gas mask were so young and anxious, a look familiar to Mary, and she thought for a moment that he may be another previous student of hers.

"I don't know," came a foreign and muffled voice from behind the mask.

The door was once again slammed shut, and Mary sat back down on the couch to eat her bread. The rain continued to rap on the roof. When Mary was young, her grandfather had told her that the rain plays a tune in the key of D. She paused her chewing to listen for it. For a moment, she rocked back and forth, eyes closed, and hummed along with the rain. The sound of her own warbling voice was almost comforting.

The hours passed and nothing changed. The rain kept up its tune, just out of key with the low hum of the lights. Either out of boredom or desperation, Mary let her mind wander to thoughts she hadn't allowed herself to think in several years, thoughts of the time before her husband disappeared before Gonzales was ruined by the collections.

He and Mary had argued about whether or not to fulfill their allotment of one child, as allowed for all married Valley residents. At that time, she was filled with hope for the Valley and its people, optimistic about the future, but he wasn't. Mary's hope was embodied in the children at the school. They were so open and innocent and ready to learn. He'd worked the Gonzales loading ramp and interacted daily with the UP. Mary knew that was the source of his lingering despair.

The fact that she finally triumphed in their argument was ultimately moot. She was unable to conceive, and although he'd been loving and understanding through the tribulations of several miscarriages, deep down she felt he was surreptitiously happy about her failure to reproduce.

Mary paced the room as she allowed bygone and painful episodes from her past to come forth in a string of surprisingly clear memories. Her thoughts strung a tighter and tighter knot in her mind that wouldn't come undone. If she was going to die in this room, she thought, what was the point in suppressing these thoughts any longer?

Knowing now what happened to her husband and all the children of Gonzales, maybe he was right, and it was best they hadn't brought another child into the Valley.

Mary's disturbing reverie was ended by the sound once again of squeaking boots in the hallway. Mary rose from the couch as a loud pound came on the door, the metal latch clanked, and the door swung open. A soldier came into the room, scanned it, and stepped to one side. Another soldier stood in the doorway holding out a gas mask.

"Put this on. You're coming with us."

CHAPTER THIRTY-SIX

Ben felt a strange aching numbness in his arm. The dilute solution of Helen Taft's blood stopped the burning instantly, but the deep pain lingered for several hours. There were still so many unanswered questions. Was the blood effective at low concentrations? Was it long lasting? Could it affect the weather? What was in their blood that killed the artificial bacteria? There was so little time for the right studies. He had to think and act fast. Within days, the Valley Manager would send the children to their demise at the border, then there would be no answers, no solutions, no saving this Valley.

He distractedly rubbed his forearm as a knock came on the lab door.

"Sir."

Ben turned to see a wide-eyed teenage soldier-boy.

"Sorry to bother you, sir." The boy hesitated to enter the lab.

"Go ahead. What is it?"

"I was told to let you know that the children's teacher has arrived."

"Okay, thank you," Ben said. "Is that all?"

"Yes, sir," the boy said awkwardly and turned to leave.

"Do you know where she's being held?"

"Yes, sir."

Ben hung his lab coat, picked up his medical bag, and followed the boy to the elevator. Many floors down, at the end of a long hallway on a lower level of the building, Ben knocked quietly on the cell door before opening it.

A woman sat with her head down, resting her chin on her forearms at a table in the corner of the room. She looked up at him with curiosity as he entered. Ben thought she might be in her late twenties, although possibly older. She had wavy brown hair pulled back into a disheveled ponytail and clear, pale skin with the remnants of two black eyes. She seemed weary and dazed. From that first moment when she looked up at him, he had a vague feeling of familiarity with her. Something about her presence felt immediately comforting.

"Hello, I'm Ben Harrison," he said, crossing the room with his hand out. "I'm the Valley Science Minister."

She rose from the table and offered him her hand. It was cold and smooth to his touch, and he let go quickly. He wanted to stare at her, to examine her closely but fought the urge.

"Mary McElroy," she said, watching Ben closely with suspicious eyes.

"Pleased to meet you."

Ben turned back to the door where the boy-soldier still stood, awkwardly waiting for a command.

"You can wait outside now," Ben said. "Please close the door behind you."

Turning back to Mary, Ben asked, "Do you mind if I sit?"

"Go ahead," Mary said and sat across from him.

"I apologize if you've been treated poorly. I can only imagine what you've been through."

With that statement, Ben noticed a softening of Mary's face, almost as if his kindness was a surprise to her. She squinted suspiciously.

"Are you feeling alright?"

"Yes, I'm fine," Mary responded. Their eyes locked for a moment too long, and she looked away.

"You must be hungry. When was the last time you ate?"

"I had bread this morning." Mary crooked her head sideways, as if she wanted to ask Ben something, then hesitated.

"It's important that I know what's happened to you. Have you been questioned by anyone else since arriving in Salinas City?"

"No. I was left in a small cell by myself."

"Can you tell me what happened at the school?"

Mary looked down at the table and said nothing. Ben waited. Finally, Mary said, "Soldiers came. They built a fence in the yard and made the children—" Mary's lip began to shake.

Ben felt the urge to reach out and comfort her, like she was an old friend, but thought better of it. "I'm so sorry, Ms. McElroy. It's a despicable thing, what happened in Gonzales. You've been through a great deal in the last few days." Ben looked around the room, leaned over the table toward Mary, and said in a low voice, "I want you to know that some of us in the Administration tried to stop it."

Mary nodded and looked back down at the table. Ben noticed her eyes shining with tears.

"Before the soldiers came to your school, did you know that any of the children could survive the rain?"

Mary shook her head.

"So, there was nothing different about the two children who survived, no way to tell them apart from the other children?"

"Not that I can think of."

"How many children were there at the school when the soldiers arrived?"

"Twenty-three."

A look of disgust came across Ben's face. He hadn't imagined there were so many children. He shook his head. "I'm so sorry." He whispered to himself, "This has to be stopped."

The air between them seemed to carry a positive charge, some unknown frequency perceived by each as a feeling of having known the other before, a familiarity, a comfort that neither fully understood. Ben wanted to ask her if they'd met before, but he knew there was no way they could have. A tear fell from Mary's eyes as she looked down. Her hands were there on the table, and Ben could've easily reached out and held them, tried to comfort her, but he hesitated.

"The two surviving children from your school are here in the building and they've been asking for you."

Mary smiled, then quickly covered her mouth with her hand as if she were ashamed. Ben realized she was just trying to hide her excitement, as if she accidentally showed it, something more would be taken from her. It was a sad and delicate gesture, and one of the most beautiful Ben had ever seen.

"We can go see them now," he stated evenly.

Mary stood from the table. "Please," she said, almost desperately.

Her excitement made him happy, infected him in a way. He was hopeful again.

Ben rose, picked up his medical bag, and went to the door. Looking back at Mary, he couldn't help but smile. He pounded on the door, and the boy soldier opened it without hesitation.

"We're headed to the children's room," Ben said to the soldier. "Make sure any of her belongings are brought there."

"I have nothing," Mary said.

Ben held the door open for Mary, then followed her out.

He led her along the hallway with the panels of fluorescent light ticking past overhead. Halfway down the hallway one of the bulbs flickered, but Ben didn't look up at it. They rounded a corner and came to a door on which Ben knocked quietly. He pushed the door open, and Mary rushed past him to where Helen sat on the couch.

Helen jumped up and met Mary halfway across the room. Jimmy stood from the table, looking confused.

"Oh, sweetheart," Mary said, her voice wavering with tears, beckoning to the boy. Helen cried and said something muffled into Mary's jacket. Ben could see her slender pale arms coiled firmly around Mary's waist.

"I thought we'd never see you again," Helen cried.

"Here I am," Mary said. "I'm not going anywhere."

Ben's heart swelled, and a knot came into his throat. He realized at that moment how rare that type of loving emotion was in that building, in that dreary city. His life had been devoid of real emotion for a long time, and the emptiness was now so obvious. He wanted to do everything in his power to help Mary and these children.

Mary turned to Ben, teary-eyed, and whispered, "Thank you."

Ben nodded. "There are other children, survivors from a school in Greenfield, being held separately. Would you be willing to stay with all the children?"

"Yes, of course."

"I can find you a larger room. I'll make arrangements now."

Ben watched while Mary kneeled in front of the couch, sitting Helen and Jimmy back down, her hands resting in their laps. He backed toward the door but realized he didn't want to leave the room. He didn't want to leave Mary.

Mary rose and turned to Ben. Their gazes met, and neither cared to break the stare.

"Thank you," she said again.

He nodded and put his hand out to her, a natural, almost involuntary gesture made between parting friends.

She took his hand as he said, "I'll be back soon."

CHAPTER THIRTY-SEVEN

Will smelled the dank smell of stale breath on the inside of the black hood. Two soldiers were on his back, pressing him against the floor while a third zip-tied his wrists together.

"Always trying to be the hero. When will you learn it does you no good?" Millard Fillmore said, kneeling next to him.

He was lifted to his feet and once again walked out to an awaiting vehicle. This time he sat with his wrists tied behind his back in the back seat with a soldier on each side. The familiar burn came to his throat as they sped through the rain on wet and rutted streets.

From the front seat, Will heard Millard's voiced muffled by a gas mask. "How's that burn feel in your throat?"

Will didn't respond. He was feeling nauseous, and his whole head and upper body ached.

"You don't have long, my friend. If it was up to me, you'd be gone already."

The engine whined above the crackle of tires on wet pavement. When they reached their destination, Will scooted out of the back seat while being pulled up by a soldier. He was then on his feet being pushed through a series of doors, farther and farther into the belly of a large building. Will counted the doors they went through, each one clicking open and locking behind him. He worked his wrists against the zip ties, trying to loosen them as he was pushed into another small room. The door swung closed, locked, and he was alone.

A single fluorescent tube was visible through the black material of his hood. He felt his way around the room slowly circling the walls past a sink in the corner, until he came to a couch. He sat cautiously and strained to step through his tied arms to bring them around to his front. After several moments of stretching and rolling on the couch,

Will brought his burning arms under his feet and around onto his lap. He rested, breathing hard, while the burning in his throat and shoulders faded.

He hadn't sat long when the door was once again unlocked.

"Are you Will Taft?" A man's voice came to him after the door closed.

"I am."

"I'll take your hood off."

A tall slender man pulled the hood gently from Will's shoulders and stood back. Will squinted while his eyes adjusted. The man was about Will's age, maybe younger, but his black hair peppered along the edges with gray gave him an older, distinguished look. He wore no uniform, and his spectacles made him look more like a librarian than a soldier. He studied Will with a look of concern.

"My name is Ben. Ben Harrison. I'm the Valley Science Minister."

Will nodded while studying the room. There was nothing in it except the couch on which he sat. The door behind the man was closed and had no knob.

The man stood near the door, keeping his distance from Will. "I understand that you've been through a lot, and I want to help you, but if you touch me you won't make it out of this room alive. You'll never see your daughter again."

At the mention of Helen, Will rose from the couch, causing Ben to lift his hand.

"You know where my daughter is?" Will saw fear in Ben's eyes.

"I do," Ben said, still holding up his hand. "And I think I can arrange for you to see her. I need you to cooperate with me."

"Where is she?"

"She's here, in the Valley Administration building."

Will felt a strange mix of fear and hope. "She's here?" Will asked, his voice cracking with excitement.

"She's with her teacher and several other children."

"Why are they being held here?"

Will could tell the question wasn't easy for the science minister to answer. He pulled his glasses off, wiped them on his shirt, and returned them to his head. "Don't you know why?" Ben finally asked.

"No," Will answered.

"Your daughter has a special ability," Ben said slowly. "Discovered at the school in Gonzales."

"Discovered?" Will shouted. His rage overcame him. Suddenly he was across the room in two long strides, with his hands on the science minister's neck, pushing him up against the wall. "I saw the aftermath at the school in Greenfield. I saw the children, the graves," he said loudly, his face right next to Ben's.

"I didn't know about that before it happened," Ben sputtered out in a whisper. "I've tried to stop all of this."

Will squeezed harder while Ben kicked against the wall.

"I saw the bodies of children being stacked up at the bottom of a hole. Then I saw more in Gonzales. A line of graves. Our children, our Valley's children," Will shouted.

"I," Ben stuttered and wheezed. "It was a mistake. The Administration is desperate, the Valley is under attack and being overrun. The rain is killing us, our way of life."

Will stared into Ben's bulging eyes. "The Valley is always under attack. I was told that as a child, then as a soldier, and now as a father. Our way of life? What way of life? You killed children."

"I didn't want it to happen, but I couldn't stop it," Ben whispered, the sound in his voice almost gone. His eyes pleaded with Will.

Ben thrashed against the wall.

The lock clanked on the door to the cell. Will released Ben and stepped away from him as he gasped for air.

"Is everything alright, sir?" a soldier asked as he came into the cell.

Ben held up his hand. "Everything is fine. Leave us be."

After the soldier had closed the door, Ben said, "There are powerful forces in the Administration who are trying to stop this. Trying to change the way we do things. A time will come when we need your help, and your daughter's life depends on you helping us."

"What do you want from me?" Will asked.

Ben held his throat, watching Will carefully, finally saying to him, "I'm sorry about all of this. I'm trying to help you. I need to know more about Helen."

"What about her?"

"Did you know she could survive the rain before the incident at the school?"

"No, I didn't. I learned about it when I arrived at the school. When I found out she'd survived." Will rubbed his head with his tied hands and looked down. The frayed leather on his boot edge was still stained with the black mud from his walk along the Salinas.

"Did you ever suspect she was resistant while she was growing up?"

Will looked up at Ben, irritated. "She's a child; she's not grown up," he said loudly.

"Did you ever suspect she wasn't afraid of the rain? Was she ever out in it as a younger child?"

"No, we never knew."

"I'm just trying to figure out if her condition was there from birth or only presented itself later in life," Ben said.

"We protected her from the rain. Like good parents."

A knot formed in Will's throat. He stood and walked to the sink in the corner of the room, then struggled to turn it on with his hands tied. He let the water run a long time, then cupped it and brought it to his face. His beard was thick, and the wound on his cheek still burned beneath the hair. He bent over and drank straight from the faucet. The sting in the back of his throat was gone. Water dripped from his beard onto the linoleum floor. He could feel he was being watched closely and finally turned to face Ben.

"I need to get to Helen immediately," Will said.

"Yes," Ben whispered. "But you also have to help me. Your daughter holds the key to us fixing the rain, saving this Valley. It's getting worse. Soon there will be no Valley, nobody left. It'll kill all of us. And quickly."

"What do you mean, she holds the key?" Will asked.

"Her blood kills the bacteria that poison the rain. It's true for all the surviving children." Ben looked at Will. "How about you? Can you survive the rain?"

Will shook his head. "No, my throat burns when it starts. It makes me sick even when I'm near it."

"You've never gotten wet?"

"No, and I nearly didn't survive getting back to Gonzales from the work camps," Will said.

"And your wife? Was she resistant?" Ben asked.

Will thought about Hannah and their times together outside, escaping to a shelter just before the rain, her always pushing him inside, always calm. At that moment, he realized he didn't know. Was it possible she was always protecting him, that the rain would never have hurt her? He couldn't remember her ever complaining about the rain, but then he couldn't remember her complaining about anything.

"I don't know," Will answered. "Maybe."

"I need a blood sample from you," Ben said.

Ben moved to the door and knocked on the inside of the door.

The soldier standing outside the room opened the door immediately. Will stayed seated, debating his next move. What was behind that door? How many more soldiers? How deep into the building were they? Where was Helen?

"I need my medical kit," Ben said to the soldier.

"Nothing can enter the room with you, sir."

"What do you mean, nothing? I need to take a sample of this man's blood."

Ben stepped out into the hallway and went through his black leather bag. "Here, a syringe. That's all I'm taking in with me."

The young soldier stood looking at the syringe in Ben's hand.

"Alright." He stood away from the door, then shut it behind Ben.

"Roll up your sleeve."

Will rolled the sleeve of his worn flannel, then pushed the roll up over his biceps.

"Please, stay still," Ben said, kneeling next to Will.

Will watched Ben closely while he drained the blood. He skillfully retracted the plunger while the dark fluid filled the barrel. He studied the lines on Ben's face and the dark rings under his eyes. Up close, he was younger than he seemed.

"There, thank you," Ben said, looking up at Will.

He capped the syringe, then pulled a scalpel from his pocket. He held Will's wrists, carefully slid the shining blade next to Will's skin under the zip tie and cut it free. As the tie fell to the floor, Will rubbed his wrists. The two men made eye contact, then looked down at the blade in Ben's hands. He set it on the couch next to Will, who snatched it up and slipped it into his pocket.

"Now is not the time to use that," Ben whispered. "But you may need to soon."

"Thank you," Will said under his breath.

Ben went to the door and knocked. He nodded to Will as the soldier let him out, then the door slammed behind him.

CHAPTER THIRTY-EIGHT

Millard Fillmore knocked on the partially opened door of the office he'd hoped to never enter again. He looked upon the Manager's office, this building, this part of the Valley, and all these weak people with undisguised contempt.

"Sit," the Valley Manager said, pointing to the chair in front of his desk.

"I think I'll stand," Millard said, brushing back his long black coat.

"Did Taft's transfer to the building go smoothly?"

"Why wouldn't it? I didn't let him die in the rain if that's what you mean." Millard rolled a toothpick in his teeth, watching his younger brother study him from behind the desk. He knew too much about how he'd come to sit behind that desk to be intimidated by any of it.

"Millie, I'm just trying to get all the information," the Manager said.

"Why did you call for me?"

"I figured since you were in the building, we may as well take the opportunity to talk. It's been long enough."

"The sooner I can get out of here the better."

"Is he as dangerous as they say?" the Manager asked while stroking the edge of one of his fingers.

"Maybe for you and your boy soldiers. I'll have no problem getting him back to the labor camp. Dead or alive."

"You have to do everything you can to make sure he doesn't affect our plans."

Millard nodded. "You know I will."

"Colonel Adams tells me that repairs to the longvalley are nearly complete. He's ready for the upvalley transfer anytime."

"Or you could just give me the order, and I'll kill him in his cell downstairs. That'd save all of us all a lot of time and energy."

"You've never followed any of my orders anyway."

Millard looked down on the Manager with annoyance. "Why would I? You have no authority."

"I have complete authority," the Manager said, his voice rising in pitch and volume.

Millard scoffed, pulled the toothpick from his mouth, studied it, and looked down on his brother. "Authority?" He scoffed again. "You have no idea about authority. Your authority comes from the politicking. Conniving. Not from strength. I could cross this room and choke you out of existence right here."

Millard saw the Manager's body tense. He continued, "You've always been too scared, too concerned about maintaining that fake authority to do the thing that needed to be done."

"What's that?" the Manager asked.

"What are you waiting for? Why are those children downstairs with their teacher? Why haven't you given the order to use them? You have a powerful weapon, yet you still hesitate to use it."

"We're waiting to run more tests on their blood."

"More tests?" Millard shook his head. "I don't know how this Valley has lasted as long as it has with you runnin' it."

"Watch what you say to me," the Manager said loudly, rising from his chair.

Millard took three deliberately slow steps toward him. He could see the fear in his younger brother's eyes.

"Sit. Down," Millard commanded. The Manager sat back down. Millard put both hands on the desk and leaned in over the Manager.

"It's time you decided. Exercise some of that authority you supposedly have."

"Send the children over the border now?"

The Manager pursed his thin lips. "You know what needs to be done. Why wait? Just make it happen, Mister Valley Manager."

Millard looked down at his brother's thin hands. They were shaking.

The Manager rolled his hands into fists and said, "You're right."

Millard pushed away from his desk and turned to the office door. Without looking back at the Manager, he said, "I have work to do, and so do you."

"Just make sure the father is controlled."

Millard nodded.

"And send Captain Wilson in on your way out," the Manager said. Millard stopped. He shook his head in disdain and disappointment. "Get up and get him yourself," he said as he walked out of the office.

CHAPTER THIRTY-NINE

As the door to Will Taft's cell closed behind him, Ben Harrison could think of nothing but returning to Mary and the children. His impatience to see her again surprised him. He looked down at the capped vial of Will's blood in his hand and knew he had a great deal of lab work ahead. *The blood is the key, but how?* he thought, excitement tainted with dread. His medical bag swung against his knee, and he could feel his heart reverberating with slight thumps against the hollowness of his throat. Outside, the rain still refused to stop.

He rounded a corner into the hallway where Mary and the children were being held. Ben slipped the vial into his pocket.

"Open the door," he commanded to the young soldier standing guard in the hallway.

He stepped inside and scanned the room. Helen and Jimmy were gone, and Mary sat on the couch with her head buried deeply in her hands.

When she heard him enter the room, she looked up at him in a way that made his heart sink. Her face was red, and her bruised eyes were watery and irritated. Her swollen face was a sheet of sadness and rage. She rose, crossed the room, and lifted a fist to pound him on the chest.

"What did you tell them?" she screamed.

Ben dropped his medical bag.

"I thought you were going to help us." Mary was now crying and hitting him weakly on his chest.

"What are you talking about? Where are the children?" Ben asked, holding her forearms.

"He came for them." Mary looked wildly around the room, then to the door, as if something terrible may come through it.

"Who came for them?"

"The captain. Wilson."

Ben's jaw grew tight. He could feel himself begin to sweat as an angry heat flushed through his body. "Where did he take them?" he asked sternly.

"He came with another soldier, made sure they had their jackets and left with them. He wouldn't tell me where they were going. I thought you were going to stop this?"

Ben let go of Mary's wrists and clenched his fists. "I was supposed to have more time."

Mary shook her head, stepped back away from him, and sat back down. "Poor Jimmy has no idea what's going on. They were hurting him, pulling on him. He didn't want to leave. He was so scared." Mary began to cry.

Ben went to her on the couch and kneeled in front of her.

"Mary, look at me. I had no idea about any of this. I'll find the children. Please believe me, Mary. We'll get them back."

Mary sat sobbing and didn't look up at him. "You're all the same," she cried quietly.

Ben stood, looked down at Mary in silence, then turned stiffly and picked up his medical bag. He was consumed with rage. He stepped out of the door, into the hallway, and ran to the elevator.

CHAPTER FORTY

Ben was panting, and his fists were clenched when he reached the Manager's office. He dropped his medical bag in the hallway and pounded on the half-open door.

The Manager looked up as if he were expecting Ben, then went back to some papers he was signing. Ben waited for him to speak.

"Sit down," the Manager said, nodding to the empty chair across the desk.

Ben didn't move. He wanted to jump over the desk and strangle him. He continued to stare coldly at the Manager as he went over his remaining papers. He saw the knife-like letter opener on the Manager's desk, the tiny white mound of spittle accumulating in the corner of the Manager's mouth, and the bright red edges of his fingernails as he worked an overly fat pen across a piece of paper.

"Sit down, Ben," the Manager repeated in a stern voice. "I have bad news."

"Where are the children?" Ben interrupted.

The Manager looked up and studied Ben, apparently surprised that he was still standing. He pushed himself back away from his desk, then swiveled in his chair to the wide window behind him. The light was drawing down under the clouds in the west. Afternoon thunder trundled along the unseen Valley walls. The unceasing rain had morphed into a foul mist.

"It still hasn't stopped. Almost two full days now," the Manager said while staring out the window.

"Where are the children?" Ben repeated.

"We'll get to that. First, you need to know something."

"What is it?" Ben asked, his jaw still clenched, his neck corded.

"A large number of people died in the rain yesterday."

"How many?"

"Hundreds, maybe. We still don't have the numbers."

"Where? How did they get caught out in it?" Ben asked.

"They didn't." The Manager rose from his chair, staring at Ben almost as if he was studying his reaction. He turned to the window on the city and continued, "They were in their houses in the Bolsa Knolls Sector when a heavy rain started. The entire sector went quiet. A convoy reported back about the incident about an hour ago."

The Manager turned from the window and approached Ben. "The convoy reported that none of those people were wet. They died in their houses."

"What?" Ben asked, stunned. He pressed his fist to his mouth, winced, and stared out at the murky city beyond the glass. His mind raced. "This is what I feared would happen."

"Damn it, Ben. What have you been doing?" the Manager asked, his eyebrows lowered, his lips tucked. "This is going to kill us all."

Ben was panicked. "It's escalating. I'm not sure how much time we have now."

The Manager stared at Ben, looking disgusted. "Our Valley will be wide open for the taking if we don't do something soon."

"Were there any survivors in Bolsa Knolls?"

"I don't know yet." The Manager sat back down behind his desk and began to nervously rub the edge of his forefinger.

Ben knew the Manager blamed him for the rain, and that only made him angrier. "What have you done with the children? Their teacher said Wilson came for them."

"He's moving them to the border."

Ben shook his head. "You told me I had more time for tests, that I would have at least a week with them," he said, his voice gaining in volume.

"There's no more time for your tests," the Manager protested loudly, suddenly angry. "I never promised you anything. If we don't use those children now, the Benicians will take our Valley easily. I've given the order. It's done."

Ben put his hand to his forehead and looked at the floor. He blinked, his thoughts scrambling. The Valley Manager bloodied yet another hangnail. Ben could smell his sour breath.

"Is the captain going to keep Helen and Jimmy safe during their mission?" Ben finally asked.

The Manager winced slightly, then stared at Ben.

"Do you remember when we vowed to give everything to defend this Valley from our enemies? Remember when we promised that again at the beginning of our time in the Administration?" the Manager asked.

"Yes," Ben replied.

"We're not the only ones who have to sacrifice for this Valley. It's only through the blood of our people that the whole Valley won't perish." The Manager stared at Ben.

"What are you talking about?"

"They won't be returning from their mission," the Manager said, his voice stiff and cold.

A chill moved along Ben's spine. "What have you ordered Wilson to do with them?"

"They'll be using their special gifts to carry something through the rain that our enemies won't see coming. We'll strike a blow at the heart of their border encampment and another in their city." The Valley Manager got more excited as he spoke. "This will be the change we need. The break from this war we've been waiting for."

"How could you do this?" Ben asked, raising his voice again.

"These are military issues. Issues of Valley security."

Ben tried to calm himself, to not expose any emotion to the Manager. "What about the blood? It was our opportunity to study how it could stop the rain."

"You'll have to make do with the younger children. The Greenfield boys are still here. We have a different mission for them. Now you have the father's blood as well. What else do you need?"

Ben looked at the Valley Manager not knowing how to answer. After a moment, the Manager nodded and said, "You're free to go now. Get back to the lab. Go do your job, and I'll do mine. Why don't you spend less effort worrying about those children and more time trying to fix the rain?"

Ben turned toward the office door, then stopped at the window. The rain had escalated again and was coming in sheets from the remaining light in the western sky.

"You need to make something work, Ben," the Manager said calmly. "Before it kills all of us."

"I'm trying."

"Try harder. The resistance is spreading like a virus, our enemies are at our borders, and now even the air is becoming toxic."

Ben stared out the window. Wide drops of water pummeled the outside of the glass. Suddenly, something clicked in his brain. He slowly faced the Manager. "What did you say just then?" he asked.

"When?"

"Repeat what you just said."

"I said the air is toxic."

"No before that, just before that," Ben said, getting excited.

The Valley Manager looked confused. "I said the resistance is spreading in this Valley like a virus."

Ben snapped his fingers. "That's it! That's what I've been missing."

"What are you talking about?" the Manager asked.

Ben looked at the Manager as if he just realized he was standing there. He felt the vial of Will Taft's blood in his pocket. "I have to get to the lab immediately."

With that, Ben rushed into the hallway, leaving the Valley Manager to stand in the doorway of his office.

CHAPTER FORTY-ONE

Will waited impatiently on the couch in his cell. For what, he wasn't sure. *Could he trust the science minister?* He didn't know, but he had the scalpel in his pocket as evidence of his commitment. His thumb rubbed against the smooth metal handle. He didn't know what time of day it was but based on his exhaustion it was likely nighttime.

A pound came on the door, and Will heard the muffled voice of a soldier from the other side. "Move to the back wall of the room."

Will rose from the couch and stepped away from the door, gripping the scalpel tightly. The door was unlocked and opened halfway. A meal tray was slid on the floor into the room, then the door was slammed shut. Will saw only the light blue sleeve of a UP soldier's uniform.

"The light will go out in twenty minutes. Eat," said the voice behind the door.

Will moved over to the tray of food. Although it didn't look appetizing, nor recognizable, he was hungry. Two piles sat on the tray, one tasting vaguely of cornmeal polenta and the other, some kind of fruit paste, gritty like pear, but with the flavor of a turnip. Somewhere in the blandness of the fruit pile, however faint, was a flavor reminiscent of the apple pies he and Zach had found in the broken-down Soledad grocery store. Will closed his eyes and breathed in deep, trying to recapture that sensation, but nothing came.

The lights went out soon after he was done eating, and the room fell nearly black save a faint strip of gray light flaring across the floor from under the door. He drifted off to sleep on the couch, still holding the scalpel. In the night, dreams of Helen fluttered and flashed like a broken movie reel. Images of her alone in the rain calling to him disturbed his sleep and blended with the darkness of the room in his brief waking moments.

At some point in the night, he awoke and went to the corner sink and drank. The water smelled of rotten eggs and tingled on his throat. He laid back down on the couch and thought of Zach. *What had become of him in the rain outside Dick Nixon's apartment? Was he still on the streets of Salinas City? Had he been captured?* Eventually, Will drifted off to sleep again until, some unknown number of hours later, the lights flickered, then flared on overhead, and the room was once again filled with stark light.

He sat up on the couch rubbing his eyes, trying to remember the content of the dreams, to get a grip on all the thoughts that had come to him so clearly in the night, but he couldn't. All that remained of those vivid images were bitter feelings of helplessness and separation from his daughter.

He rose and stretched his sore muscles. He had several darkening bruises along his side and neck. Finally, he heard steps in the hallway, then muffled voices. A knock came on the door before it swung open slowly. Will stood rigidly gripping the blade in his pocket.

The science minister peeked through the open door, saw Will then came in and closed it behind him.

"Bad news," Ben whispered. A bleak expression spread across his face. "Your daughter's been moved to the border."

Will felt his face flush hot and his fist clench. "When?" he asked in a loud whisper.

"They left last night."

"What do you mean, *they*?"

"Jimmy, the other child from the school. Captain Wilson brought them."

At the mention of the captain's name, Will could feel himself begin to sweat. He paced back and forth looking around the room.

"Why the border?" Will asked, suddenly feeling disconnected from Helen and trapped. He looked around the room, panicked. The thought of his daughter being sent to that grim and embattled crossing gave Will a chill along his spine.

Will faced Ben, waiting for a response, but none came. Finally, Ben made eye contact with Will and whispered, choosing his words carefully. "Your daughter is in grave danger."

Will felt the temperature in the cell go up by ten degrees instantly. The walls seemed closer, the ceiling pressing down on him. "I need to get out of here. You have to help me."

"I'm going to." Ben was wide-eyed and frantic.

"Now?"

"Yes. But you'll need a vehicle and gas mask to get to the border. You won't survive long out there without one. I'm working on how to make that happen. The rain hasn't stopped in three days."

"Is it getting worse?"

"Yes, and quickly. People are dying without getting wet. I don't know how bad it is throughout the Valley, but it's escalated in parts of Salinas City."

Will noticed that Ben seemed to be lost in thought for a moment, distracted, looking at the wall behind Will. Finally, Ben said, "I may have a solution. It's a long shot, but it could work." He looked up at Will, and there was a glimmer of excitement in his eyes. "I worked through the night. It's our only chance. The Valley's only chance."

Will put his hand back into his pocket and felt the blade. "I'm ready when you are."

The science minister took off his glasses and rubbed his tired eyes. He put his hand to his mouth and seemed to be lost in thought.

"What do we do now?" Will whispered loudly. "How do we get out of here?"

"I'll get what you need ready, then come back for you. One more question about Helen. Do you ever remember her getting a bad fever or flu growing up?"

"Maybe once when she first went to school," Will said impatiently. "Why do you ask?"

Ben's expression shifted, his eyes widened. "Her blood may protect her from the rain, but it's not so much her blood as what's infected her blood. Last night I was able to—"

A loud pound on the door interrupted Ben. It swung in violently. Millard Fillmore slinked through the door with his gun raised at Will's chest. He turned the gun on Ben, who instinctively put his hands up, then back to Will.

"You," Millard said to Ben. "What are you doing in here?"

Ben's mouth hung open. Finally, he stuttered, "I, I was talking to the prisoner about his blood tests and his daughter."

Millard squinted and watched Ben with skepticism and contempt. He rolled a frayed toothpick in his mouth.

"You done?" Millard asked Ben with his gun still on Will.

"I guess so," Ben said, caught off guard.

"Go on then. I'm sure you have better things to do. Hero boy here is due for another trip upvalley."

Will watched as Ben stood frozen, unmoving. Millard shifted, raising the gun from Will's chest to his head while his heavy leather jacket squeaked.

"Go on," Millard repeated.

Ben's eyes met Will's.

"I, I need more of his blood," Ben stuttered, his voice wavering. "You can't take him yet. You'll have to come back later."

Millard turned from Will to Ben, a pinched expression of disbelief coming across his face. Will saw Ben's chest heaving as he breathed.

Millard moved toward Ben slowly and purposefully as Ben backed up against the cell wall. When he was right up on him, breathing in his face, Millard raised his gun to Ben's neck. Ben pulled his head back away from Millard, looking to the side. Millard leaned in, pressing his body against Ben's. He was so close that the toothpick in his mouth touched Ben's cheek.

"You need more blood, huh?" Millard asked in a clear sarcastic tone.

Ben didn't respond. He was frozen.

"Maybe you could use your own." Millard scoffed at his own joke as he pressed the gun harder into Ben's neck, pushing his head harder against the wall. Millard waited, seemingly studying the side of Ben's head, then said, "You shouldn't be in here, science man. You're gonna end up gettin' hurt."

He backed away from Ben and a smile crossed his face. Ben raised his hands, palms facing Millard, his eyes wide and watery under his glasses.

"Go on now," Millard said, motioning to the door with the gun. "There's nothing more here for you."

Ben stepped carefully around Millard, his hands still raised. Will saw him glance back, then disappear into the hallway.

Millard turned to Will, reached into his long coat, and threw a pair of handcuffs onto the linoleum in front of Will. They slid across the floor and clanked to a stop against Will's boots. "You know the drill. Put 'em on."

Will stared at the open silver rings on the floor and didn't move.

Millard cocked the hammer of his gun. "I've been told that I can get you back to the labor camps in any fashion that I'd like. That includes in a body bag. I'm fine with going that route if you are. If not, lean down and fasten those cuffs."

Will bent to retrieve the cuffs. He made eye contact with Millard as the rings clicked closed around his wrists.

Millard smirked. "Alright, here we go. Out to the jeep." He stepped farther into the cell while the soldier at the door backed out behind him. "Move over to the corner." Will obeyed his command. "Now, I'll follow you. Try anything stupid and I'd be happy to paint this hallway with your brains."

Will came around Millard, who kept his distance and stepped out into a long hallway. "Go to the right, slowly," Millard commanded.

A soldier stood next to the door at the end of the hallway. As Will approached, he stood back and opened the door into another short hallway where a second soldier wearing a gas mask manned a set of doors that led to a covered parking lot at the back of the building.

Will walked slowly, considering his options. He could hear Millard's purposeful steps trailing him and the doors clicking shut as the soldiers let them through. As he got to the end of the hallway, he could hear the rain outside, pounding the road beyond the covered parking area and running in wide thin sheets along the surfaces beyond. Water bounced off the pavement, shuddered, and died in the deluge of new drops. The smell of rotten garlic hit Will like a punch in the chest. With a single breath, he felt his throat thickening and burn while his cheeks numbed.

He stopped at the end of the hallway a short distance from Millard's parked jeep and turned around to look at Millard. While they walked, Millard had slipped a gas mask over his face. With his gun in front of him and a muffled voice through the mask, he said, "Go on. Get to the truck."

Will knew that once he was handcuffed to the jeep, his chances of seeing his daughter were gone. In four hours, he'd be in a high-security wing of the San Ardo labor camp, exactly where he was a week earlier, but now with a dead wife and daughter in mortal danger. He couldn't get into that truck. With his hands cuffed in front of him, he reached for the pocket with the scalpel, but couldn't get a hand in. He stretched his fingers out just far enough to feel the steel of the blade handle. Each breath seemed to burn more, and it occurred to him that in this rain he may not survive the ride back to the labor camp anyway. He felt dizzy.

"Come on. What are you waiting for? I said move to the truck." Millard stood back away from Will, expressionless underneath his mask, the canister pulsing in and out. His eyes cold and calculating, too careful and too smart to get close to Will.

Will turned back to Millard's jeep, feeling weak in the knees, thighs burning. He thought he may not even be able to make the short walk through the open air. Beyond the building was a toxic shower like none Will had seen. His vision narrowed.

"I'll just shoot you right here and drag your body into the cargo hold of the truck," Millard's muffled, and irritated voice came from behind. "Go on now. Walk."

While the slow seconds passed, Will's mind raced through a dismal analysis. *Run toward Millard and get shot. Walk forward to the truck, and even if you make it, end up back in the labor camp.* His options were few, and none involved any scenarios in which he survived to see his daughter again.

Will took his first careful steps out of the building to the truck, and in that moment something from the side knocked him off his feet. A sound came to him like air being sucked through a pipe, then the pounding of a low drum. The next thing he knew he was on the ground, his only sensation was of his throat burning and his ears ringing. The world had compressed to a silent tunnel, a small segment of pavement just beyond his face.

He lifted his cuffed hands to his ears, and they came away bloody. He tried to focus but couldn't. He was on the pavement just outside the building where a short distance from his face was half of a brick. Broken bricks were everywhere, raining with violent clinks onto the walkway. Will looked up and saw a wide, jagged hole in the side of the Administration building. He tried to stand, but his muscles weren't responding.

He rolled onto his side and looked out beyond Millard's jeep. There was a dark silhouette coming toward him, backlit by the bright haze of the clouded sky. Zach came into focus. He stood motionless, a ghost blending with the mist and water, soaked through, with an awestruck expression. Will pulled a hot burning breath into his lungs and writhed in pain. His eyes went out of focus again, and he felt like he was drowning.

Seconds later Zach was standing over him, yelling something at him. Zach pushed a mask onto Will's face and helped him to his feet. Will leaned on Zach, and together they limped to Millard's jeep. Zach helped Will into the passenger seat, slammed the door shut, and ran back toward the building. Will took deep, controlled breaths through the mask. From his seat, he turned toward the building. Bright blue sparks lit up the gloomy morning, and bricks continued to fall from the upper part of the hole in the building. Millard Fillmore was sprawled face-down on the sidewalk where Will was blown off his feet. Will saw Zach kneeling over Millard, frantically searching through his overcoat. Will's heavy head flopped forward. He closed his eyes and lost consciousness.

CHAPTER FORTY-TWO

Will awoke feeling worse than he could ever remember. Wipers squeaked and slashed back and forth across a foggy windshield. Water sprayed in all directions. A gas mask was pulled securely onto his face, and the filter canister moved in and out with each breath. He reached up with handcuffed hands and lifted the mask off his head.

"You'll want to keep that on," Zach said, not looking at Will. He was hunched over the steering wheel, focused on the wet road ahead.

Will's head pounded. His throat was swollen, his eyes awash with tears, and the smell of garlic hung thick in the car. He pulled the mask back over his face and took deep breaths.

"What happened?" he asked through the mask.

"I found the keys to your cuffs in his jacket. There," Zach said, pointing to the dashboard.

While Will worked the round key from Millard's key chain into the keyhole of the handcuffs, Zach slowed the car, jerking the jeep into a lower gear. A loud grinding sound came from the transmission.

"Do you know how to drive?" Will asked.

"Never drove a car before. Spent lots of time on my daddy's tractor, though. Seems like the same basic concept."

"Where are we headed?" Will asked.

"I have no idea. I just drove so we could get out of there while everyone was distracted."

Will freed himself from the handcuffs and looked down at his hand-gun, which Zach had set in the Jeep's center console. He pulled the scalpel out of his pocket and set it next to the gun. He stared at the blade, pondering the small and ineffective weapon that had been so important for him while in the holding cell. The scalpel was a pact between him and the science minister, whom he figured he'd never see again.

As they drove the rain slackened.

"There's water in the pack on the back seat. You should drink," Zach said.

Will reached around and extracted the plastic bottle from the pack. It was the same pack he'd taken from the dead boy by the river, now empty of its explosives.

"Thank you," Will said while lifting the mask from his face and sipping the water.

He returned the mask to his mouth and breathed evenly, starting to feel his senses returning. He looked out the windshield to see if he could determine where they were. They were headed east into the morning sun, which was beginning its cold transect above the obstructed downvalley sky.

As far as he could tell, they were on a side shoot of the longvalley freeway somewhere in the eastern suburbs of Salinas City. Another grind of the gears and Zach halted the jeep on the edge of the road. The rain had slowed to a mist. With the diesel engine clucking its idle underneath them, they turned around, peered through the rear window, and surveyed the road behind them. Will could hear Zach panting quietly.

"Doesn't look like we were followed," Zach said.

"What happened? How did you get here?"

"I'll explain, but should I keep driving?" Zach asked.

"They'll be looking for us and this jeep," Will responded. "We need to get to the border camp immediately. They took Helen there."

"Which way?"

Will used his sleeve to wipe the condensation off the inside of his window. He stared at the mountains, trying to focus.

"There. See the old Fremont communications tower?"

"Yeah, I see it."

"That's to the east of us. We need to keep heading downvalley. We're in the Natividad District. Keep going straight. We can take the Old Stage Offshoot if it isn't blocked."

"Do you want to drive?" Zach asked.

"No, you're doing great."

Zach stepped on the clutch, jammed the gearstick forward, and raced the engine. The tires screeched on the wet pavement as they lurched into motion.

Will pushed the mask tight to his face as they came into a cloud burst and thunder clapped above them. Even breathing through the filter, he felt nauseous. What the science minister had told him about people dying even when they were dry formed a pool of fear in the pit of his stomach. He sunk back into the seat and closed his eyes again. As the sickening rush of water flowed over the jeep he tried to breathe calmly through the mask.

Zach glanced at him. "You alright?" he asked.

"I'll be fine," Will said, but he didn't feel fine. He was feeling claustrophobic. He suppressed the fear in his gut and asked, "How did you get to the Valley Administration building?"

"Dick Nixon."

"Dick Nixon?"

"When you and Mary were taken, I sat out in the rain on the fire escape below his apartment until all the soldiers had left. I had the gun and the explosives in the pack, and I didn't know what to do. I was going to force Dick to help me find you, but when I came back into the apartment, he was there at the table and didn't even resist me. He was partly shocked by me coming in from the rain, but also he felt terrible."

"What do you mean?"

"I guess he was trying to find out about your daughter, but they were on to us and came to the apartment without him knowing."

"But the three knocks on the door; that was his system."

"He told me they held him at gunpoint."

Will breathed steadily through the mask, trying to keep his head clear. "Hmmm. Not sure I believe any of what he says."

"Yeah, I guess it doesn't matter. I was going to shoot him right there in his apartment, but he helped me devise a plan to get to you. I waited for him to find out what was going on. I had no choice but to trust him. He didn't know I had the explosives."

Will stared forward as the rain once again abated.

"Where's Mary?" Zach asked.

"What?" Will's ears were still ringing.

"What happened to Mary?" Zach asked loudly.

"I'm not sure. She was with the children in the Administration building until they were moved to the border."

They raced along the raised causeway between inundated fields. Areas of rich soil, once so productive, now only flooded wetlands invaded by cattails and pickleweed from all sides.

"Dick turned out to be a good guy. He has a lot of loyalty to you and felt terrible about what happened. He helped me get to the building and find out when and where you were being transferred. I didn't have a plan other than to break you out of there somehow. I guess I got lucky, recognizing this jeep. The timing just worked out."

"Yes, it did."

"I was outside in the rain at the back of the building all morning, trying not to be seen, as it got lighter. When Millard pulled up and went inside, I placed the explosives next to the door. I thought they'd create a distraction while I grabbed you from Millard. I didn't know how big the explosion would be. It damn near tore off half the building. At first, I thought I killed you."

"You almost did."

"Was Millard alive?"

"I didn't check. He wasn't moving."

Will and Zach drove on. A wake of toxic mist swirled behind them. The rain had ceased by the time they were on Old Stage Road. Dead snags of trees lined the road, bark concrete gray and smooth, still standing, but naked of their leaves. Will watched patches of sunken fields pass by, abandoned long ago to flooding. Lines of water pooled in ancient furrows reflecting white against the sky. Strawberries were farmed here once but had long ago become impossible to grow in the soggy fields.

The jeep was the only car on the rutted road in any direction. When they came upon a knoll at the eastern edge of the Valley, Will asked Zach to pull over onto the muddy shoulder, where they got out and surveyed the Valley. Salinas City, where it was still raining, rose out of the low clouds.

"There," Will said, pointing downvalley to a clear narrowing between rolling hills. "See the trucks? Beyond that is the encampment, and beyond there is the border. That's where all the crossings happen. If Helen's here, that's where we'll find her."

"I see it," Zach said, squinting into the haze.

"You can barely make out the wall crossing the hills beyond the trucks." Will's tone and expression changed to something darker, and he spoke almost to himself, "I thought I'd never be back here."

"What's our plan?" Zach asked.

"We're near the camp. We need to get rid of this jeep and head the rest of the way on foot. As we get closer, there could be soldiers everywhere."

"What about the rain?"

"We can't keep this thing. They'll find us if we do. We need to get to Helen as soon as possible. We'll find shelter. If they send her over the border, in the rain or not, she won't come back."

Zach drove the jeep down off the hill back onto the Valley floor, where they left it on a dirt side road behind a stand of live oaks. As Will closed the door, wind rustled through the trees, and water fell from leaves and drummed against the waterlogged ground. He looked up beyond the leaves to the thick clouds skirting across the sky.

Zach pulled his pack from the back seat, then stood and looked up at the sky, blinking his bloodshot eyes. Will wondered how he could have ever considered not saving him at his grandparents.

"Ready?" Will asked.

Zach nodded, then slammed the door.

"At this point, if it rains, if anything happens to me, don't worry about rescuing me. Go straight to Helen. Do whatever you need to do to get her as far away from the border as possible. At least you can both travel in the rain."

"Understood."

"Thank you," Will said.

"Of course," Zach said. "Sorry about the explosion."

"I mean for all of it. Thank you," Will repeated, holding his gaze on Zach.

"I know," Zach said with a nod.

As they stepped away from Millard's jeep, a troubling wind rose over the low hills in front of them, moving the leaden squall line of sky over the border in their direction. Will turned into the caustic breeze, snugged the gas mask onto his bearded face, and jogged in the direction of the border. Zach limped beside him, one leg strong and limber, the other weak and stiff, straining to keep pace.

CHAPTER FORTY-THREE

Ben Harrison was in the lab when he heard the explosion. The whole building shuddered underneath him, and the lights went down for a moment, then flickered back on. He held onto the countertop while the room ceased its swaying. He rushed to the window where he could see white smoke rising in the rain from the base of the building.

The power outage caused the centrifuge he was standing by to turn off and whine to a stop. He untwisted the lid from the rotor, lifted a tube of clear fluid out of the machine, and held it up to the light. A beige coagulate hovered at the bottom of the tube. He carefully placed the tube back into the rotor with eleven others just like it and went back to the window. The white smoke was still rising.

Back at the centrifuge, Ben worked quickly, pulling tubes out in succession and carefully decanting the clear liquid off the thick plug at the bottom into an opaque plastic bottle. He poured each tube in succession, filling the bottle.

A knock came on the lab door as he screwed down the lid. Before he could answer, the door swung open. It was Dick Nixon standing in the doorway, a surprised expression with sweat rings staining an area of his shirt far beyond his armpits.

"Dick," Ben said, not surprised to see him.

"What are you doing? We have to go immediately," Dick replied, speaking like he couldn't catch his breath. "Everything is starting."

He approached Ben and continued in an urgent whisper. "There's been an attack on the building. The whole south side is blown open."

"Calm down," Ben whispered loudly. "Stick with our plan or we'll both get caught."

"This wasn't expected," Dick said. The whites of his eyes were bright and made a full circle around the irises. "Are you still in contact with the colonel?"

"No, but we talked yesterday. Are you ready for what you have to do?"

"Is that it?"

Ben nodded.

"Have you been here all night?"

"I had to be. The pilot should be waiting for you. Don't stop for anything, stay out of sight, and make it there as soon as you can."

"What's in the bottle?"

"Our only hope. It has to work. This is all we have." Ben held the bottle up to the light and swirled its contents. "It should be enough."

"What about the children? The teacher?"

"I'll get to them." Ben looked at his watch. "There isn't much time," he said, handing Dick the opaque plastic bottle.

Dick took it with both hands.

"Be careful. Make sure you tell him exactly what we went over."

"Will the colonel come?"

"I hope so."

"Okay, my friend, stay dry," Dick said, holding out the hand that wasn't carrying the bottle. They shook hands.

Ben nodded at him. "You, too. We'll meet in a few days. You have the most important job of all of us."

"I know. I'll be careful." Dick smiled, then said, "For the Valley."

"Yes. For the Valley," Ben said.

He watched Dick hurl his great weight forward and lumber off with his precious plastic bottle down the hallway.

Ben Harrison wanted to waste no time getting back to Mary. He pulled down the coat hanging on the back of the lab door and scanned the room for anything he thought he'd need to take with him. He paused at the door of the laboratory, a room in which he'd spent the better part of his life and surveyed it one last time. *Nothing will ever be the same again*, he thought.

Out the door, he went, down the long hallway to the elevator. He hit the button to call the elevator, but no light came on. He rushed back down the hallway to the stairwell where he went down eighteen floors and came out into another hallway, sweating and breathing hard. All the doors were closed on both sides of the deserted hallway, and the shiny floor reflected the strip of fluorescents on the ceiling. He moved quickly down the corridor, around a corner to where a soldier stood near an open door.

"Move aside," Ben said in a stern tone as he approached the young soldier. The soldier stood back, exposing the doorway to the room. He scanned the empty room. Adrenaline surged through his veins. Mary McElroy was gone.

"Where is she?" Ben asked the soldier, gritting his teeth.

"She's been moved, sir."

"Were the three boys taken?" Ben asked, trying to catch his breath.

"Yes, sir. My commander came and took them all after the explosion."

"Where were they taken?"

"I don't know, sir. He took them down the hall to the stairs, headed to the first floor."

"Why are you still here?"

The young man looked at Ben, confused. "I wasn't given any orders, sir."

Ben left the soldier standing next to the open door and went back to the stairwell. He skipped down the stairs, landing on every other, to the ground floor. When he pushed open the metal stairwell door, he was hit by the bitter smell of rotten garlic from the outside rain, combined with smoke that smelled of burning plastic.

He was in a foyer at the front of the building. To one side, a long hallway ended at a set of doors leading out to a covered parkway at the back of the building. That back exit was now a wide-open hole. Soldiers were scrambling about randomly. Someone out of Ben's sight was yelling commands. The front doors were propped open with chairs, and the smoke was clearing from the hallway.

Ben went to the front of the building and slipped out the door at the main entrance. He'd entered this building five, sometimes six, days a week for over fifteen years and had so rarely come through the wide, guarded glass doors at the front. A short distance outside the entrance he saw two military vehicles, each loaded with UP soldiers and a white van parked between them. Just beyond the covered parking area, the damp sky sagged, and rain roared on the pavement.

Ben felt the sickly sting of the rain in each of his breaths. Mary McElroy stood outside the door of the van helping the last of the children inside. He moved in her direction but was approached by a young soldier who guarded the first vehicle. The soldier put his hand up.

Ben looked over his shoulder and caught Mary's eye as another soldier pushed her into the van after the children. She looked panicked.

As the van door slid shut, Ben focused on the wide-eyed boy in front of him. His light blue uniform was impeccable as if he'd never been out of the headquarters building. "Stand aside, soldier," Ben said loudly. "I'm the Valley Science Minister."

The boy soldier had an anemic look about him and red rings around his eyes. His pursed lips were a pale green color. He was clearly feeling ill, even under the covered area at the entrance of the building. The boy mustered the strength to stand up straight and put his hands on his rifle. "Sorry, sir. My orders are to not let anyone near the vehicles."

Ben turned to see the Valley Manager in the back seat of the lead vehicle. He had a gas mask on and a soldier on both sides. The mask had two thick filter canisters at angles to his mouth and a clear plastic hood attached to the back of the mask draped over his head.

"What is this?" Ben yelled over the soldier at the Valley Manager, holding both his hands up. "Where are you taking them?"

The Valley Manager stared at Ben. He was barely recognizable, distorted under his plastic hood. His cold eyes, like little black caves above the mask, stayed on Ben. He turned his head away, keeping his eyes on him, and tapped the driver of his vehicle on the shoulder. They rolled forward, and the van carrying Mary and the children followed.

Ben stepped in the direction of the van, but the soldier put his hand on Ben's chest.

"Sir, I can't let you come any closer."

The vehicles rolled away from the front of the building, and as the Valley Manager passed, he continued to stare. Ben felt a sinking feeling inside as he stood silently watching the sparse convoy disappear into the dirty mist beyond the tall buildings.

He turned back to the entrance of the building to see Millard Fillmore limping out of the front doors. His long black trench coat was covered with white dust, and blood ran down his left cheek onto his neck. His eyes wandered the distance like a dazed crazy man.

As he got closer, Ben could see that there was a gash on Millard's head, just above the hairline, from whence all the blood was falling. The back of one of his hands looked badly burnt and a pant leg was torn open.

"What did you say?" he asked loudly when he was close to Ben.

"Nothing."

"My ears are ringing. I can't hear shit. My vehicle was taken. I need another one immediately."

Ben shrugged. He smelled burnt hair as Millard pushed his way past him.

"Soldier," Millard yelled, "bring me a vehicle." The boy hesitated. "Now," Millard said, taking a step forward. The boy looked at him for a moment, then hustled off toward the back of the building.

"Where are you going?" Ben asked Millard.

"What?"

"Where are you going?" Ben yelled over the roar of the rain.

"I have an appointment with your new friend Willie Taft at the border," Millard said with a tight grin on his wretched, bloodstained face.

"How do you know he's headed there?" Ben asked.

"I know where his daughter is. He'll come to me."

A black military jeep came out of the rain and screeched into the covered entrance. The vehicle sat idling and dripping, puffs of white smoke dissipating out of the tailpipe. The young soldier stepped out and stumbled away from the driver's door. His face was ashen, and he had a wide-eyed, dumbfounded look with visibly trembling lips. He bent over and vomited onto the pavement. Millard stepped away from him.

"Isn't this rain a bitch?" Millard asked, looking at Ben. Millard went to the boy, who was still bent over on the sidewalk and kicked him gently with the toe of his boot. "Stand up, soldier. Give me your sidearm." He stood, shaking, his eyes wide with fear, peering back and forth between Millard and Ben.

"Give me your gun, and don't make me ask you again."

The boy was apparently too weak and scared to resist. He pulled his handgun out of the holster on his belt and held it out. Millard skillfully popped the clip from the handle, examined the chamber, then reassembled the gun.

While tucking it under his coat, Millard said to the boy, "Go on now, get back into the building and get some fresh air." The boy just stood there, still bent over, holding his stomach.

Millard got into the jeep and pulled a gas mask from the passenger seat over his bloody head. He stared out at Ben through the open window.

"There'll be repercussions for you. I promise," Millard yelled.

"There will be for all of us," Ben yelled back, but there was no way Millard could have heard him.

The tires of the jeep squealed, and Millard sped off into the rain.

CHAPTER FORTY-FOUR

The world surrounding the border camp was soggy and washed out, only muted tones of steely gray. The frequent rains had stolen anything vibrant from this place. As the border shifted, pushing forward, then pulling back, the only consistent loser was the land, beaten by man's ceaseless warring. The sun was never more than a chalky diffusion, whose position in the sky remained obscure throughout the day.

Great sheets of mist sat over the fallow fields, and the smell of sodden leaf mold contended with the remnant rotten rain. Will and Zach walked cautiously toward the contested crossing. A thick duff of fallen leaves muted their hurried passage along the edge of the road. Will's feet were cold and wet, and he could hear the hum of the border encampment's generators in the distance. At one point he turned to see his distorted reflection in the dark and oily water in the roadside ditch, masked and hard, with eyes sunken and backlit by the weak daytime glow.

Will heard a vehicle approaching.

"Quick, get down," Will yelled at Zach.

The whine of the vehicle got louder as Zach lurched in Will's direction. They both laid on the edge of the abandoned irrigation ditch. A black military jeep roared by them sending aloft a fetid mist from the tarmac. Will buried his face into the gas mask until the spray settled and the sound of the jeep had faded and blended with the hum of the camp.

They drug themselves out of the ditch and continued along the road. After a short distance, they moved up a hill, through an oak woodland to the edge of a clearing where they could see the sprawling UP military encampment below.

Down in the camp, the pavement ended abruptly at a roadblock constructed of old broken concrete traffic barriers with a moveable pole laid between them. Will and Zach knelt in the sour duff at the edge of the clearing watching the guard shed and the activity in the encampment beyond.

A tall wire fence ran along the back edge of the camp and into the chaparral on both sides. Will knew that a short distance beyond that fence, scared and exhausted San Benician soldiers were hunkered down in their damp hovels waiting for their opportunity to advance. Somewhere far beyond those soldiers were their leaders, warm and dry, plotting and scheming in the tall buildings of Hollister City.

The oldest and most permanent buildings of the camp were four long, wooden rectangles laid out in a square. From this core of central buildings, many smaller hastily built structures spread out randomly in all directions. A row of diesel generators at the camp's edge belched forth a muffled hum. Stained wooden poles supported wires running from the generators, like a chaotic spider web, to various buildings throughout the camp. Several ground-level hatch doors lined the camp's edge, the entrances to flooded and abandoned underground tunnels.

Walkways covered by rotting plywood crisscrossed the camp between buildings. The heavy chocolate mud of the Salinas Valley was everywhere, staining the sides of each building. The scene struck Will as more of a shantytown than a military camp. He thought back to his time in this exact camp and wondered if it was as dilapidated back then.

Will watched the sky. "I hate this place," he said quietly, his voice deeply muffled in the gas mask.

"What'd you say?" Zach asked.

"Nothing," Will said, speaking louder. "I thought I'd never have to see this place again."

"It looks like a hellhole. I guess this is where I was headed." Zach looked down at his leg as he rubbed it.

Will studied the sky beyond the camp, then turned toward Salinas City. He thought for a moment he saw an airplane dip briefly below the clouds above the city, then disappear into the ash-colored mist just as fast.

"Did you see that?" he asked Zach.

"See what?"

"I'm not sure. Never mind."

Will slipped the gas mask off his face and took a shallow breath. It burned, and the sour stink coated the inside of his throat. A needling pain

resided at the base of the back of his head. It had started as a dull head-
ache and was now growing sharper. He knew the mist-laden air was
slowly poisoning him. He secured the mask again, pulled the straps
tighter, palmed the filter canister against his face, and inhaled deeply.
The dirty filters gently sucked in with each of his troubled breaths.

She could be so close, Will thought. *Just on the other side of a few
UP soldiers. She never should have seen this place.* Anger began to
seethe deep inside him. *Captain Wilson.* He had to be patient. They'd
have one opportunity, and only one, to get her out. They'd wait for the
cover of night, which meant rain was likely.

"There, see that large building along the edge?" Will asked Zach.

"Yeah."

"That's where she'll be. It's the old mess hall and officer's
quarters."

The jeep that had passed them on the road was parked with the
other muddy trucks in front of that building.

"How do we get down there and get her out?" Zach asked, squinting down into the camp.

"We'll need to go around that edge of the camp and come down
over there. It'll have the least number of soldiers around. It'll be best to
wait until dark."

Zach turned his chin up to the sky.

"We need to find shelter and wait. Come on."

They hustled their way up through the twisted grove of live oaks
surrounding the camp. Each crack of a dried stick underfoot, each loud
crunch of old bark or brittle leaf made Will nervous. They moved
through the woodland to another clearing near a well-worn path that
circled the camp.

"That shed at the edge of the camp looks abandoned," Zach said,
pointing down into the camp.

Will grabbed Zach from behind, pulling him back against the
trunk of a tree as he drew his handgun. "Shhhh. Don't move."

Two UP soldiers were coming along the path headed straight for
Will and Zach. They could hear the soldiers talking before they saw
them. The soldiers hurried around a bend in the path into the opening,
their light blue uniforms muddied below the knees. Both wore gas
masks and had rifles drawn.

CHAPTER FORTY-FIVE

Ben Harrison watched the back of Millard Fillmore's jeep fade into the pallid haze beyond the Administration building, disappearing into the murky rain below the ceiling of heavyset clouds. Soldiers rushed chaotically around the building's entrance while someone yelled commands. Around the edge of the building, the metallic blue light of a severed and arching electrical conduit regularly flashed against the falling rain, buzzing over the roar of water on the pavement. The air was nauseating, and his throat ached and burned with each breath.

Ben went to the soldier, who was still sick from having retrieved Millard's jeep in the rain. He was still bent over, seemingly studying the small pool of vomit on the pavement below. His spotless uniform and young age betrayed him as a new recruit. Ben placed a hand on the boy's back.

"Hey, you alright?" Ben yelled over the rain.

Black smoke was rising from broken windows on the front of the building, and there was another loud boom somewhere around the back. More soldiers and administration workers came streaming out, looking dazed and directionless.

The boy didn't answer, and Ben could feel him shaking.

"Come on, we need to get you inside."

Ben lifted him upright, and the shaking boy took uneasy steps toward the main entrance of the building.

"Hold that door open," Ben commanded another soldier as he helped the boy up the steps.

"We're evacuating the building, sir. You sure you want to go inside?"

"He needs to get away from the rain," Ben said while crossing the entrance threshold.

There was smoke in the foyer and a fine layer of dust over everything. Ben studied the wide hole at the rear of the building. The damage was much greater than he originally thought. There were several soldiers sprawled on the linoleum floor while others stood over them.

"What happened to them?" Ben yelled to one of the standing soldiers.

"Don't know, sir. They just passed out."

"He's not breathing," another soldier screamed, kneeling over one of the bodies. "What's happening here?" he shouted at Ben.

"The rain is getting worse. Some of them must be more susceptible," Ben shouted, dread gripping him. "Get them away from the openings. Drag them to the center of the building."

Ben pulled on the boy, and they limped together down a hallway away from the entrance. The rotten smell of the rain and smoke faded.

"You'll be alright," Ben said, as the boy leaned harder and harder on him.

"What's happening to me?" he asked, still shaking. His voice was desperate and breathy.

"Sit down, try to breathe slowly," Ben commanded, lowering the boy onto a chair in the hallway.

"Thank you, Minister," the boy said, looking up at Ben with panicking watery eyes.

"I was supposed to guard the Valley Manager," he said slowly, straining on each word. The boy's face cringed like it hurt him to speak. "I was too sick." The boy grabbed his stomach and bent over. Ben could hear his short, shallow breaths.

"Stay calm. Try to slow your breathing."

"I was supposed to go with them to the Boronda. You have to tell someone. I, I abandoned my post," the boy stuttered.

"That doesn't matter now." Ben kneeled and grabbed the boy by the shoulders. "Are you sure that's where they were headed."

The boy's face had turned a pale blue color, and he panted rapidly.

"Something is wrong." His face was twisted in pain. "I can't breathe." The boy gripped Ben's knee. "Can you smell that?"

"Your orders were to go with the Manager to the Boronda?" Ben asked loudly.

"Yes, then upvalley." He strained to get the words out.

"Where upvalley?" Ben was now holding the boy's head up, staring into his frightened eyes.

"I don't know." The boy's eyes rolled wildly, and beads of sweat were forming on his green forehead. "What's happening to me?" The boy cringed in pain. "I'm not wet," he cried. "I'm not wet."

"Lie down." Ben helped the boy off the chair onto the floor as he began to convulse.

"Can you smell that?" the boy screamed. "I can't breathe. What is that?" Foam was forming on the edges of his mouth. Ben held him as he continued to shake violently. The boy's eyes rolled back into his head, the shaking stopped, and he collapsed onto Ben's lap, no longer breathing.

"Help!" Ben yelled down the long hallway to a group of soldiers running by. "Help." None of them stopped.

Ben rolled the boy onto his back and leaned over, pressing his ear to the boy's mouth. No breath came forth. He pumped on the boy's chest, occasionally breathing air into his open mouth for several minutes, but he remained unresponsive. Ben quickly surveyed the empty hallway. Sweat was dripping from his brow. Black smoke had entered the narrow stretch and was moving along the ceiling in his direction.

He rose, took one last look at the dead boy at his feet, and ran down the corridor to the back of the building.

The stink of rotting garlic and burnt plastic intensified in waves as he approached the opening torn in the building's rear wall. Twisted rebar, bricks, and dust lay everywhere. Severed electrical cables hissed and sparked above him.

Ben covered his mouth with his sleeve as he leaped through a wall of smoke and came out the back of the building. A group of panicked looking soldiers made a semicircle under the covered parkway around a boy who laid twisted and unconscious on the ground between them.

"Where's your commanding officer?" Ben shouted as he approached them.

"Don't know, sir. All the officers are gone."

"Gone?"

"They were called away on a special mission this morning. What do we do?"

"Anyone who has passed out needs to be brought back inside away from the rain. Everyone else should get out of the building." They all looked at him, stunned. "If you can breathe okay, help others. Find as many masks as possible and put them on people who are having a hard time breathing."

Ben nodded to one of the soldiers. "Will you lend me that?" Ben asked, pointing to the gas mask hanging on one of the soldier's belts.

The young man unclipped the mask and proudly handed it to Ben, who pulled it over his head, knocking his glasses onto the ground. A soldier bent to retrieve them and handed them back.

"Are you okay, sir?" the soldier asked.

"I'm fine. Now get this man inside and help the others," Ben said, pushing his glasses back on top of the gas mask.

Moments later, Ben was in the driver's seat of a jeep, panting through his mask, realizing he was a young soldier the last time he was behind the wheel of a vehicle. Before starting the ignition, he pushed and released the clutch, moving the gearshift between positions. The rain was letting up as he lurched past the guard station on his way out of the Valley Administration complex. A wake of septic mist swirled about the vehicle as he sped through the deserted streets of Salinas City.

CHAPTER FORTY-SIX

Will held his breath, perfectly still, pushing Zach against the mud-stained tree trunk. They were less than five feet off the path.

The soldiers were talking loudly and laughing.

"How many girls were there? Tell me there were two." Both soldiers laughed.

"I guess we'll see when we get back home."

Will considered stepping out and shooting them both but thought it best to stay still. Maybe the soldiers wouldn't see them.

"I hope one of them is tall," one of the soldiers said as they passed by.

"But not too tall," the other soldier said, and they both laughed, low and muffled, through their masks.

"This must be the perimeter patrol path," Will whispered when the soldiers were out of sight. "We need to get off this path immediately and move down to that shed. Keep an eye out. There'll be more of them."

They watched the camp below from the edge of the woodland. A twisting spire of white smoke rose from the end of the mess hall and the generators hummed away. A soldier emerged from a low barrack and laid his blue jacket on the railing. Will impatiently studied the buildings for any sign of activity. Any sign of Helen.

From one end of the building a door swung open, and someone stepped out on the walkway. The slow pulsating of Will's mask stopped as he realized that the dark figure was Millard Fillmore. Will stiffened and involuntarily bore his teeth under his mask. One of Millard's hands was in his coat, and he rubbed the side of his head with the other as he looked up at the hills around the camp. He paused when he was facing their direction.

Will froze, and the hairs rose on the back of his neck. Even though Millard was too far away, and the mist made the visibility poor, Will was afraid he could see them. Millard continued his survey, turning slowly, looking at all the edges of the camp, then went back inside.

"Was that?" Zach began to ask.

"Yes, it was," Will said, cutting him off. "He must have been in the jeep that passed us on the road."

"I hoped the explosion had got him."

"Obviously not," Will said, his fists still clenched.

They moved downhill until they came to the edge of the camp. The shed was a short distance into the camp and dark on the inside of its three walls.

"I'll go first. Don't come down unless you see my signal," Will said.

Will was about to head for the shed when a soldier walked out from behind a nearby building, crossed under a covered pathway, and disappeared into the camp. Will and Zach stood motionless on the edge of the bank they had just descended. The soldier hadn't noticed them.

Will moved cautiously into the exposed clearing of the camp, jogging toward the shed with the handgun held down. He came upon the shed and ducked under the low roof on the open side. His eyes adjusted to the low light, and he could see it was empty. He looked back at Zach, who was crouched awkwardly against the bank waiting for his signal. Zach's straw-colored hair contrasted with everything dark and drab in the camp. Will leaned out of the open side of the shed and waved at Zach, who came running.

They crouched under the shelter, panting. A fine dust floated up from the dry dirt floor, and the shed was empty except for a tall stack of burlap sacks along one of the corrugated steel walls. Will went to the stack and felt the contents of one of the swollen sacks.

"Wheat," he said to Zach. He untied the end of one of the bags and wheat berries flowed out onto the ground. He lifted the gas mask to his forehead and bit down on one of the small grains between his front teeth. The air stunk in the shed with a mixture of sour rain, mildew, and old diesel fuel. The wheat berry crushed easily into a sweet, earthy powder.

Will scooped the golden pellets into the cup Zach formed with his outstretched hands.

"Let's move these sacks onto the ground in front of the others so we can sit," Will said.

After they had stacked several of the heavy brown sacks, they settled down onto the soft material. Will kept his gas mask on while he continued to chew.

Zach handed Will his canteen, and he took a long drink, then another.

"Reminds me of home."

Zach turned to him.

"That's probably where all these sacks came from," Will continued. "Gonzales, King City, Greenfield. Upvalley. All the food that's eaten in this camp. Harvested by hand at upvalley farms, loaded on the longvalley highway and trucked down to this hellhole." Will shook his head and was momentarily distracted by a memory. "I loaded so much of it myself."

"What a waste."

"Have you ever met someone from San Benito."

"No. I've heard stories, though."

"I don't know what you've heard, but almost everything I heard was lies. I've been in their territory, seen Hollister City. We hid out there for weeks. I saw San Benicians with my own eyes. Saw the way they live. I've talked to a San Benito soldier captured by my unit."

"Talked to him about what?" Zach asked, shocked.

"Doesn't matter. The point is, they're the same. The same type of people. They come from us and us from them. They have less land than we do. Maybe less food, but they're the same, suffering in the same way."

Zach's mouth dropped open while Will spoke.

"What's all this about then? Why are the soldiers here? The wall?"

"I'm not sure anymore."

"My whole life I was told about the San Benicians," Zach said. "About how dangerous they were."

Will sat in silence, breathing slowly through his mask. Finally, he said, "None of that matters now. You and I can't fix anything. We can get Helen and get out of here. That's all."

Will leaned back on the soft sacks and listened to the hum of the generator in the distance. He watched Zach, rubbing his leg. In the dappled late afternoon light in the dusty shed, Zach seemed tired and older.

Will twirled a wheat berry between his fingers. "What happened to your leg?" he asked.

Zach turned to him, seemingly surprised by the question. He looked back down at his leg and didn't respond. Will knew he'd heard his question but had no interest in pushing Zach to answer if he didn't want to.

Finally, Zach said, "It wasn't that long after my brother died." He peered down on his thigh again as if he was waiting for it to agree to his story. "I was supposed to be cleaning in the barn, but I was out in the dry creek that ran along my grandparents' property. I was hoping to see another animal or anything, anything moving, anything like me that could survive in the rain. It was cloudy, but I thought I had time. Then the sky just opened up. I suppose I should have been more careful, but at that point, I just didn't care. I ran along the boulders in the creek, looking for anything moving in the rain. I slipped, and my leg caught between rocks, but my body kept moving."

Zach winced as if the pain was coming back to him. His face turned dark. "The bone came right out of my thigh. I remember the blood soaking my pant leg and dripping onto my shoe."

Will shook his head. "Oh, man."

"I was so afraid that they would find out that I could survive in the rain, that I was responsible for my brother dying. I thought they'd ship me away or something worse. I crawled back to the barn. Laid there for hours, trying to get dry. I was so cold and losing blood. I remember thinking I was going to die that afternoon."

Zach flicked a wheat berry across the shed, and it pinged off the inside of the tin siding. "Eventually they found me, hours later. I don't remember that part all that well."

"Your grandparents never found out where you were when it happened?"

"No. I'd dried out by then, and they thought I'd fallen from the barn's mezzanine."

"I'm sorry, Zach."

"It never healed right. I'm not sure it would have even if I hadn't laid there all those hours. I'll never know. Sometimes I feel like being unaffected by the rain is a curse."

Will got up, went to the edge of the shed, and peered out. The clouds hung heavy, their bellies dark with liquifying water.

"One of us should rest while the other stands watch. I'll start," Will said, turning to Zach. "You lie down for a bit. It'll be a few hours until it's dark enough for us to move again."

"Alright. I feel like I haven't closed my eyes in days. I was up all last night in the rain."

"You rest. I'll wake you if anything happens."

Zach leaned over against the soft sacks and was asleep within minutes, breathing hard with his mouth open. Will stood next to the door in the shadows of the shed and watched the woodland slopes at the edge of the camp. From where he stood, he could see the unchanging, bleak sky above. Somewhere far away there was a faint rumble of thunder barely perceptible over the diesel generators.

He stood next to the door watching the sky for an hour, maybe longer, occasionally looking back at Zach, who was fast asleep. Soon he would leave this hellhole with his daughter or die trying. Millard would be waiting for him and who knew what else.

Kneeling beside the open door, Will could sense no change in the sky for the entire time he watched it. He could see by the movement of trees at the camp's edge that the wind was picking up. He lifted his mask to his forehead to smell the air. It stunk, but not as bad as it had earlier. He waited for the first spits of rain to come, but they never did.

The wind increased, and the air changed in an unfamiliar way, ceasing to stink altogether, then something happened that Will didn't expect, something he'd never seen during his time in the camp as a soldier.

Not only did the typical afternoon rain never come, but the clouds thinned and pull apart. Beyond their wispy edges, sweeping across the sky above him, Will saw what looked like late afternoon blue sky. He blinked and cleared his eyes to make sure what he was seeing was real.

The clouds morphed and rolled in the wind as the sun continued to sink over the downvalley hills to the west. A new light came over the camp showing golden and yellow on the woodland embankment. The trees swayed in the warm wind.

"Zach," Will whispered loudly, gently nudging him awake. "You have to see this."

"What is it? What's wrong?" Zach asked, getting up quickly, confused about where he was.

"Nothing's wrong. Look at the sky."

"What is it?"

"It's a sunset."

"A what?"

Zach stood shoulder to shoulder with Will at the door of the shed and looked out at the sky. The clouds had broken apart, and their lower edges were fringed with orange. At first, the change was incremental and subtle, almost imperceptible. Red eruptions faded to gold, and a white arch ran through it. The clouds, whose edges were now on fire, grew purple and the sky beyond a deep midnight blue. Will looked at Zach. He was smiling with his mouth open in amazement at the colors.

"Wow," Zach said after a long time of silence, more to himself than to Will. "I never saw anything like that before."

"Very strange. I've never seen it not rain in the afternoon at this camp."

"Well, that's good for us."

"Maybe."

As they sat and watched, somewhere out of sight the sun dipped below the hills, and the magenta and orange of the clouds faded back to dark brown and finally black. Nothing of that electric sky was left, except what was burned into their memories. The winds increased and changed direction rattling the tin of the shed, and the clouds closed in around them.

"You smell that?" Will asked.

"Yeah."

"Here it comes," Will said, pulling the mask down onto his face.

CHAPTER FORTY-SEVEN

Ben Harrison stopped at the curb down the block from a complex of dilapidated one-story buildings in northern Salinas City. He turned the engine off and wiped the inside of the windshield so he could get a better view. He was breathing hard through his mask. The Administration holding facility was a converted school from a long-ago era of Valley peace. He'd been there once before, many years earlier during his training, and it hadn't noticeably changed. He saw the van that had carried Mary and the children in front of the building. *What did the Valley Manager have planned for them?*

He cranked down his window and looked around nervously. Except for the distant hum of activity in the city, the afternoon was calm, no sign of anyone. He lifted the mask from his face and took a cautious breath. As the rain had died down, the stench of the air had mostly passed, leaving only the unpleasant but bearable scent of sulfur. He checked his watch.

He was about to open his door when the rear window exploded open in a loud crash. Tiny cubes of glass rained down on the back seat. He froze, eyes wide and darting around, trying to determine the direction of the danger. He felt the blood drain from his face as he turned to see a wide hole shattered in the center of the rear window. He ducked down in his seat just as a second shot rang out with a deafening crack, and the back window on the passenger side exploded. He bent over in the seat, not breathing, his chest pushed into his thighs. No further shots came. He wanted to look up but feared to make any movements. He waited. Silence.

A rumbling baritone voice came over a bullhorn from the direction of the holding facility. "Exit the vehicle." After a moment, the voice came again, "Exit the vehicle. Now."

He rose, hands shaking, opened the door, then stepped out onto the street. He still couldn't see anyone. He felt vulnerable, frozen in terror, adrenaline spiking in his blood, and assumed he would soon be shot. He slowly raised his empty hands, fighting the urge to run.

Again, the voice came over the loudspeaker, "Put your hands on the hood of the vehicle."

Ben complied. The palms of his hand felt numb on the droplets of water beaded on the warm surface of the hood. There was a rush of footsteps behind him.

"Put your head down."

He was grabbed from behind, his arms zip-tied at the wrists, and a black hood was forcefully slid over his head. When the darkness of the hood came over him, Ben began to panic. *Had he been betrayed? Why hadn't they been there to meet him? The plan was ruined.*

Ben was pulled from behind and, when he resisted, twisting away from the grip of his captors, he was flipped around and punched hard in the stomach. The blow doubled him over and he went down on his knees, unable to catch his breath.

"Stand up," commanded a muffled voice.

Ben stayed on his knees. His eyes were open on the inside of the dark hood. He could see nothing but the black material, which smelled of burlap and rotten eggs. A second blow came from a boot to the side of his head. His neck wrenched backward, and bright pops of light danced across his field of vision. He felt the cold wet pavement below him, the distant and vague sensation of being lifted, then blackness.

CHAPTER FORTY-EIGHT

Will stepped back from the opening as to not be splashed with mud. Occasional clicks on the tin roof grew to a steady patter, then moments later a downpour was consuming the shed and camp beyond. He felt a burning sensation on the back of his neck and looked up to realize that he'd been dripped on through a small hole in the corrugated tin roof. The skin numbed as the water worked its way down his shirt collar. He moved away from the drip and let it thump the dusty ground while rubbing his neck.

The hillside beyond the shed had grown black. The generators hummed their night song above the rain, a song that had lulled Will to sleep on so many miserable nights. He despised those generators and everything it took to run them. Lights came on, and an orange glow from the buildings illuminated the vertical lines of falling water.

"When the soldiers return to their tents and there's a break in the rain, we'll go," Will said.

"How long?" Zach asked.

Will crouched at the bottom of the shed opening and looked into the camp and the dark hillside beyond. "Should be less than an hour."

"Well, it's dark enough. I should look around while it's raining."

"Alright, but be careful not to be seen, and don't stray far from the shed or this side of the camp. Stay out of the light."

"Okay," Zach said as he buttoned his jacket.

"Take this," Will said, handing Zach his handgun. "Just in case."

Zach put the gun into his pocket and stepped out into the rain, his shoulders darkening with streaks of water. He turned back to Will, nodded, then faded like a ghost in the downpour.

The wind calmed, and the rain fell steadily as Will crouched near the entrance of the shed. *Just a few more minutes of waiting.* He pushed the mask against his face and ignored the pain in the back of his head. *Be patient*, he told himself, knowing the time was soon. Through stinging watery eyes, he watched the rain form small pools on the ground outside the shed. The pools filled and ran together while he listened carefully, nervously waiting for Zach to return.

When he did, not a shred of light remained from the day. The hillsides beyond the camp had receded into blackness, and the sky was a dark and shapeless mass, invisible except for the cold toxin it spits forth.

"Did you see Helen?" Will asked, speaking through his mask as Zach ducked into the shed.

"I saw Millard," Zach said in a loud whisper while breathing hard. His eyes were wide and bloodshot. "He's in the main building. I think I saw a child there, too."

"You saw her?" Will asked, excitedly grabbing Zach's wet coat.

"It was hard to see. All the windows were fogged up, but there was a child."

"A girl?"

"I'm not sure," Zach replied.

His hair was soaked, and he stepped away from Will to shake off what water he could. Will stood in the darkness, waiting for more answers.

"The camp seems deserted," Zach whispered.

"What else did you see?"

"That's all. I watched the mess hall for a while. Nothing happened."

"Were there any soldiers guarding the buildings?"

"Not that I could tell. Everything seemed quiet."

Will and Zach stood shoulder to shoulder in the darkness at the opening of the shed, peering out. *She's here,* Will thought.

"See that covered walkway? Once we get to it, it'll give us a covered path to the mess hall," Will said, pointing.

Will put his hands up to his gas mask and looked into the dark rain beyond the shed opening, beginning to feel nervous. "Once there's a break in the rain, I'll make a run for the walkway."

"It doesn't seem to be letting up."

Will heard a strange noise of wind rustling through leaves. The pitch of the diesel generators changed, then the whole camp seemed to shudder and move at once. Sheets of rain were pushed horizontally on a blast wave, and the shed was pounded from all sides. Will braced himself against the wall, and the ground moved beneath their feet. The sky lit up flame orange, glowing momentarily under the dark murk above, then faded brown to black. The light was burned into Will's eyes, and he blinked to clear the remnants. An instant later, a concussive boom the likes of which Will had never heard came to them from the direction of the border.

"What was that?" Zach whispered loudly, clinging to the wall of the shed, his face frozen in horror, still upturned to the sky.

"An explosion just over the border."

Zach scanned the area outside the shed. "Wow, that was close."

As Zach spoke, Will thought of the special mission he'd been told about for the children. Goosebumps rose on his entire body, and he was consumed with panic. *Had Helen already been forced across the border in the rain? Was he too late?*

"We have to go now," Will yelled, his voice cracking with fear.

"But how? The rain? You'll—." Zach fell silent.

Will raced to the back of the shed. "Tear open these sacks and dump the wheat out. I need three or four of them."

They worked on the sacks, straining to lift them and dump out their contents. The wheat berries fell onto the dirt floor in mounds and cones.

"We have to go now." Will's voice was desperate under the mask. "We can't wait for a break in the rain. Put the sacks over my head and back."

"They won't keep you dry," Zach said in disbelief and shock.

"They'll have to do. I'm not staying here, trapped in this shed while Helen is sent across the border."

A vision of bodies lying in a line in the mud flashed through Will's mind. He saw them all clearly as Zach draped the burlap over his back, Zach's younger brother, the children at the school in Gonzales, and Mary's student whom they found next to the Salinas after the rain, all with their mouths open to the sky, rain pouring in. He suppressed the thoughts and moved to the entrance of the shed.

He was bent over with the sacks draped over him. He didn't need to see Zach's face to know the worried look. "Pull them up over my head," Will yelled at Zach, shouting over the noise of the rain.

"We can wait, see if it dies down," Zach said, pulling the burlap up onto Will's bent back.

The roar of the rain was steady on the shed, and drips fell across the open door.

"We have to go now. There's no time."

Will could hear Zach's voice growing frantic. "I don't think you should do this. You might not make it. We should wait."

Please let her be alive, Will thought. There was no time to think, no time to reconsider. Will took rapid forced breaths through his mask.

"You lead the way. Make sure not to get ahead of me. Go straight to that covered walkway." Will shoved Zach through the opening into the rain. "Go on," he shouted.

The instant he was in the rain, Will could feel it. On his first breath, his legs began to grow numb and weak. He wondered if the mask was working at all. The feeling hit him like a punch in the chest, and he held his breath. Rain fell off the burlap sacks over his head as he ran, watching Zach's feet moving through the darkness and mud in front of him. Will felt like he was falling and was overcome by dizziness.

Seconds after they'd left the shed, halfway across the opening between shelters, Will began to stumble. He willed his legs to move, but he was losing control of them. He tried to stay on his feet, but the wet burlap seemed to weigh too much. He watched the backs of Zach's boots and the ground in front of him.

Zach began to slow. Will bent lower, his vision drawing in, darkening on all sides. Closer and closer, the wet ground was coming up to meet him. He could no longer see as he felt the wetness on his forearms and chest. *Push up, crawl. Crawl for Helen* was the last thing Will thought.

CHAPTER FORTY-NINE

Ben Harrison awoke with a gasp as if he'd been holding his breath. As he regained consciousness, he blinked rapidly to clear his stinging eyes. Still, there was only the damp darkness of the inside of the hood. He felt groggy like he'd overslept. He tried to lift a hand to soothe his aching temple, but his arms were tied behind him.

"You didn't think I'd find out what you were up to?" The voice of the Valley Manager was cold and emotionless and close to Ben. "Remove the hood."

The material was gripped from above and yanked from Ben's head. He shut his eyes against the brilliance of the overhead lights. Upon opening them, he saw the twisted face of the Valley Manager seated across from him. A stout soldier with a proud, smug look stood behind the Manager, holding the hood in one hand. A sickening knot formed in Ben's stomach, cutting through his grogginess. He had no idea how long he'd been unconscious.

"Give us the room," the Valley Manager said to the soldier without turning to him.

After the door was closed, the Manager stared at Ben, occasionally running a nervous finger over the back of his hand. Neither man spoke. Ben's head was throbbing, and he thought for a moment that he may throw up. He turned his face to avoid the stink of the Valley Manager's breath.

"How long have we worked together?" asked the Manager, then instantly answered his own question. "Fourteen years, maybe fifteen. Everything we've done for this Valley. We've built so much. All those sacrifices." He fell silent again, then asked, "You want to throw that all away?"

Ben didn't respond.

"What do you have to say for yourself, traitor?"

For a long time, Ben watched the spittle glistening in the corners of the Manager's mouth and the sepia circles under his eyes. In the light of the single bulb above them, the Manager's head was skeletal.

Finally, Ben asked, "Where are Mary and the children?"

"You answer *my* questions, not the other way around," the Manager screamed at him, losing what little control he had over his temper.

Ben looked around the empty room. "This has to be stopped." His words came out in a croaked whisper as if they were his first in years.

"This has to be stopped?" the Manager yelled, trying to conjure up a laugh, but failing. "Stopped? Nothing's going to be stopped." He was now shouting at full volume. "We have to defend our people and our way of life in this Valley, whatever the cost. Have you forgotten that? We're on the verge of being destroyed."

"No, we aren't," Ben said calmly.

"I'm not going to have this conversation with you. You're a traitor. You've conspired to ruin this Valley, and for that, you will soon die."

The words turned Ben's blood to ice. He'd lost track of time, of his plan. He sucked in a breath through his teeth and looked at his long-time colleague with disgust. Ben's voice turned harsh. "You're no longer running this Valley properly. You haven't been for some time."

A slight smile came across the Manager's face as if he'd won a game. He looked down at Ben in his chair, arms tied back, sweat glistening on his brow, and scoffed.

"The girl's father will be captured and killed soon. Who else have you conspired with? I need the names of all the traitors."

"Where are Mary and the children?"

"You will never see any of them again. You won't leave this room again." The corners of the Manager's mouth curled. "Each of those children is a powerful weapon against our enemies. They each have an important mission to carry out."

The Manager answered Ben's look of disdain with one that could only be interpreted as pure hate. "How many years have you been trying to fix the rain? How many?" he yelled. "I should have replaced you long ago. I never ran short of patience with your incompetence. And what thanks do I get? Your betrayal." The Manager's brow creased as he attempted a look of sorrow.

"The violence must end," Ben said.

The Valley Manager grew calm. "The violence is what makes us Valley people," he said, his voice hissing. "It's what makes us work. Without the fear, there would be chaos."

Ben shook his head. "We're not who we used to be. Look around. All the soldiers left are barely teenagers. And now, using children? You've led us astray."

The Manager's face became rigid as if he'd made some final decision. He rose from his chair.

Ben scanned the room. There were no windows to the outside. His watch had been taken while he was unconscious. He had no way of knowing the time. He looked up at the Manager and said, "It'll be over soon."

The Manager pursed his lips and regarded Ben coolly. "It'll be over when I say it's over."

He stepped back and knocked on the door behind him. It swung open, and the hulking soldier stepped into the cell, ducking as he entered. His poorly fitting uniform gave him a thuggish appearance, jacket too tight over his massively rounded chest and pants too short. He looked down at Ben tied to his chair, and a smug expression of pleasure flickered across his face.

The soldier turned to the Manager. "Sir?"

"We need to deal with this traitor." In a strained and inflectionless voice, he said, "Do it in a way that doesn't make a mess."

Ben panicked, and he struggled against his restraints as the soldier came around behind him, gripped his neck, and pulled him back firmly against his chest. Ben's fingers clawed against the chair, the zip ties dug into his wrists, and breathy, ragged gasps escaped his throat. The soldier squeezed harder on Ben's windpipe, cutting his air off.

The Manager turned away. Facing the door, he said, "Goodbye, Ben."

Ben's face turned bright red, and his eyes bulged as he thrashed in his chair. White lines crossed his field of vision. His sight darkened, and his movements slowed.

The sound of boots pounding in the hallway came through the open door, then two soldiers ran into the cell.

"Stop," a winded soldier yelled. "Sir, you need to come to the front of the building."

The soldier let up on Ben's neck, and his lungs pulled in a hoarse breath. Ben let out a scream.

"Damn it," the Manager said under his breath. He looked back at Ben in disgust. "You stay here and watch this traitor," he commanded the large soldier.

After the Valley Manager had stalked impatiently from the room, Ben sat tied to his chair, panting loudly. His eyes watered, and drool was on his chin. He focused on the two soldiers left standing at the door of the cell. The large soldier remained behind him with a heavy hand on his shoulder.

"What were your orders?" Ben yelled, his voice weak and raspy.

The soldiers stared wide-eyed at him, not answering.

"What were your orders?" Ben repeated. "Your commanding officer told you to take me out to the front of the building with the Valley Manager, didn't he?"

One of the two soldiers stuttered, "Yes, sir, but, but the Manager told him to keep you here. To watch you."

"That won't do," Ben said sternly. "I'm the Valley Science Minister. You'll follow your orders. Do as you've been told by your commanding officer."

The soldiers hesitated, then looked at each other.

"Do as you were commanded by Colonel Adams," Ben yelled in a gravelly voice. "Do it now."

One of the soldiers lifted his rifle to the soldier standing behind Ben.

"Stand back away from the Minister," he commanded.

The large soldier scoffed, removed his hand from Ben's shoulder, and stepped aside. "Fine, take him," he said.

The soldier lifted Ben from the chair, and with his arms still aching and zip-tied behind him, Ben stumbled out into the hallway. He peered back through the door into the cell where the burly soldier was still standing behind the chair. The light from above cast dark shadows over his proud brow into the deep pocket of his eyes.

"Which way to the front?" Ben asked as the two soldiers came out behind him.

"There," one of the soldiers said, pointing.

At the end of a dark hall, they came through a pair of closed doors, which Ben pushed open with his shoulder. When he came out of the entrance of the building, he was instantly disoriented. It was dark outside, yet no rain was falling. A thick fog surrounded the building, and the air was wet and smelled faintly of diesel exhaust. His throat felt hot and swollen, and he knew his adrenaline was the only thing keeping it from aching.

The Valley Manager was standing next to Colonel Adams and Dick Nixon. The three men were surrounded by a wide circle of UP officers.

When the Manager saw Ben come out, he shouted, "What is this?"

Ben looked at Dick, who was studying him carefully, then to Colonel Adams.

"It's over," Ben said.

"You traitor," the Manager said, baring his teeth. He glared at the men around him, turning, making brief and uncomfortable eye contact with each. "You're all traitors," he screamed, his voice loud and cracking. He turned to Colonel Adams. "And you, what are you going to do?"

"I'm relieving you of your command," Colonel Adams said. "As of this moment, you're no longer the Manager."

"A coup? Are you joking?"

"This isn't a coup. We're just ending your tenure as Valley Manager."

"No, you're not," the Manager yelled, each word coming after a long pause. The Manager turned in a circle. "Who's with me? Who's loyal to the Valley? Seize these three men."

Nobody moved. The soldiers looked at the ground in front of them.

Colonel Adams nodded to some of his men, two of whom stepped toward the Manager. The Manager pointed an accusatory finger. "Don't touch me." They looked at the colonel, who nodded again.

While the Manager continued to shout, the two soldiers wrapped up his weak arms and led him to the back of one of the many military trucks now parked outside the holding facility.

"This isn't over," was the last thing they heard the Manager yell, muffled by the closing of the doors on the truck.

Colonel Adams nodded to another soldier who came around behind Ben and clipped the zip-ties off him. Ben brought his hands up to his sore neck to survey the damage. He took several deep breaths through his nose and instantly noticed the smell in the air. He turned to Dick and asked excitedly, "Did you get the bottle to the plane?"

"I did." Dick smiled. "It was deployed this afternoon."

Ben looked up at high clouds overhead. "Do you smell that?"

"Smell what?" Dick asked.

"Something's different. It should be raining now, but it's not." Turning to Colonel Adams, Ben said, "I was afraid you weren't going to find us here."

"We were delayed in Bolsa Knolls. The rain was devastating there."

"It might start to improve," Ben said, still peering skyward. "What will you do with him?" he asked, turning back to the truck.

"He's about to enjoy some manual labor."

The sky to the northeast flashed orange and reflected in Colonel Adams' sunken eyes. Everyone turned as a low rumbling boom trundled over them seconds later.

"That was at the border," Colonel Adams yelled, looking around at his men, his mouth hanging open in shock.

"There are still children at the border camp," Ben said, his voice frantic. "We need to get to them as quickly as possible. Have you been in contact with soldiers in the camp?" he asked the colonel.

"No. There aren't many stationed there, but we're headed there now." Turning to his men, he yelled, "Load up," and waved his hands as the soldiers around him scrambled for the vehicles.

"Where are Mary and the children?" Ben asked over the roar of igniting diesel engines.

"They're back in the van." Colonel Adams nodded to the van parked behind the other vehicles. "That soldier's been instructed to not let anyone in or out until he hears from you."

Ben stepped close to Colonel Adams. "Thank you."

"Thank me later. We have to go." The colonel nodded at Ben. "For the Valley," he said loudly.

"For the Valley," Ben repeated.

The colonel jumped into the passenger seat of the running vehicle awaiting him, and the military convoy roared off into the foggy night.

Ben turned to Dick, who was watching the fading red lights of the convoy. "Thank you for all you did today."

"Do you think it will work?" Dick asked, peering up into the darkness.

"It's all we've got. Either way, I need to get Mary and the children back upvalley as soon as possible."

"I'll see you soon, my friend," Dick said, drawing Ben into a hug and slapping his back. He lumbered off across the lot toward his vehicle, carrying a gas mask at his side.

Ben approached the young man guarding the van. "Thank you, soldier," he said.

"Yes, sir. Is there anything else I can do?"

"Is there fuel in the vehicle?" Ben asked.

"There is, sir. I checked it myself."

"That'll be all then."

"Yes, sir. For the Valley, sir," the boy said, almost as an afterthought as he rushed off.

Ben grabbed the handle and slid the van's door open. Mary McElroy sat on the inside with the three boys, two of whom were leaned on each other, completely asleep. The oldest boy met Ben's gaze with scared, dark eyes. Mary smiled when she saw him. Ben couldn't remember ever being happier to see another person.

Mary lifted her finger to her mouth and whispered to the awake boy, "Be quiet and wait right here. We'll be right back. Everything is fine."

She stepped out, and Ben gently slid the door closed behind her. He followed her as she walked away from the van. Mary turned and raised her eyes to Ben. He wanted to embrace her but hesitated. A smile came across her face, and she lifted her arms to him, pulling him close.

"Are you okay?" he asked in a whisper.

"Yes. I'm sorry for the way I treated you earlier. I know you were just trying to help us."

"I'm glad you're safe."

"I was so happy to see you come out of the building," Mary said.

He felt her small frame against him, and she was shaking. Her closeness caused tingling electricity to move through his body. She was much shorter than he remembered, her face more delicate, more beautiful. The strange freshness in the air accentuated Ben's sense of smell. Above the dissipating diesel exhaust, he breathed in the musty sweetness of Mary's hair. They held each other for a long time.

"Are the boys alright?" Ben asked her.

"They're fine," Mary said, stepping back and looking up at him. "They're scared and they want to go home."

"Let's take them then," Ben said with a grin.

"Now?" Mary asked, her face lighting up.

"Yes, now. We need to get as far from Salinas City as we can. We can be in Greenfield before morning."

"What about Helen and Jimmy?" Mary asked.

"They're still in the border camp. Colonel Adams is headed to them now."

"And Willie?"

"Hopefully he's there, or he's on his way there now."

"I hope he and Helen are okay. What about Zach?" Mary asked.

"Who?"

"The boy Willie and I were traveling with?"

"I never saw him," Ben said. "Are you ready to go?"

"Yes," Mary replied with a smile.

Ben watched her look down at the ground, then all around. Her face was illuminated. "Look at that," she exclaimed.

"What is it?"

"Look at that," Mary repeated. "It's everywhere."

"A moon shadow," Ben whispered, his mouth open in amazement.

Both looked up into the clearing sky. The clouds had slid apart and exposed a nearly full moon, brighter than anything either of them had seen in the night sky. The orange glow of Salinas City paled in the distance as the luminous moon cast daytime shadows beneath every object. Maybe it was the sight of Mary smiling in the new light or the distinctly different, almost sweet, smell in the air, but Ben was overwhelmed with hope. He felt like the change he had worked for all those years might be finally happening.

"Have you ever seen anything like this?" she asked him, her long neck craned up to the sky.

"Not since I was a child." Ben met her gaze and grinned. He stared down into her eyes, glistening in the light. She smiled back at him.

"It's so beautiful," Mary said as she made a slow, full turn, peering upward.

Although he hadn't seen that luminous celestial body for most of his adult life, Ben's attention wasn't skyward. All he cared to see were the soft shadows on Mary's face as she turned in the moonlight.

CHAPTER FIFTY

Will felt hands on his face, then nothing but cold wetness. Once again, something poking at his eyes and forehead above his mask. He groaned involuntarily. He had a vision of himself perched above the edge of the longvalley highway, and tears were streaming down his cheeks. A truck roared by. Muffled sounds were everywhere, then he was consumed with the sharp feeling of fear with no known reasons behind it. The world swirled and roared around him.

"Hey, wake up." Zach had thrown the wet burlap off him and rolled him over onto the covered walkway. He was pulling open Will's eyelids, slapping his face gently in desperation.

Will squinted, trying to return his stinging eyes to the shut position.

"Hey," Zach whispered loudly. "Breathe." He pushed the mask tightly onto Will's face.

Will's lungs drew in a long breath. He blinked rapidly.

"You're dry. You made it. You're alive," Zach said.

Made what? Will thought. He stared at Zach, then in a rush of thoughts and memories, everything came back. *Helen!* Will lifted a hand to Zach, who pulled him onto his feet. He felt lightheaded, and his legs were still weak. He leaned on Zach as they moved along the covered walkway toward the mess hall.

"Let's stop here," Will said, his voice only a low groan.

He bent over and breathed deep. His hands were on his thighs, and he waited for the nausea and dizziness to pass. The rain quickened, and water came off both sides of the walkway's roof in steady streams. Wind-blown drips formed small domes on the dry wood at Will's feet and were quickly absorbed.

Will pounded his thighs with his fists and fought off the sickness, willfully deciding to push forward no matter how bad he felt. He stood tall and surveyed their situation. They were a short distance from the covered porch at the back door of the mess hall. No soldiers were outside. He felt the cold rage of a dispassionate killer, a feeling he learned to cultivate inside himself during those many nights in this same camp years earlier.

Will yanked the handgun from the back of his belt and made a sign for Zach to come close. Through the mask, he said, "Circle the building again and let me know what you can see inside. Meet me there by that back entrance."

Zach stepped off the walkway into the mud and rain, disappearing into the wet darkness. Will proceeded carefully along the last part of the walkway to the covered porch at the back of the mess hall. He stood in the shadows with his back pressed against a walkway post. He hadn't waited a minute when Zach appeared again.

"What did you find?" Will asked.

Zach shook his head. "I couldn't see anyone inside."

"Where is everyone?" Will wondered out loud. "I'm going inside. You stay here and watch the door."

"Careful," Zach said.

The handle was cold to the touch as he turned it and cautiously pulled the door open. The mess hall was poorly lit by yellow light bulbs, half of them blown out, strung along the walls. The floor was covered with wide pine boards that creaked under his feet. Even through his mask he could tell the room had the same smell it had always had, the sour scent of rotten linseed oil repeatedly used to treat the wood.

Long tables with benches on each side lined the room in two rows with an open walkway between them. Will stepped inside, and the door squeaked closed. He nervously scanned the room while creeping toward the front area that led to the officers' quarters. He'd gotten halfway across the room when he sensed something behind him.

"That's far enough."

Will froze in his tracks as he heard the click of a gun.

"Don't turn around. You so much as bat an eye and I'll blow you right into hell. You're gonna drop that gun real slow like."

Even though his voice sounded less human, almost mechanical, behind a mask, Will recognized it as Millard Fillmore's. He bent forward and set his gun down with a thud on the floorboards in front of him. With his hands out wide, Will slowly turned to face Millard. He looked haggard. His pant leg was torn open, and his hair was matted with dried blood. His long coat was partly burnt along the bottom, and his eyes above his mask cast a hateful and irritated look.

"Where is she?" Will asked.

"Willie, Willie, Willie," Millard said slowly, shaking his head back and forth. "You *are* a survivor. I'll give you that. You're making me regret not killing you when I had the chance."

"Where's my daughter, Millie?"

"That mutant daughter of yours has a job to do for this Valley, and so do I. I'm gonna ensure you don't get in her way. You and I are headed back upvalley."

Will took a step in Millard's direction. "Whoa," Millard said, raising his gun from Will's chest to his head. "Don't try it."

"Where is she?" Will's jaw was clenched so tight, his mask no longer suctioned onto his face. He tried to stay calm, but he was frantic, his mind racing through dismal options.

"You don't want to get in the way of your daughter's mission. It's for the Valley, Willie," Millard spoke in a mocking tone. "You and I are a couple of patriots. We gave everything for this Valley."

Millard was silent, and the two men stared at each other behind their masks.

"For the Valley, Willie. For the Valley," Millard said, and his eyes squinted above his mask.

Will heard a quick yelp from behind the open doors at the front of the hall. It was just a split second of sound, barely a peep, but he recognized it instantly. He turned away from Millard to the front of the hall.

"You move, I'll shoot you in the back. You don't want to die in front of your daughter, do you, Willie?"

Helen stepped from behind the open doors at the front of the room with Captain Wilson holding onto her shoulder. In his other hand, the captain was holding a dark blue backpack.

When Will saw his daughter, he held his breath. It'd been several weeks since he'd seen her. Her face seemed thin and hard, and he didn't recognize the clothes she was wearing. From across the dimly lit room he locked on to her wide eyes, scared and bloodshot. He pulled his mask onto his forehead, and a wave of recognition came across her face. She brought her hand to her mouth and looked like she would cry. A lump instantly formed in Will's throat, thinking of the horrors she'd witnessed, and tears pricked his eyes.

"It's okay, it's okay," he said with his hand out to her. "You're alright."

She tried to run to him, but Captain Wilson held firmly onto her shoulder. She let out another involuntary yelp.

"Take your hands off her," Will commanded.

The captain didn't move. He stood, gripping Helen's shoulder, returning Will's cold stare. Will lowered the gas mask back onto his mouth and watched the captain. He looked at Helen, who mouthed the word, *Daddy*.

"Hold your weapon on him," Captain Wilson commanded Millard. "She needs to go across before the rain lets up."

"With pleasure," was Millard's cold response.

Will heard the handcuffs hit the wooden floor behind him. "Third time's a charm," Millard said. "Turn around slowly and put 'em on."

Will turned to face Millard, his muscles clenched in rage. He knew he would die this time before putting those handcuffs on, but not in front of Helen. As he kneeled to pick up the cuffs, the back door of the mess hall burst open with a bang. It was Zach, a streak of blond hair, soaked to the bone, his red eyes wide and crazy. He went straight for Millard, who swung around and fired at him. As Zach went flying off to one side, Will lunged at Millard and tackled him from behind before he could turn.

Will felt his whole body pulse with adrenaline. A strength he didn't know he had surged through him as he landed on top of Millard. Weeks of rage and frustration pumped through his powerful muscles. His mask was pulled to the side, and he could smell the leather of Millard's coat collar through the stinging air. He pushed down hard on the back of Millard's head, compressing it into the floorboards. He struggled for the gun clutched in Millard's outstretched hand while wrapping an arm around his neck. Millard grunted and bucked his whole body.

Will bore down hard on him, squeezing tighter and tighter on his neck. He let out a growl and twisted Millard's head back with all his strength. He heard a muted, yet distinctive click somewhere deep inside Millard's neck. Millard's whole body shuddered, then went limp.

Will roared again and slammed Millard's limp head twice in quick succession against the wood floor. Blood burst onto the floorboards where Millard's forehead had caved in.

Will laid on top of him, his gas mask pulled to one side, gulping in air. The subtle rusty smell of Millard's blood met his nose and warred with the rotten linseed oil and sulfur in the air.

Will rolled to one side, rose quickly to his feet, adjusted his mask, and looked to the front of the mess hall. Helen and the captain were gone. He turned to Zach, who was on his back a short distance away. Will went to him and kneeled beside him. Zach's eyes were wide open but focused far away on something beyond the ceiling in the hard, rainy sky. Magenta blood soaked through the front of his wet shirt and grew in an oblong patch.

"Zach," Will said, reaching down to his shoulder.

"Will." Zach tried to reach up to him but couldn't. "What happened?"

"You'll be fine. Just hold on."

"Did I get him?"

"You did."

A halfhearted smile came across Zach's face. "Did you get your daughter?"

"Not yet."

"Go get her then," Zach said. Will put his hand gently on the wound on the side of Zach's chest. It was warm and wet. Zach winced.

"I'll be fine," he said, and Will heard a gurgling sound to his voice. "Go on now, get your daughter."

Will lifted Zach's hands and placed them on the wound. "Hold your hands here, and I'll be right back." Zach flinched at the weight of his own hands.

Will looked down into Zach's bloodshot eyes. He was so young. Fear and bewilderment flashed across his face. "You're coming back for me, right?" Zach asked, with a slight cough that exposed blood on his lips.

"Of course. I'm not going anywhere without you. Hang on right here. I want you to meet Helen."

Zach's lips curled into a smile and glistened with brown blood in the yellow light. Will stood, bent to pick up his gun, then looked back at Millard's motionless body, his head face-down in the middle of a widening pool of blood. He wiped Zach's blood from his hand onto his pants, then adjusted his mask.

CHAPTER FIFTY-ONE

The clamor of rain on the building's roof got louder as the clouds spewed their putrid thirst. Will went to the front of the mess hall. Raising his gun, he peeked cautiously around the door. The entrance area was empty, with a hallway leading to the officers' quarters on one side. Through a window, Will saw the back of Captain Wilson's head on the front porch. He ducked down, snuck to the front, opened the door quietly, and stood frozen in the threshold with his gun trained on the captain. Captain Wilson didn't move. He was focused on something beyond the porch, in the darkness and rain.

Will let the door close behind him. When he heard the click, Captain Wilson turned to face Will.

"Easy now," he said, lifting his arms away from his sides. "See this thing in my hand? It's a detonator. You shoot me, we all die."

Will looked past the captain. Helen stood in the rain with the heavy backpack over her shoulders.

"Don't move, Hellie," Will yelled to her. She seemed strangely calm, her tiny legs barely supporting the weight on her back. She looked up into the darkness and rain above her, lost her balance momentarily, then took a step to brace herself.

"There are ten cubes in that pack. Enough to destroy this whole camp. She knows exactly where to take it."

"No," was all Will could think of to say.

Captain Wilson, who wore no mask, turned to Helen. "Do as you were told, Helen," he yelled. "You know where to take that backpack. This is for the Valley. Your dad will be here when you get back."

"Hellie, stay right there." Will trained his gun on Captain Wilson's head, watching the black detonator in his hand.

"Don't do anything stupid. You'll kill all of us. She'll drop the backpack and be back here in half an hour."

"They'll kill her. She can't just walk into the Benician camp."

"In this rain, she can. Did you see the first explosion? There probably aren't any of them left anyway. This one will destroy the rest." A closed-lip smile came across the captain's face.

"They'll kill her. You know it."

"We'll see."

"Where's the child who carried the other explosives?" Will asked.

"We had to detonate that one before he could make it back." Captain Wilson looked at the detonator, then down at his boot. "I won't push this button until Helen returns. You'll be free to go after that." After a long hesitation, he said, "You have my word."

Will turned to his daughter. "Hellie, take that backpack off slowly."

"You'll do no such thing," Captain Wilson yelled at her. "You touch that backpack and I'll blow all of us up. You'll be responsible for killing your own father."

Helen stood frozen, shivering in the rain, looking up at both men on the porch. Water dripped from her bangs.

"Go on now," Captain Wilson yelled at her. "Do what you've been told to do. Save your father and this Valley."

Will watched over Captain Wilson's shoulder as Helen walked into the darkness toward the crossing. He stared down the sights of his gun barrel at the shortly cropped orange hair on the back of the captain's head. He drew a deep breath and took one long step forward. The drips of rain from the porch roof slowed in their descent, and Will's vision narrowed to the target at the end of his gun barrel. He felt the trigger and the weight of the gun in his two hands.

The captain turned back to face Will. He squinted down the barrel of Will's gun and lifted the detonator.

"Drop that gun or I'll push this button as soon as she gets far enough away."

Will continued to stare across the top of the barrel at the captain's forehead.

"Drop it," the Captain yelled, raising the detonator. "You may shoot me, but not before I push this button."

Will bent his elbows and brought the gun back to his chest, then tossed it onto the porch in front of him.

The captain stepped forward, close to Will, and kicked the gun under the railing out into the rain. As he went for his holstered firearm with the hand not holding the detonator, Will lunged forward and shoved him backward off the walkway into the rain. His eyes grew wide as his light blue uniform was darkened by the torrent of water falling from above. He let out an abbreviated groan, then crumpled down onto one knee and was still, with his head down and his free hand in the mud in front of him.

Will watched in terror as the captain lifted his head and looked up into the night sky, the rain soaking his face. He pulled his massive frame up onto his feet and stood tall in the rain, wolfishly smirking at Will.

Rage consumed Will as the captain walked out of the rain, back up the lower steps and under the covered walkway.

"You coward," Will said in disgust.

The captain set the detonator on the railing next to him and pulled his gun from his holster.

"You're sending children over the border to do a job you could do yourself."

The captain shrugged. "I just do as I'm told." He lifted the gun to Will's head. "Now it's your turn to go for a walk in the rain," he said, his voice icy, his face still dripping with water.

Will's eyes darted between the barrel of the captain's gun and the detonator resting on top of the railing.

"Turn around. Walk," the captain commanded, gesturing with his gun to a second set of stairs behind Will.

"Face the stairs. Go on. Turn around," the captain shouted.

Will twisted around slowly and stepped to the edge of the short stairs, then stopped.

He could sense Wilson standing impatiently at his back. "Go on now, step out into it."

Will's legs were being splashed with the water dripping from the covered walkway. He stood unmoving. The canister of his mask pulsed under his squinted eyes.

"Move," the captain commanded, "or I'll shoot you in the back."

Will waited.

He heard the wooden deck creak as the captain shuffled forward to kick Will into the rain. In one continuous movement, Will ducked and swung around, catching the captain's leg in the middle of his kick. The captain fired while losing his balance, missing Will and shattering the wooden handrail near his head. The gun's explosive crack was muffled by the roar of the rain but left Will's ears ringing. As the captain fell, Will came down on top of him. He held the captain's wrist and swung his free hand with all his force in the direction of his head. Will's fist landed in the middle of the captain's wet throat, and he could feel the windpipe collapse within.

The captain let out a groan as his face contorted in pain. He tried to turn the gun on Will, but the blow to his neck had weakened him. Will knocked the gun out of his hand, then brought his elbow down hard onto the captain's jaw. He rolled off him in the gun's direction, grabbing it as the captain sat up.

Will fired. An instant later, a dark hole formed at the center of the captain's forehead as his head jerked back. Will saw pieces of the back of his skull splatter onto the wooden post behind him. His mouth fell open, a stunned look solidified on his face, then his whole body buckled.

Will pushed himself to his feet and rushed for the detonator. He scooped it up off the railing and held it carefully. With the gun in his other hand, he swung around, surveying the walkways for other soldiers.

He ran to the edge of the walkway where he last saw Helen.

"Helen," he yelled into the roaring rain beyond the porch. "Helen."

He lifted the gas mask to his forehead. "Helen," he screamed again as loudly as he could, her name cracking in his throat. "Come back," he said, his voice coming forth as a hoarse croak. The river of rain that fell around him dampened his voice.

Will looked around in a panic. Captain Wilson laid dead in the fetal position on the raw wood walkway. He carefully set his gun and the detonator on the railing, then put both hands around his mouth and yelled again into the darkness. No answer came back. He ran around to the other side of the walkway and, leaning as far as he could over the handrail without getting wet, yelled again into the void.

He stared into the blackness, then down at the steps to the mud beyond the porch. The surface of a puddle churned and boiled as water splashed out of the sky onto it. He felt trapped and helpless. The rain scorched his throat with each breath, but he left the mask on his forehead.

He fell to his knees on the walkway, eyes red and watering. "Helen," he cried. "No."

"Daddy," Helen yelled, coming out of the darkness. "Daddy!"

Will saw Helen's small figure coming toward him in the rain. As soon as she was under the overhang, he grabbed her.

"It's okay. It's over," he said, pulling the backpack off her tiny shoulders.

He lifted her cold wet body into his arms and pulled her close. She seemed so small and bony, much lighter than he remembered. Hugging her firmly, he felt the ladder of her tiny ribcage squeeze inward. Her fawn-like legs dangled in front of him, and she shook and sobbed. He carried her inside, removed his mask, and sat on a bench.

"It's over now," he said, while she cried, his eyes and throat burning. "You're okay."

She looked around the room, then up at him with wild bloodshot eyes and tried to say something but began to cry again. He thought of all she'd been through, and it hadn't occurred to him until that moment she'd also lost her mother. In trying to process these thoughts, all his hard-fought control over his emotions finally slipped. His lip quivered, and he pulled her against his chest.

"Can we go home?" she cried. "Is Mommy at home?"

Will pulled her tightly to his chest and was silent. "We have to get out of here," he said. "My friend's been hurt. We need to check on him."

Will knelt next to Zach while Helen stood behind him. His eyes were closed, and his face twitched slightly. His hands still covered his gunshot wound, and blood formed a gelatinous film between his fingers. Will put his hand on Zach's forehead, which felt cold and clammy.

"Hey, buddy, how're you doing?" Will asked softly.

Zach's eyelids fluttered, then opened. His pale blue irises were consumed with red, and he looked possessed and confused.

"Hang in there. We'll get you out of here," Will said.

"Did you find her?" Zach asked, his voice soft and strained.

"I did. I want you to meet her," Will said, turning back to Helen.

Helen kneeled next to her father. Zach opened both eyes and strained to lift his head so he could get a look at her. A smile lit his face, then his head fell back onto the floor. The smile remained.

"Nice to meet you," Zach said, mouthing the words with barely any sound coming forth.

CHAPTER FIFTY-TWO

Zach was dead. He'd died in the back seat as they drove out of Salinas City, and Will knew it. While his daughter slept in the front seat, the jeep heater blowing its warm dry air, Will talked to Zach. As they passed Colonel Adams' caravan of military vehicles, he told him of his early years in the UP. Will talked to Zach about how he'd learned to be alone as a young soldier, not without people around him, but to be alone in his thoughts.

He spoke of how he coped during his time in the border camps and patrolling the wall by thinking of his parents and the people of Gonzales. For the first time, he talked about his visions and how much they'd frightened him. He apologized to Zach for not having been more talkative during their time together.

As Will drove through the downvalley darkness, the rain began to clear, and the moon was revealed through the clouds. The paddocks of rice reflected the strange white light under the longvalley causeway, and Will felt like they were gliding above a lake.

He told Zach about his wife, how they'd met, and about their days by the river. He told him how afraid he was to tell her about the things he'd done as a soldier. How he thought she'd be ashamed of him, but instead, when he finally told her, she held him and didn't say anything.

He continued to talk to Zach as the Salinas City skyline dwindled in the side mirror. He discussed the Salinas and his love for that river. He made promises to Zach. To visit his grandparents at their upvalley farm and tell them of the heroic things he'd done, to help care for his grandfather. He promised to honor his memory, then he promised it all again. Willie Taft used more words on that drive through the early morning hours than he'd used in the previous year.

Over the roar of the engine, Will couldn't hear when Zach stopped breathing, but he knew it'd happened and that nothing could be done to save him. As early morning light framed the Gabilans to the east, Will reached back to where Zach laid on the back seat and held his cold hand. When he couldn't untie the knot forming in his throat, Will pulled the jeep to the side of the longvalley freeway, left it running, and stepped out onto the edge overlooking the expansive black agricultural plane below. While the sun rose, long shadows pulled back across the fields, and Willie Taft cried as silently as possible.

Through watery eyes, he cursed the ugly buildings of Salinas City in the distance. He cursed the Administration, the Manager, the fantasy of a strong and warring Valley, and his willful participation in the system that had caused the suffering of so many innocent people. He pounded the railing of the longvalley as the tears came. He cried for Zach, for his wife, for the boys he'd killed, for what his daughter had been through, and for the news he'd have to share about her mother. When all the frustration and sadness settled, he looked back at the idling jeep.

Helen was still peacefully rolled up in a ball on the front seat. A wave of relief came over him, and he felt his chest loosen as if to make room for the slightest bit of hope. When there were no more tears, he felt he could finally breathe for the first time. He drew in a deep breath and noticed something different. The smell was gone. Some vaguely rotten odor that had lingered in the Valley for his entire lifetime was missing. He couldn't remember a time when the air seemed fresh, but it did on that morning. He wiped tears from his cheeks and returned to the jeep.

CHAPTER FIFTY-THREE

For six days after Will drove Zach and his daughter away from the border camp, a golden haze sat behind voluptuous thunderheads in the downvalley sky. A battle raged inside billions of minute droplets, throwing burning reflections from their disordered surfaces across the Valley skyline. Great clouds welled up one day, threatening rain but never delivering, then flattening on the following day, yet, by virtue of an epic microbial struggle therein, even at midday, the clouds never lost their golden hue.

For six days, a type of cloud never before observed by Valley residents settled into the Valley. They were more robust, stable, and not prone to rain. People stood in the newly shadowed streets and bright daylight of Salinas City and bore witness to an unfamiliar sky above the tall buildings, which altogether altered the feel of their dreary metropolis. Workers balanced on their hoes and rakes in the mid-Valley fields and studied the sky, waiting for the typical afternoon change that never came. Each early morning, as workers tied up rows of rapeseed and twisted sugar beets from their birthplace, colors in the sky unknown to them oozed out from behind the eastern hills. In the dry upvalley wheat farms, oil fields, and labor camps, people huddled in small groups and watched the brilliant colors in the distant sky while whispering rumors of a sweeping change overtaking the Valley Administration.

The moment the concentrated viral fluid from Helen's blood entered the clouds, precipitated by Ben Harrison, carried to the airport by Dick Nixon and flown aloft by a young soldier, those skyward bodies of water were never the same. For six days they churned, the skyline on fire, refusing to rain, as Valley residents watched awakening orange and purple reefs of light in awe and confusion. As the toxic air was cleared, parts of the Valley fell into a six-day-long sunset that would be the seed of legends for generations to come.

The sun would rise, a bloody globe, wavering in the haze, then hanging in the amber sky for hours. They watched the color pool up along the horizons, then drain, then flare out again across the sky. The Salinas pulled back from its muddy banks and braided tranquil through the sandy bottom into the cold and calm Pacific.

At night countless stars and a full-bellied moon swung overhead in a slow procession. Fires were lit, and Valley residents suffered from lack of sleep as to not miss a moment of the slow arch of the night sky. Constellations were renamed.

On the seventh day, the sun rose into a brilliant cobalt morning sky the likes of which no living Valley person had ever seen. The entire length of the Valley sat burning in the sunrise. The afternoon of that seventh day was warm and golden. The sun seared the Valley floor, and steam rose everywhere. Years of sogginess and sickness rose in distorted clear lines and were carried out into the eastern deserts on a sweetly scented wind. That night, no clouds formed in the early evening sky. There was nothing to block the view of the Milky Way as it stretched out a path above the Valley, the infinite heavens, so much closer than previously imagined, perfectly parallel with the long edges of the Valley.

While Will and Helen Taft stayed at the old Salinas Valley State Prison, nearly two weeks passed without even the hint of a cloud in the sky. When the lost seasons returned to the Valley, it was early spring, and another week passed before any rain fell.

When it did, the crops drank greedily, and Valley residents praised the thing they'd feared and cursed. The bravest among them hazarded moments in the wetness and were left unscathed. The rain had changed, void of any poison, only sweet water rising from the Pacific on the cold orographic air of the Santa Lucias and condensing around fertile Valley dust.

The End.